Royal Festival Hall
on the South Bank

The World's Best Writers, Artists and Orchestras come to the Royal Festival Hall and Hayward Gallery - Why Don't You?

Join the **Royal Festival Hall** and **Hayward Gallery.** For just £8 you will receive a monthly diary and advanced booking for all events

To join, call the Membership Department on **0171 921 0655** or send a cheque payable to:

South Bank Centre
Membership Department
Royal Festival Hall
FREEPOST
London SE1 8BR

GRANTA 57, SPRING 1997

EDITOR Ian Jack
DEPUTY EDITOR Robert Winder
MANAGING EDITOR Claire Wrathall
ASSISTANT EDITOR Karen Whitfield

CONTRIBUTING EDITOR, DELHI Urvashi Butalia

CONTRIBUTING EDITORS Neil Belton, Pete de Bolla, Frances Coady,
Ursula Doyle, Will Hobson, Liz Jobey, Blake Morrison, Andrew O'Hagan

Granta, 2–3 Hanover Yard, Noel Road, London N1 8BE
TEL (0171) 704 9776, FAX (0171) 704 0474
SUBSCRIPTIONS (0171) 704 0470

FINANCE Geoffrey Gordon
ASSOCIATE PUBLISHER Sally Lewis
SUBSCRIPTIONS John Kirkby, Rhiannon Thomas
PUBLISHING ASSISTANT Jack Arthurs

TO ADVERTISE CONTACT Jenny Shramenko 0171 704 9776

Granta US, 250 West 57th Street, Suite 1316, New York, NY 10107, USA

PUBLISHER Rea S. Hederman

SUBSCRIPTION DETAILS: a one-year subscription (four issues) costs £24.95 (UK),
£32.95 (rest of Europe) and £39.95 (rest of the world).

Granta is printed in the United States of America. The paper used in this publication
meets the minimum requirements of American National Standard for Information
Sciences—Permanence of Paper for Printed Library Materials, ANSI Z39.48-1984. ∞

Granta is published by Granta Publications and distributed in the United Kingdom by
Bloomsbury, 2 Soho Square, London W1V 5DE, and in the United States by Penguin
Books USA Inc, 375 Hudson Street, New York, NY 10014, USA. This selection
copyright © 1997 Granta Publications.

Cover design by The Senate
Cover photographs: Derek Henderson, Sebastião Salgado (front);
Dayanita Singh (back); film poster from the collection of Nasreen Munni Kabir

ISBN 0 903141 04 3

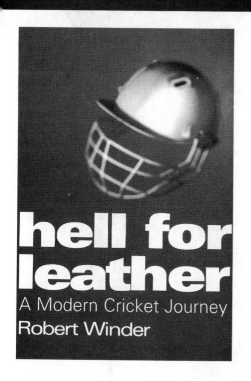

The Best Contemporary Story-telling

**Love
and
Longing
in Bombay**
Vikram
Chandra

Five haunting stories
which paint a remarkable
portrait of modern Bombay.
17 March 1997.

A Fine Balance
Rohinton Mistry

*Winner of the Commonwealth
Writers Prize. Shortlisted for
the Booker Prize.*
'Remarkable . . . Wonderful . . .
Enthralling . . . A majestic epic of
modern India.' *Observer*

Red Earth and Pouring Rain
Vikram Chandra

*Winner of the Commonwealth
Writers Prize Best First Novel*
'Chandra is imagining
and writing with
such originality
and intensity as
to be not merely
drawing on
myth but
making it.'
*Sunday
Times*

faber and faber

INDIA

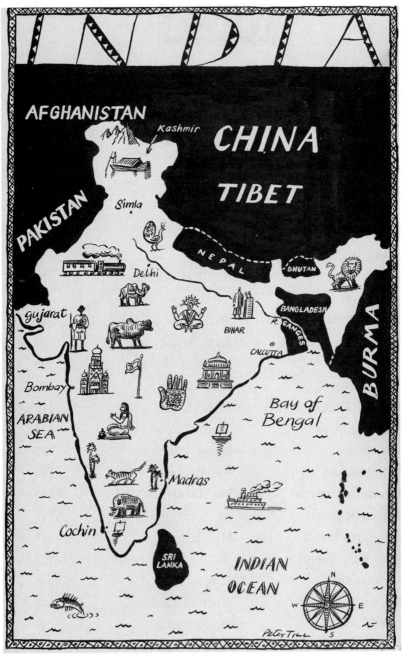

PETER TILL

INTRODUCTION

I first went to India twenty years ago as a reporter. It was late 1976, in the last months of what India knew as 'the Emergency'. In the summer of the previous year, fearing anarchy and more particularly a threat to her own position, Mrs Indira Gandhi, the prime minister, had imposed a form of dictatorship. Troublesome members of the opposition were locked up, the constitution was suspended, the press censored, foreign correspondents withdrawn. I got a visa because I promised to write about subjects which weren't obviously political: the country's great and romantic railways; cataract operations for the poor that were conducted thousands at a time in tented villages called 'eye camps'; and of course those relics of the British Empire—summer hill resorts, graveyards, gentlemen's clubs—that survived to touch the colonial heart. Like many people in Britain, I saw myself sentimentally connected to India. My grandmother had been born there, the daughter of an army sergeant. We had Indian mementoes in the house: pictures of soldiers lined up in ranks on sun-baked parade grounds, a small stuffed crocodile, a book in Urdu which had been presented to my great-grandfather for his imperative skill in Hindustani, the mixture of Hindi and Urdu which the British used when they wanted their orders understood and obeyed. Of modern India, of Indian India, I knew almost nothing.

Before I went on that first trip, a newspaper colleague who was Indian gave me some tips. 'Take some Marks & Spencer's nylon shirts,' he said. 'They never go wrong as presents. Indians love them.'

I didn't, but in Delhi in that winter spanning 1976 and 1977, I could see that his was not bad advice. India then seemed remote and austere, resolved to cope with its problems and fulfil its aspirations in its own way. It called itself a 'sovereign socialist secular democratic republic' (it still does, though few people now take the second word seriously) and bought arms and steel mills from the Soviet Union. It was 'non-aligned', the leader of the movement of that name in the Third World, and believed in economic independence. No Coca-Cola then, or foreign cars, and certainly no shirts from M & S. Foreign goods, especially those defined as luxury goods, faced stiff tariff barriers. I remember being invited to a dinner party at Golf Links, the smartest 'colony' (i.e. housing estate) in New Delhi. 'You must come,' said the hostess, 'there will be wine.' Pretty well everything that was sold in India had to be made in India. Jawaharlal Nehru had made that one of the founding principles of the state, remembering how in the previous century cheap imports made by British technology had destroyed native crafts and native employment. Nehru wanted his India to build 'the temples of industry' and initiated a series of Soviet-style five-year plans. Sheltered behind import controls, subsidized and licensed by the government, Indian industry would grow, and out of its taxes, profits and employment would come both the creation and the redistribution of wealth, the abolition of illiteracy, disease and poverty. It was called 'Nehruvian socialism'.

Agriculture had prospered—thanks to irrigation schemes and new strains of wheat, India could feed itself—but the quality of India's manufactured products was often poor. There were scarcities, a thriving black market and corruption. Many things did not work; the middle class was exasperated. But the political rhetoric focused on the poor, for whom a collapsing telephone system was hardly a priority compared to the price of rice and onions. The poor matter in India as they do not in many other developing countries—China, say. They are, of course, a majority. They also have the vote.

This was the kind of India I came to in 1976, though politics had been temporarily suppressed and replaced by Mrs Gandhi's 'twenty-point programme', in which people were exhorted to plant trees, restrict their families to two children, inform on black marketeers and, most of all, to work. There were slogans everywhere—in hotels, on the sides of buses and trains, fluttering above the wide avenues of New Delhi: A SMALL FAMILY IS A HAPPY FAMILY . . . BE INDIAN, BUY INDIAN . . . WORK IS WORSHIP. They had an urgent, last-gasp ring to them, as though Mrs Gandhi had woken in a panic and decided to save her country from the five horsemen of its apocalypse—poverty, overpopulation, corruption, disease, bureaucratic sloth—by stamping her feet and shouting a lot (like an empress—there was a saying then, 'Indira is India'). There were mistakes and cruelties, particularly in the family-planning programme, where official zeal about meeting quotas sometimes meant that poor people were sterilized against their will. It was difficult to separate fact from rumour. In a censored state, rumour becomes news.

I travelled for six or seven weeks and met no other foreign correspondent—perhaps only the staff of *Pravda* had been permitted to stay—and few foreigners of any kind. I had never been anywhere so beautiful, so disturbing, so hospitable, so foreign. It never felt physically threatening. One of its attractions was Anglophilia. In railway compartments, I would be asked about my education.

'You must have gone to Oxford.'

'No, actually.'

'Ah, the other place then.'

I had not studied at Cambridge either, but it seemed a shame to disappoint. I invented, for these casual encounters, a career which included punts and creeper-clad Gothic buildings, and also children, though I then had none, because to be childless was to be unblessed. Honesty about this lack would evoke concern and often the blunt query: 'Why?'

Then, in January 1977, Mrs Gandhi announced that she would end the Emergency and hold elections, and my newspaper asked me to stay on to cover them. It became an exciting time. I went to my first village and asked a very poor, skeletal man, an Untouchable, how he would vote. 'Well, sir,' he said with no irony, 'how would you advise me to vote?' India's starkest division, between those with power and those without, could be seen in his deference. Words which in Britain sounded quaint and dead—'the élite . . . the common man . . . the masses . . . feudals . . . lumpens'—were used in India unselfconsciously; they applied to the living in their white cotton shrouds, to what V. S. Naipaul has called 'the white crowd of India'. But as the election campaign gathered strength and vast outdoor audiences listened to opposition speakers, in what Indian newspapers called 'pin-drop silence', you could also see the force and meaning of political freedom and universal suffrage, with a clarity that is sometimes obscured in the West. Poverty and illiteracy do not equal stupidity. Mrs Gandhi and her Congress party, the party which had ruled India since its independence, were swept to defeat.

For the next thirteen years, India became my second home. I made friends there and married one of them. I acquired in-laws in Calcutta and, for a year or so, a landlord in Delhi. Throughout the 1980s India gave journalists plenty to report. Elections returned Mrs Gandhi to power in 1980, and her son Rajiv in 1985; both were assassinated. A Sikh revolt broke out in the Punjab. India sent troops to Sri Lanka. A leak of poisonous gas from a factory in Bhopal killed thousands; in terms of the dead, it was said to be the largest industrial accident in history. And, the most ominous change, 'communalism' and 'secularism' replaced the phrases of Marxist analysis as the key words in political debate. Perhaps the rich-versus-poor division had been too simple. There had always been in India 'fissiparous tendencies'—an opaque term that stood mainly for regional alienation from the central government—but the politics of religious identity had been more or less held at bay since the creation of India and Pakistan in 1947. That was the success of the Congress party, which drew its support from Muslims and other religious minorities, as well as from the Hindus who comprise more than three-quarters of the population. Now many Hindus began to feel, without much supporting evidence, that the secular state caved in too often to minority pressure. What was India, after all, but a Hindu country? Hindu nationalism moved from the margins to the centre of politics.

These were the broad forces at work, as I understood and tried to convey them, but by then I had moved into a narrower and kinder world. India as a clamouring frieze had been replaced in my sight by a collection of quiet and individual miniatures: the homes and the people that I knew;

the names of domestic servants; gardens and rivers lit by the winter sun of Delhi and Calcutta—all the familial privacies of India which are such a vital strength of the Indian novel. When my wife and I separated, in 1991, I did not think that I could easily go back. For six years I stayed away, and missed a great turning-point in Indian history.

On page 159 of this issue, the English writer Trevor Fishlock meets an ordinary member of the Indian middle class in Gujarat. Talking about his country's future, this man tells him: 'We are taxiing on the runway. We will leave America behind. Nothing will stop us becoming the greatest economic power in the world.' As a prediction it looks fantastical. In 1994 the Indian national income was $279 per person; in the US, $23,063 per person. For every hundred Indians there was 0.3 of a car, one telephone, four televisions; for every hundred Americans fifty-six cars, sixty telephones, eighty-one televisions. And yet in India now you can sense the ambition and therefore the possibility of it. The siege economy has been largely dismantled; 'Nehruvian socialism' is going down the tubes. The making and lavish spending of money, which for forty years was inhibited (though not prevented) by an official morality of social justice and redistribution, has won open respect. Much of India has become like the rest of the world.

Before I went back in November last year, I telephoned one of my oldest friends in Delhi. Was there anything she would like me to bring? She mentioned a kind of dishcloth that was peculiar to Woolworths. Nothing else? No disposable nappies (in great demand at one time), colour film, wine, replacement parts for word processors? 'No,' she said, 'everything is available in the market here.'

We met at Delhi airport and drove in her car (Japanese-designed; no longer the old lumberer made from the jigs and tools of post-war England) towards her house in one of Delhi's southern colonies. At the entrance to the colony I noticed that high steel gates had been erected. Guards stood beside them in a sentry box. This was new. 'Every colony has them now—crime,' said my friend.

That night we met her younger brother, Rahul. When I first knew him, Rahul worked in a bank. Sometimes I'd go to see him there, to cash foreign cheques and drink tea among his stacks of cardboard files, each containing sheaves of yellowing stenographer's paper, each tied with a purple ribbon. His was not a particularly convenient branch to get to, but it was better to suffer the inconvenience of the travel rather than the inconvenience of a bank where I knew nobody—to queue, to wait, to find another queue, to sign, to wait, to countersign, to find a third queue, to wait, to sign again, to collect the cash, and later to find some notes in the middle of my bundle so worn, torn and stuck together again with tape that even a beggar might hesitate before accepting one.

But now, as well as working in the bank, Rahul was helping to run an export business in rubber toys. He produced some samples from a bag. There was Noddy, there was Big Ears, there was Mr Plod the Policeman. But who was this duller rubber figure in a suit and large spectacles?

'That's Bill, Old Bill, Billy Boy,' Rahul said. He held the doll fondly to his cheek. 'Don't you know Bill Gates?'

It is said—one of those uncheckable things—that villagers in the remotest part of India know who Bill Gates is, would recognize him if he stopped by at the well one day to beg a glass of water. He is famous partly because he has said, or is said to have said, that South Indians are the smartest people in the world after the Chinese. With that remark, India felt that greatness had been conferred upon it from the highest and most modern authority—at long last someone had recognized the truth.

The measurement here was computer programming—Bangalore, in south India, has a burgeoning software industry—but smartness in India is not confined to that particular skill or region. India has smart restaurants, smart clothes, smart cars, smart magazines, three dozen television channels which range through a spectrum of smartness and vulgarity. Expenditure on advertising, a good index of urban prosperity, rose by forty per cent every year in the first half of the 1990s; last year, when it rose by only twenty per cent, advertising agencies talked of a slump. Cars, auto-rickshaws, motor scooters, lorries and buses choke the avenues of Delhi, and new hoardings stand high above the flyovers to shine palely in the fumes. The Emergency was only twenty years ago, but it seems an unreachable era. The public are not to be instructed, but seduced. WORK IS WORSHIP has long since been replaced by slogans for mobile phones, saris, fans, faxes, airlines. One that I liked read: BEFORE AIR POLLUTION KILLS YOU SLOWLY, CHOOSE 'FOREST AIR' AIR FRESHENER.

Perhaps for the first time, an averagely prosperous western visitor can feel poor here, at least in some parts of Delhi and Mumbai (as Bombay is now called). Certainly, he can no longer think of himself as a herald of popular fashion, an advance party for the changing tastes of the West. These have already reached here from California without stopovers in Europe, directly by the Internet and via the satellites that cross south Asia. America is the model now; slowly, inevitably, the old Indo-Anglian upper class, the anglophone India which had such attractive gentleness, voices courtesy of the BBC, pipes by Dunhill, politics from the Fabian Society, is retreating towards its pyre. An MBA from Harvard is worth three BAs (Oxon).

Nobody really knows how many people this new upper class contains. Figures range between one hundred and two hundred million—between just under ten or twenty per cent of the population—though if a telephone is taken as the index of prosperity, it would seem to be smaller than that. It may also be unwise to overestimate their comfort. In Delhi, which has almost doubled its population (to about ten million) since I first knew it, services which depend on public funding are close to collapse. To get reliable supplies of water and electricity people who have money sink their own tube wells and buy their own generators; the level of groundwater, already dangerously low, sinks further, and generator smoke adds its small quota to the growing population of asthmatics.

And India's poor? The figures for them are even more debatable than for the rich. In 1979 the Indian government set a calorific measurement as the line below which people could be defined as poor—the poverty line. Below it fell the people who could not afford to buy food equivalent to 2,100 calories a day in urban areas and 2,400 calories in rural areas—the rural poor do more physical work. For many years, the figure for this category was about forty per cent of the population. Then in 1996, to jubilation, the government announced that it had fallen to nineteen per cent. Some months later, however, it was revised upwards after further calculation to thirty-eight per cent. Other agencies, which take factors such as stunted growth and the illiteracy of female children into account, estimate it at fifty-two per cent.

More than ever, they and the people just above them seek political action to meet their demands: more subsidized food, more government jobs. They vote for the people who are most like them. In this sense, India has never had such *representative* politicians. Patrician, English-speaking leaders have almost disappeared, though English is the language of the new commercial vitality and many of the people who have benefited from it. The forces of economics and democracy are opposed.

In 1983 I spent a week in Dhanbad, a colliery town in Bihar, and there got to know the man who managed its railways, supervising the movement of the long coal trains which fed power stations all across northern India. I have forgotten almost everything about him, apart from his question. Could I think of any country, at any time in its history, which had achieved these three things simultaneously: one, a dynamic economy; two, a redistribution of wealth and justice; three, a fair and law-abiding democracy?

Sometime in the next forty years, India will overtake China as the world's most populous country. The question remains the greatest conundrum of its future, and ours.   IAN JACK

URVASHI BUTALIA
BLOOD

Muslims leaving India after Partition   ILLUSTRATED LONDON NEWS

URVASHI BUTALIA is a co-founder of the Kali women's press in Delhi. Her book, a collection of memoirs about Partition, will be published later this year by Penguin India.

The political partition of India caused one of the great human convulsions of history. Never before or since have so many people exchanged their homes and countries so quickly. In the space of a few months, about twelve million people moved between the new, truncated India and the two wings, East and West, of the newly created Pakistan. By far the largest proportion of these refugees—more than ten million of them—crossed the western border which divided the historic state of Punjab, Muslims travelling west to Pakistan, Hindus and Sikhs east to India. Slaughter sometimes prompted and sometimes accompanied their movement; many others died from malnutrition and contagious disease. Estimates of the number of dead vary from 200,000 (the contemporary British figure) to two million (a later Indian speculation), but that somewhere around a million people died is now widely accepted. As always, there was sexual savagery: about 75,000 women are thought to have been abducted and raped by men of religions different from their own. Thousands of families were divided, homes were destroyed, crops left to rot, villages abandoned. Astonishingly, the new governments of India and Pakistan were unprepared for this convulsion. They had not anticipated that the fear and uncertainty created by the drawing of borders based on headcounts of religious identity—so many Hindus and Sikhs versus so many Muslims—would force people to flee to what they considered 'safer' places, where they would be surrounded by their own kind. People travelled in buses, cars and trains, but mostly on foot in great columns, called *kafilas*, which could stretch for dozens of miles. The longest of them, said to comprise 800,000 refugees travelling east to India from western Punjab, took eight days to pass any given spot on its route.

This is the generality of Partition; it exists publicly in books. The particular is harder to discover; it exists privately in the stories told and retold inside so many households in India and Pakistan. I grew up with them. Like many Punjabis in Delhi, I am from a family of Partition refugees. My mother and father came from Lahore, a lively city loved and sentimentalized by its inhabitants, which lies only twenty miles inside the Pakistan border. My mother tells of the dangerous journeys that she twice made back there to bring her younger brothers and sister to India.

My father remembers fleeing to the sound of guns and crackling fires. I would listen to these stories with my brothers and sister and hardly take them in. We were middle-class Indians who had grown up in a period of relative calm and prosperity, when tolerance and 'secularism' seemed to be winning the argument. The stories—looting, arson, rape, murder—came out of a different time. They meant little to me.

Then, in October 1984, the prime minister, Mrs Gandhi, was assassinated by one of her security guards, a Sikh. For days afterwards Sikhs all over India were attacked in an orgy of violence and revenge. Many homes were destroyed and thousands died. In the outlying suburbs of Delhi more than three thousand were killed, often by being doused in kerosene and then set alight. Black burn marks on the ground showed where their bodies had lain. The government—headed by Mrs Gandhi's son, Rajiv—remained indifferent, but several citizens' groups came together to provide relief, food and shelter. I was among hundreds of people who worked in these groups. Every day, while we were distributing food and blankets, compiling lists of the dead and missing, and helping with compensation claims, we listened to the stories of the people who had suffered. Often older people, who had come to Delhi as refugees in 1947, would remember that they had been through a similar terror before. 'We didn't think it could happen to us in our own country,' they would say. 'This is like Partition again.'

Here, across the River Jamuna, just a few miles from where I lived, ordinary, peaceable people had driven their neighbours from their homes and murdered them for no other readily apparent reason than that they were of a different religious community. The stories from Partition no longer seemed quite so remote; people from the same country, the same town, the same village could still be divided by the politics of their religious difference, and, once divided, could do terrible things to each other. Two years later, working on a film about Partition for a British television channel, I began to collect stories from its survivors. Many were horrific and of a kind that, when I was younger and heard them second or third hand, I had found hard to believe: women jumping into wells to drown themselves so as to avoid rape or forced religious conversion; fathers beheading their own children so that they would avoid the same dishonourable fate. Now I was hearing them from witnesses whose bitterness, rage and hatred—which, once uncovered, could be frightening—told me that they were speaking the truth.

Their stories affected me deeply. Nothing as cruel and bloody had happened in my own family so far as I knew, but I began to realize that Partition was not, even in my family, a closed chapter of history—that its simple, brutal political geography infused and divided us still. It was then that I decided I would find my uncle Rana—Ranamama as we called him, though he wasn't mentioned often.

Nobody had heard from Ranamama in almost forty years. He was my mother's youngest brother. In 1947 my mother, who was working in the part of the Punjab that became Indian, had gone back to Lahore to bring out her younger brother, Billo, and a sister, Savita. Then she went back a second time to fetch her mother—her father was dead—and Rana. But Rana refused to come and wouldn't let my grandmother go either. Instead he promised to bring her to India later. They never came, but my family heard disturbing news.

Rana had become a Muslim.

My family didn't think that God had played much part here. They were convinced that both Rana's refusal to leave and his conversion were calculated decisions which would allow him to inherit my grandfather's property—a house, land, orchards—when my grandmother died. Letters were exchanged for a while but they began to draw the attention of the police and intelligence officers. They were opened, and questions were asked. Pakistan and India had so much in common—if not religion then certainly language and ways of life—that the barriers of a nation state became especially important to their governments as proof of difference and nationhood. Travel between the two countries, for the people who lived in them, became nearly impossible. My mother gave up hope of returning to Lahore and soon abandoned correspondence. What was the point of trying to communicate with someone who was so mercenary? And so, though Rana continued to live in my grandfather's house in Lahore, which is fewer than three hundred miles from Delhi, forty minutes in a plane, he might just as well have been on another planet. We heard rumours that my grandmother had died, but no one really knew. My mother's grief at losing her home, her mother and brother, gave way to bitterness and resentment, and eventually to indifference. The years passed; Pakistan and India fought two wars; Ranamama's fate remained obscure.

Then, in the summer of 1987, I managed to get a trip to Pakistan, to Lahore. I told my mother I wanted to meet her brother. She was sceptical. Why? What was the good? I felt as though I were betraying her; once in Lahore, it took me three days to pluck up the courage to go to my grandfather's house. I first saw it late one evening—an old and crumbling mansion set in a large bare garden—and found it hard to believe that this was the house we'd heard so much about. Through a window I could see a bare bulb casting its pale light on cracked green walls.

I rang the bell, and three women came to the barred window.

Yes, they said, this was Rana's house, but he wasn't in—he was 'on tour' and expected home later that night. I said I was his sister's daughter, come from Delhi. Door-bolts were drawn, and I was invited in. The women were Rana's wife—my aunt—and her daughters—my cousins. For an hour we made careful conversation and drank Coca-Cola in a luridly furnished living room, and then my friend Firhana came in her car to collect me. I'd met her sister in Delhi and was staying at their house.

At midnight, the phone rang. It was my uncle. He called me *beti*, daughter. 'What are you doing there?' he said, referring to my friend's house. 'This house is your home. You must come home at once and you must stay here. Give me your address, and I'll come and pick you up.'

This was a man I had never seen, who had last seen my mother five years before I was born. We argued. Finally I managed to dissuade him. But the next day I went to his house and stayed there for a week.

Rana looked like a solid citizen of Pakistan. He was six feet tall, strongly built and always dressed in a long cotton shirt

17

and pyjamas—a style Zulfikar Ali Bhutto, the former prime minister who was deposed by the military and executed, had popularized as the *awami*, or people's, suit. He had a deep, enjoyable voice, which I heard a lot that week. I asked questions, he answered them; some facts emerged. My grandmother had died in 1956 (the seven of her eight children who lived in India dated her death variously as 1949, 1952 and 1953), and Rana had married a Muslim.

Why had he not left with his brother and sisters at Partition?

Well, Rana said, like a lot of other people he had never expected Partition to happen in the way it did. 'Many of us thought, yes, there will be change, but why should we have to move?' He hadn't thought political decisions could affect his life and by the time he understood otherwise it was too late. 'I was barely twenty. I'd had little education. What would I have done in India? I had no qualifications, no job, nothing to recommend me.'

I had enough imagination to understand those reasons. In Lahore, Muslims, Hindus and Sikhs had lived alongside each other for centuries. Who could have foreseen that as a Pakistani rather than an Indian city it would become so singularly Muslim, that 'normality' would never return? But his treatment of my grandmother was harder to forgive. She had lived on for nine years after Partition—nine years in which her six daughters heard nothing of her—hidden, alone, isolated. Why had he forced her to stay with him?

'I was worried about your mother having to take on the burden of an old mother, just as I was worried when she offered to take me with her. So I thought I'd do my share and look after her.'

I didn't believe him. What about his decision to become a Muslim?

'In a sense there wasn't really a choice. The only way I could have stayed on was by converting. I married a Muslim girl, changed my religion and took a Muslim name.'

But did he really believe? Was the change born out of conviction or convenience?

He said he had not slept a single night—'no, not one night'—in forty years without regretting his decision. 'You see, my child,' he said, and this became a refrain in the days we spent

18

together, 'somehow a convert is never forgiven. Your past follows you; it hounds you. For me, it's worse because I've continued to live in the same place. Even today when I walk out to the market I often hear people whispering, "Hindu, Hindu". You don't know what it is like.'

That last answer chilled me and softened me. There is a word in Punjabi that is enormously evocative and emotive: *watan*. It's a difficult word to translate: it can mean home, country, land—all and any of them. When Punjabis speak of their *watan*, you know they are expressing a longing for the place they feel they belong. For most Punjabis who were displaced by Partition, their *watan* lay in the home they had left behind. For Rana, the opposite had happened: he continued to live in the family home in Pakistan, but his *watan* had become India, a country he had visited only briefly, once. He watched the television news from India every day; he rooted for the Indian cricket team, especially when they played Pakistan; he followed Indian soap operas.

By the end of my week with him I had a picture of his life. As forty years had gone by, he had retreated into himself. His wife and children, Muslims in a Muslim nation, worried for him; they couldn't understand his longings and silences. But perhaps his wife understood something of his dilemma. She had decided early in their marriage, sensibly I thought, that she would not allow her children to suffer a similar crisis of identity. Her sons and daughters were brought up as good Muslims; the girls remained in purdah and were taught at home by a mullah. One of his younger daughters told me once: 'Apa, you are all right, you're just like us, but we thought, you know, that *they* were really awful.' She meant a couple of distant relatives who had once managed to visit and who had behaved as orthodox Hindus, practising the 'untouchability' that Hindus customarily use in Muslim company. They had insisted on cooking their own food and would not eat anything prepared by Rana's family. They were the only Hindus this daughter had met. Who could blame her for disliking them?

One day, as Rana and I talked intimately into the evening, stopping only for some food or a cup of tea, I began to feel oppressed by him. 'Why are you talking to me like this?' I said. 'You don't even know me. If you'd met me in the marketplace, I would have been just another stranger.' He looked at me for a long time and said, 'My child, this is the first time I have spoken to my own blood.'

I was shocked. I protested: 'What about your family? They are your blood, not me.'

'No,' he said, 'for them I remain a stranger. You understand what I'm talking about. That is why you are here. Even if nothing else ever happens, I know that you have been sent here to lighten my load.' And in some ways, I suppose, this was true.

I went back to India with gifts and messages, including a long letter from Rana to his six sisters (his brother had died by this time). They gathered in our house and sat in the front room in a row, curious but resentful. Then someone picked up the letter and began reading, and soon it was being passed from hand to hand. They cried, and then their mood lightened into laughter as memories were shared and stories recounted. Tell us what the house looks like now, they demanded. Is the guava tree still there? What's happened to the game of *chaukhat*? Who lives at the back these days? Rana's letter was read and reread. Suddenly my mother and my five aunts had acquired a family across the border.

We kept in touch after that. I went to visit Rana several times. Once he wrote to my mother: 'I wish I could lock up Urvashi in a cage and keep her here.' Then, before one of my visits, my mother said to me: 'Ask him if he buried or cremated my mother.'

Muslims bury their dead. Hindus burn them. I looked at her in surprise. Hinduism has never meant much to her—she isn't an atheist but she has little patience with orthodoxy.

'What does it matter to you?' I said.

'Just ask him.'

When I got to Lahore, I asked him.

'How could she have stayed here and kept her original name?' he said. 'I had to make her a convert. She was called Ayesha Bibi. I buried her.'

L ate in 1988 I took my mother and her eldest sister back to Lahore. One of Rana's daughters was getting married, and there was a great deal of excitement as we planned the visit. They hadn't seen their brother, their home or Lahore for forty-one years. They had last seen Rana as a twenty-year-old. The man who met them at Lahore airport was in his sixties, balding and greying, and the reunion was tentative and difficult. We made small talk in the car until we reached Rana's house, which had once been home to his sisters but was now occupied by strangers, so they had to treat it politely, like any other house. The politeness and strain between brother and sisters went on for two days, until on the third day I found them together in a room, crying and laughing. Rana took his sisters on a proper tour of the house: they looked around their old rooms, rediscovered their favourite trees, and remembered their family as it had once been.

But as Rana and his sisters grew together, his wife and children grew more distant. Our presence made them anxious— understandably so. A girl was being married. What if her in-laws objected to Hindus in the family? What if the Hindus were there to reclaim their land? What if we did something to embarrass the family at the wedding? Small silences began to build up between the two sides. I was struck by how easy it was to rebuild the borders we thought we'd just crossed.

After that, I managed to go to Pakistan to see Rana again. But it wasn't easy. He began to worry that he was being watched by the police. His letters became fewer and then stopped altogether. For a while my mother continued to send him letters and gifts but eventually she stopped too. I went on sending messages to him via my friends, until one of them returned with a message from him. Try not to keep in touch, he said; it makes things very difficult. The pressure he felt was not just official but came also from inside his family. His sons urged him to break contact with his relations in India. And then the relationship between India and Pakistan, which had grown more relaxed in the 1980s, became stiffer again, and it was more difficult to travel between the two.

It's been many years now since I last saw Ranamama. I no longer know if he is alive or dead. I think he is alive. I want him to be alive. I keep telling myself, if something happened to him, surely someone in his family would tell us. But I'm not sure I

Urvashi Butalia

believe that. Years ago, when he told me that he had buried my
grandmother, I asked him to take me to her grave. We were
standing by his gate in the fading light of the evening. It was, I
think, the first time that he'd answered me without looking at me.
He scuffed the dust under his feet and said: 'No my child, not yet.
I'm not ready yet.'

On the night of 14 August 1996 about a hundred Indians
visited the India–Pakistan border at Wagah in the Punjab.
They went there to fulfil a long-cherished objective by groups in
the two countries: Indians and Pakistanis would stand, in roughly
equal numbers, on each side of the border and sing songs for
peace. They imagined that the border would be symbolized by a
sentry post and that they would be able to see their counterparts
on the other side. But they came back disappointed. The border
was more complicated than they thought—there is middle
ground—and also grander. The Indian side has an arch lit with
neon lights and, in large letters, the inscription MERA BHARAT
MAHAN—India, my country, is supreme. The Pakistan side has a
similar neon-lit arch with the words PAKISTAN ZINDABAD—Long
live Pakistan. People bring picnics here and eat and drink and
enjoy themselves.

The suffering and grief of Partition are not memorialized at
the border, nor, publicly, anywhere else in India, Pakistan and
Bangladesh. A million may have died but they have no
monuments. Stories are all that people have, stories that rarely
breach the frontiers of family and religious community; people
talking to their own blood. □

FREEDOM

PHOTOGRAPHS BY
SANJEEV SAITH

'Long years ago we made a tryst with destiny and now the time
comes when we shall redeem our pledge, not wholly or in full
measure, but very substantially. At the stroke of the midnight
hour, while the world sleeps, India will awake to life and
freedom . . . A moment comes, which comes but rarely in
history, when we step out from the old to the new, when an age
ends, and when the soul of a nation long suppressed finds
utterance.'

Jawaharlal Nehru, India's first prime minister, in his speech to the
Constituent Assembly in Delhi, 14 August 1947

SHAM LAL, *journalist, Delhi*

August 1947 was an exciting time; a kind of euphoria had come upon all of us. Delhi was lit up, and we stood around in the streets, waiting for the appointed hour to come. Crowds filled the streets. We had gathered at the Imperial Hotel and were listening in to all that was happening. There was a sense of achievement in the air. And then, a couple of weeks later, there were riots and curfew.

At the time I was working for the *News Chronicle* and I lived right in the centre of Delhi, in Connaught Place. I saw people rushing out of shops—the looting had begun. I saw someone running out of the opposite house with a sewing machine. He was shot dead. South Indian troops had been called. And then a curfew was imposed.

The riots happened because the police and army were themselves communalized. North Indians and Punjabis were excited, and feelings were running high. I have a number of images in my head—middle-class people looting things; Nehru driving by in a car; the fires I could see from my flat. For the next few days we couldn't go out.

I had attended the session in Lahore when the Congress party passed its Independence resolution in 1930. Now Lahore was a city in a foreign country. That was very sad. When Partition came, hundreds of families were herded like animals. There were so many stories of people being killed. It was chaos really.

After Independence people thought it was only a matter of time before we caught up with western countries. But the years of Independence became the years of the population explosion. Then there was the process of politicization. Before Independence there was no universal adult franchise: only fourteen per cent of people voted. Then people's demands grew: there was a growing labour force; tribes, scheduled castes and others, all wanted a share in political power; and this brought what one might call a revolution of expectations. There were so many expectations . . . we hoped against hope that things would work out . . . then there was the disillusionment that followed. But I guess that happens everywhere.

PACHI BEWA, *housewife, Calcutta*

I'm not sure how old I was in 1947—I know that I was married then and had two or three children. I married when I was thirteen. Independence meant little to us—we women, what could we know? We hardly ever moved out from inside our houses. Yes, there was some shouting here in Calcutta, some sounds of rioting, and we could see smoke. Although we are Muslims from Bihar we have lived here, in Calcutta, all our lives . . . What was there to celebrate? Half our people lost their lives; the whole place was destroyed. Many of our relatives left to go to East Pakistan and after that, well, between us there was no going and coming. Yes, people would send greetings via someone or other who was visiting, but that was all. What's there to feel happy about? We have no peace, there's looting and killing—we were here in the 1964 riots. There is no sense of belonging. If a person has given birth to a child, and then the child does not even get to see his birthplace—what kind of freedom is that?

R. P. GUPTA, *writer, Calcutta*

I slept through our tryst with destiny at midnight on 15 August 1947. And I didn't feel very thrilled the next morning that we were independent. We had no faith in the Indian National Congress, and that Lord Mountbatten was a superior sort of gangster. We became independent semantically, but in reality we were still tied to the British. Why do you need a political structure when you support everything economically? The president of the Bengal Chamber of Commerce was as powerful as the president of India. The British gave up power because they thought they could not hold on as political rulers, but their basic interest was intact. Independence had been preceded by a number of traumatic experiences, and these were at the forefront of our consciousness: the famine of 1943, the communal riots and Partition. And then many of us, though we hadn't signed on the dotted line, were fellow travellers of the Communist Party.

TARA CHAND, *shopkeeper, Meerut*

I come from Uttar Pradesh, but my wife's family lives in Chandni Chowk in Delhi. On 14 August 1947 I came to stay with my in-laws to see what was happening in this city. Hundreds, thousands of people had crowded the streets; there were people even hanging off the trees. You won't believe it. There was one man who had foolishly brought a bicycle with him, and he simply could not wheel it along, so he had to carry it on his head. And we were all waiting for the time when India would become free. It was strange—you'd think they would do this in the morning, but for some reason they planned to do it at night. I think I know why this was: the British, you see, are a very strange people. Unlike Indians, their day does not begin in the morning, it begins at one minute past midnight. So that's what that Mountbatten was waiting for. And because there were huge crowds on the streets, he was actually quite frightened to come through them because he thought he might get shot. So he came early and hid inside the Viceroy's palace waiting for Nehru and the others to come. He must have brought some bedding with him because he was there the whole day and he must have been tired and wanted to sleep. And then, we knew that he sent someone out to the market to get him tea and something to eat. So he just hid there till Nehru came and then he waited for the English day to begin and then he started the whole business of handing things over. He had to give all the accounts, the books; everything had to be listed and given to Nehru. This took him almost till four in the morning, and we all waited and watched from outside. The place was lit up, and there was a lot of excitement. The next day we went all over the place, walking, talking, just feeling free. Even the tonga wallahs were giving free rides to everyone.

JEAN SIMEON, *teacher, Pune*

From 1942 onwards I was somewhat ostracized by my community because I was the only Christian who joined the nationalists—the Quit India movement. I used to wear khaddar [homespun cloth], even the straps of my chappals were made of khaddar. I was full of rage and believed fiercely in the glory of anti-British India. People in my community found this strange—they thought of themselves as English—and kept asking, how can you team up with *them*?

When the trouble started around Independence, my husband, Eric, was away with the army. Things got very bad, and people took refuge with us because the college where I was teaching was Christian, and they thought we would not get attacked. There was a Muslim school nearby which the Hindus set on fire; they roasted girls alive, and those who jumped out of the fire, they beat. There was so much hatred, so much evil, no reason or logic, and between two sets of people who used to be such good friends. As we drove down the road we saw bodies stacked up; the whole thing reminded me of Dante's *Inferno*.

ERIC SIMEON, *army officer, Pune*

I was one of those who joined the army early on. Many of us joined to get employment—at the time there weren't many jobs around. But gradually we became more and more aware of India and Independence. When Independence was declared, we were away from Delhi, so we were a bit distant from all the excitement. By that time a state of emergency had been declared, and Hindus and Muslims were preparing all night for a showdown—the army had declared a red alert. Within a few days martial law was declared, and things were brought under control. British troops took over Calcutta; Indian officers were not allowed to do anything because the army could not be certain of their loyalty. The Bengalis think of themselves as great nationalists, but at the end of the trouble, when some Green Howards marched down Harrison Road, all the locals—Bengalis—came out and cheered!

30

C. NARAYANI, *domestic worker, Madras*

At the time of Independence I lived in Madras—our family had come there from Kerala. I was one of five children. We got to know what was happening from the papers: they said there was a lot of fighting, and people were dying. But there was no special occasion to celebrate. For us every day was the same. But someone gave us flags, and we celebrated. It was raining—even the farmhouses were full of water.

The country has changed now; there are all sorts of bad people. I don't like it. I don't do anything except my work. I just stay in this house. I don't want to meet anyone. I just don't feel like it.

32

DIPTI CHAKRAVARTY
housewife, Calcutta

I came to Calcutta from East Bengal in July 1947. At the time we knew nothing of Partition. I didn't realize then that I would not be able to return when East Bengal became East Pakistan. My two-year-old daughter, Gouri, was ill, and I came so that she could be treated and because my husband was working in Calcutta. Soon after I arrived, there were riots. We lived in a mixed Hindu-Muslim area, so there were always disturbances. I couldn't get food for the baby.

After Partition my father went back, we kept up contact, and I did not realize that soon it would be all gone. After four years or so one of our relatives had to flee from there as Hindu houses were being taken over. Soon, our houses became like hotels, with relatives and friends arriving the whole time; all were fleeing and needed a place to stop. Independence? People hardly spoke of it. Everyone talked of Partition. We were all losers, so there was no mention of Independence, of gaining anything. We spoke only of what we had lost.

SHAH JEHAN BEGUM
women's activist, Mathura

In 1947 I was a child, maybe seven or ten years old, I did not understand much, not even which country had become independent. I saw a lot of looting and killing, there was noise, but I wasn't sure who was killing whom. We're Muslims and we lived in Mathura at the time, in a place called Choti Bazaria. Even today there is a mosque there. In the killing we lost my brother Musthaq, my parents, but the two of us, my sister and I survived and we were given away to someone else to bring up. Later, when I became aware of what was happening in the world around, I began to think and to search. Some memories came back, and with those a need to understand who we were, where we belonged. It was only then that I began to understand about Pakistan and Hindustan.

My father took us to Raichur; I remember hiding in the folds of my mother's sari. People were shouting, 'Show us, show us who is in there.' Finally my mother opened her *pallav* and said, 'Look, it's only a girl,' and I was saved. We fled into the jungle, a wild place, but there were some temples, and people in those gave us shelter. After some days people began to go home. We went back to Raichur—there was nothing left there. The houses were empty.

I used to ask myself, why did all this happen? Then my father explained: he said in our country there are mixed people. There, the Muslims have dug their heels in and they are killing Hindus, and here it's the opposite. But why this separation? It was this that started me searching. And I found a diary in my first father's papers. From there I learned about our family. Then in 1990 I went back to Mathura, to my birthplace. There were still some people who remembered him. I saw the old mosque. It was beautifully made. I was told my family had spent a lot of money on having it done. I wept when I saw that. But I was also glad we had not gone to Pakistan. In Mathura I met a Panditji, and he said to me: 'Daughter of Mathura, how can your home ever be elsewhere? You belong to this land.' And he was right. This is my home. How can I die—and live—anywhere else?

34

JOGINDER BUTALIA
journalist, Lahore

We were in Lahore at the time. I was working on the *Tribune*. Our editor had left on 7 August, but the rest of us—the machine men, the sub-editors—were all there and bringing out the paper every day. We virtually lived on the premises. There was gunfire and noise all around. In the last few days even our security guards had run away, so our sports correspondent picked up the guard's rifle and he would hold it and parade up and down looking menacing though he had never fired a gun in his life! On the 14th we heard a rumour that our building was to be attacked, so we thought it's time to go. But we thought we'd print the paper anyway, so we did, and then at eight a.m. on the morning of the 15th we all piled into an old one-and-a-half-ton truck that was used for freighting newsprint rolls—we spread some rugs on the floor and piled in. And then, in the middle of the night, we set off towards the border. I drove, though I'd never driven a truck in my life.

All the way we heard pro-Pakistan slogans. Just outside Lahore, near the Shalimar Gardens, we were stopped. I was asked for my licence. The Lahore police chief, Qurban Ali, who was a Muslim, had given us a permit to pass which we showed, and we were allowed to go. We came to the new India–Pakistan border at Wagah and crossed over into Amritsar, where we stayed in the house of Satpal Dang, a leader of the Communist Party of India. Fifty of us slept on a factory roof, in string cots.

Then we left for Jullundur where our general manager, P. L. Sondhi, had gone. We went and reported to him, and he welcomed us. I went to the house of a friend of my father and told him I had no clothes. So he opened his wardrobe and told me to take what I wanted: six pairs of trousers, shirts and some underclothes. We then got to Delhi. We had permission to break into the house of an MP, Chaman Lal, in Windsor Place and there we stayed for a month. When we were driving from Jullundur to Delhi—in the same truck—all the way along we saw bloated corpses floating in the canals. No one was bothered about them.

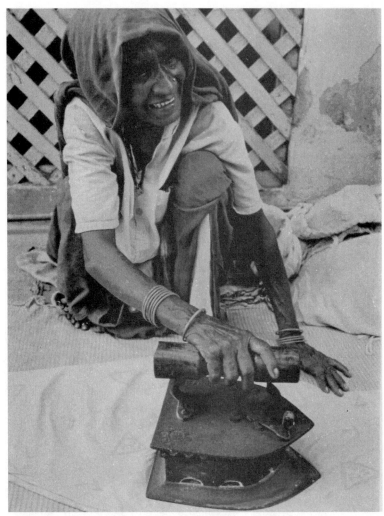

HARPIYARI, *washerwoman, Aligarh*

I can't say what my age was in 1947—even now I don't know my age—but I was quite small. In my village there were a few poor Muslims, and they were very frightened. They thought that people were coming to kill them so they ran away. But there was no rioting or killing, so things were back to normal. The poor Muslims never came back though. And then one day someone gave us flags and we waved them around.

INTERVIEWS BY URVASHI BUTALIA

EDWARD HOAGLAND
WILD THINGS

TOPHAM

EDWARD HOAGLAND, whom John Updike has described as the best essayist of his generation, was born in New York City in 1932. His books include the novels *Cat Man*, *Seven Rivers West*; the travel books *Notes from the Century Before: a Journal of British Columbia*, *African Calliope: a Journey to the Sudan*; and the collections of essays *The Courage of Turtles*, *Red Wolves and Black Bears* and *The Tugman's Passage*. His most recent work is *Heart's Desire*.

I was lucky as a child. I not only had books in the house that allowed me to conceive of myself as Mowgli, Dr Dolittle, Little Black Sambo and other people whose lives were intertwined with those of animals, I also knew a whole spectrum of animals myself. Living in the country, I could read *The Wind in the Willows* and encounter live toads and moles as well as woodchucks and muskrats. And in 1951, at the age of eighteen, I got a job working with real tigers, elephants, monkeys and panthers in the menagerie of the Ringling Brothers and Barnum & Bailey Circus, crossing America from Connecticut to Nebraska for fourteen dollars a week, all I wanted to eat at the cookhouse and half of a triple-decker bunk on the first of the three trains (seventy cars) that carried the show to the next town on its nightly hops. We didn't realize then the rarity of what we were doing: that in 1956 the big circus would close, and that tigers would become desperately endangered—their ground-up vitality used as a potion for human fertility (which the world hardly needs).

We would arrive in each town about four-thirty in the morning, which meant that we were on duty, in a casual fashion, for sixteen hours a day, interspersed with naps or swims, if the circus lot lay alongside a river, or playing with the animals. There were twenty-four Indian elephants, led by Ruth, Babe, Jewel, Modoc and other matriarchs, plus some ninety horses. Being allergic to hay, I didn't take care of them. Instead I was assigned to an old chimp and a baby orang-utan, a black rhinoceros, a pygmy hippo and a gnu, a mandrill, several mangabey monkeys, the two giraffes and a tapir. But I yearned to commune with the big cats, and eventually was apprenticed to 'Chief', the Mohawk Indian who had charge of them. The next summer, when I came back, I found he had been clawed in Madison Square Garden, had married his nurse from the hospital and stayed in New York. So I had them to myself till I went back to school.

Lions are straightforward, sociable animals, easy breeders and blessed with a humdrum, sand-coloured coat that people have not wanted to strip from them and wear on their backs. Also they're lucky enough not to share a continent with the crazy Chinese, inventing mystic applications for their pulverized bones. I had a pair of lions, a maned male and a splendid female, who patiently

managed to share the cramped cage, five feet by five, that
Ringling Brothers provided for them. That companionship, with
their bodies overlapping, seemed to calm them so much you
hardly felt sorry for them, compared to our solitary, pacing tigers.
I used to sleep under the lions' cage at night, if we stayed over in
a large city, both because of the protection that their paws,
hanging out between the bars, afforded me from wandering
muggers, and for the midnight music of their roars—glorious-
sounding guttural strings that they exchanged with the circus's
other lions, performing in the centre ring under the whip of Oscar
Konyot (a man so highly strung he sometimes had to stand and
whip one of the side poles after his act, in order to decompress).

Tigers are more moody and less predictable. Unlike lions,
they don't form gangs, or prides, and can't be herded in the ring
by somebody who knows their group dynamics and can turn the
leaders and stampede them. They're more willowy and
individually explosive and must be dealt with singly, persuaded
subtly, in a sort of time-fuse confrontation. You can apply
affection, but it's more a matter of slow seduction, one-on-one in
the training sequence, than just becoming pals with a bunch of
fractious, energetic, snarling lions. I was only a cageboy, not a
trainer—a dreamer, not a player—but I regarded my tigers as
God's cymbals when they roared and God's paintbrush when they
didn't, and though of course I thought their captivity was a kind
of travesty, the idea that wild tigers might not even outlive my
own lifespan wouldn't have occurred to me.

There was a store in downtown Manhattan I used to visit,
near where the banana boats came in, that sold pythons, tiger
cubs, pangolins, parrots, ocelots, leopards—what couldn't you
buy? For all the looting of the earth's wild places, there seemed to
be no end to such trophies. I remember how little fuss was made
when I went backstage at the circus during a performance in
Boston, and two little baby tigers had just died in the cage with
their mother. The bosses were sorry about it (as about the
cagehand who was lying on the cement floor in a pile of straw
with high-fever pneumonia), but there was no sense of a
significant financial or gene-pool loss. On the books, I notice from
the circus's archives from the early 1950s, adult tigers were carried

41

Edward Hoagland

at a valuation of only about $1,100 apiece; a polar bear, $1,200; a sun bear, $200. Chimpanzees were about $600; orang-utans about $2,000; and 'Toto', the star-attraction gorilla, $9,800. Giraffes were worth $2,200; cheetahs $1,000.

Most of our cages were old army ammunition wagons from the Second World War, eleven feet long and partitioned so that, for instance, the two lions were housed with an enormous yolk-yellow, black-striped male Bengal tiger who must have weighed a quarter of a ton. In the tiny space allotted to him, he ignored the two lions on the other side of the dividing screen and seemed the very picture of dignified placidity. The lions didn't ask for trouble, but, sprawling over each other's legs in their claustrophobic cage, were plainly prepared to shred anybody who reached inside. They bristled and snarled, their handsome lips contorting into gigantic peach pits, if you had to disturb them while cleaning their cage with the long iron rod that pulled the dung out. But the tiger just lay on exhibit, stuffed unjustly into his narrow cage, with an extraordinary tranquillity that was much more seductive than the bluff normalcy of the two lions. In his peacefulness he was cryptic, like a hostage king. You felt sorry for him, yet respectful.

Occasionally, some neophyte, one of the new workhands who had joined the circus because they were hungry (gulping that first meal down), would show off for the townie girls after the afternoon show. After prodding old Joe, the ruddy-maned lion, to roar, he might move the few feet on to silent, watchful Rajah, Joe's still bigger counterpart in the adjacent cage, and instead of tormenting him, might tentatively begin to pet that beautiful black-and-yellow coat through the bars, which were spaced wide enough to get even your elbow through. And—about once a year—when that young man, half-soused, did so, while the girls oohed and aahed, Rajah would wait till his hand moved up past his ribs to his magnificent shoulder, then whirl in a flash and grab and crunch it, pull the arm all the way in, rip it out of its socket and claw it off. The stump would be sewn up, and he'd get a free night in the hospital, then be put on a Greyhound bus for wherever his home was, still howling in agony at every jounce.

We used to scratch the rhino's itchy cheeks and the jaguar's risky flank, the cheetah's reluctant scalp, the hippo's willing

42

tongue and the four leopards' luxurious coats. It was complicated fun. Bobby, the rhino, for example, wouldn't have deliberately hurt somebody, but he didn't know his own strength when playful, or particularly care, and might inadvertently have crushed an arm against the bars in lurching about. For him, as for Chester, the large hippo (Betty Lou, the pygmy hippo, was rather unfriendly), who gaped his huge maw so that you could stick your hand in and scratch his tongue and the walls of his mouth, it was a natural procedure, akin to how the tick birds along the Nile would have searched both their bodies for parasites. The cheetah, by contrast, growled softly if touched—didn't like it, but probably wouldn't bite—whereas the jaguar objected with a mild rumble, and undoubtedly would have if he could have done so without bestirring himself. He was a frank, solitary animal, like the tigers but less complex than them, and a night-roarer like the lions, but less bold and various in how he emitted his messages, maybe because he had no other jaguars to answer him. He was penned in a cage three-and-a-half feet wide, alongside the cheetah's similar, pathetic space (the fastest animal on earth!) and a Siberian tiger confined in the third compartment of the wagon, who appeared to have gone mad, he was such a coiled spring of rage. The two giraffes, Edith and Boston, leaned down and licked the salt on my sweaty cheeks every hot day; but the Siberian would have minced me, as he tirelessly made plain.

I believed at this point in my life that no man was complete without a parrot on his shoulder, or at least a boa constrictor looped partly over him like a friend's arm. So when I say that tigers were my first love, I mean simply sexually. I was a bad stutterer, still a virgin, could scarcely talk to other people, and felt at home in the circus partly because aberrancies were no big deal there. I would not have masturbated a pet dog or cat because it would have seemed like an imposition, a perversity. But we had two great big orange female tigers compartmented in the two halves of an eleven-foot ordnance wagon, who regularly, when they were in heat, presented their vulvas to me to be rubbed. So, standing at chest-level with the floor of the cage, I used to reach in and gingerly do it. Chief had shown me how. There was also an ex-con who, like so many other hoboes, materialized one day in Ohio and worked a little while before vanishing in Indiana. The idea that caged creatures needed some solace came naturally to him. He even rubbed the old chimp's penis; not the least bothered by what's now called 'homophobia'. I *was* bothered by that and also by the fact that the chimpanzee was infinitely stronger than me and very disgruntled—being, after all, an individual who had been raised closely with people to perform as a cute baby in the centre ring, and then abandoned to solitary confinement when he outgrew his childhood. Though he was lucky, in fact, not to have been sold for experimentation like the rest, he didn't know that, and I thought I fathomed his resentment clearly enough to steer clear of his hands and teeth, which you would be at the mercy of while masturbating him. But this fiftyish guy just out of jail went to the cage and talked to him sympathetically, when he happened to be working nearby, and then reached in and massaged him a bit, much as you might ease the nerves of a murderer and be in no danger, nor even ask for a cigarette in exchange afterwards.

The white-ruffed lady tigers, however, needed to come to the bars, swing around, squat down, and present their hind ends to be rubbed, which meant that, unlike the chimp, they weren't in a position to grab me—their mouths faced away. Then the one I was doing would stand (the other tigress in the meantime observing edgily), pace off and turn and come back and try to kill me, swiping downwards with one tremendous paw extended through the bars and a roar like the crack of a landslide that brought tears to my eyes. Knowing what was coming, I liked to step back far enough that her paw just missed me but the wind made my hair hop on my head, and her open mouth three feet away ended up in a deliciously subliminal snarl that she could ratchet up to motorcycle volume if she wished to. The other tigress might share her agitation and chime in, while Rajah wheeled and sprayed pee, scent-marking the ground outside his cage.

Yet this was not much more furore than when tigers mate naturally. Soon she would return and squat peaceably for me to put my fingers into her vagina again; then maybe roar, swipe at me and come to the water pan when I slid it under the bars. I'd talk to her in her own language by making a soft chuffing sound, blowing air over my lower lip, and she'd answer—as zoo tigers also would, in New York or wherever I went, as long as I kept in practice. The secret lies in relaxing the lips; it's the opposite of a trumpeter's embouchure.

Intimacy; and I believed that I had a sixth sense. At Mabel Stark's little zoo in California, I once climbed into a mountain lion's cage. She was another female in heat whom I had been petting through the bars. She bounded at me immediately, thrusting her paw straight into my face, keeping her claws withdrawn. I also used to chance my arm with one of our leopards. She was called 'Sweetheart', and was the most handsome leopard I have ever seen, with a splendid, white, breastly undercarriage and a rich, dazzling top coat, like camouflage for an empress. She loved caresses: with her you didn't have to move gingerly. You could simply donate your arms to her and push your face against the bars while she crouched over them, licking them like long hunks of meat with her thrillingly abrasive tongue, or else twitching her tail and purring like steady thunder as you scratched her stiff-napped, oriental-carpet back. Her two grown daughters milled and whirled over and about your arms and next to your face, as swift and electric as four-foot fish—the tails an extra length, lolloping up and down like puppets. The daughters purred also; and the yearling male, who was unrulier because he was beginning to shed the docility of kittenhood, would vault around and sometimes seize my hand in his teeth and pull it as far into the cage as it would reach—without breaking my skin, but pressing down threateningly if I resisted him. Then, when he had my arm under control, he would flip over on his back underneath it and in mock fashion 'disembowel' it, like a gazelle that he had caught by the throat, with all four paws bicycling upwards against the flesh. But just like that mountain lion in California, instead of destroying my arm, he kept his claws in.

In East Africa, as a tourist, you watch lions from the safety of a well-roofed Land-Rover, comprehending, nevertheless, as soon as a lioness stalks towards you, why early people invented spears. And you grieve for the thoughtful-looking, suffering elephants existing in shattered little herds, who have obviously witnessed so many other elephants being butchered for their ivory. Safaris are a well-oiled industry now, tooled for an ever-shrinking theatre of operations; but these days you have to reach into your mind's eye for the intimations of our origins that came quite easily in Africa even twenty years ago.

When I went to southern India in 1993—flying from Nairobi to Bombay and taking an overnight sleeper from there to Madras—I found that wildlife-viewing, like everything else, was very different. In this vast disorganized democracy, the remnant wilderness preserves were shrinking, strangling really, and the larger beleaguered animals knew it. The crush and kaleidoscope of people was unlike anything I was used to. But it did not involve mass anarchy and the collapse of tribal certainties, cruel politics and looming starvation. Democracy is invigorating.

Forty years had passed since I was a mute young man who could speak freely only to animals and had played with Ringling Brothers' elephants and tigers. Yet though I had become more interested in people, I was still typecast as a nature writer, and sent off to wild places to pursue old loves. In Bombay, Madras and the newly industrial city of Coimbatore, I was lingering and lagging to walk the raucous, mysterious streets, thereby disrupting the schedule of my local handlers, who wanted me out of town and up in the mountain scenery as soon as possible, where they hoped to make money from my visit. They were travel agents— Air India had given me a free plane ticket on the assumption that I would go up into the Nilgiri Hills and write about sambars and sloth bears, tigers and tahrs—and figured that if I publicized their eco tours, then lots of rich Americans might follow me, enabling them to accomplish what they each aspired to do, which, because they were young men, was either to pay for a marriage to a Brahmin or else fly to California and go hang-gliding in the Sierras.

I wasn't enthusiastic about the idea and said that I hoped they'd protect the area as best they could from what might happen if it became a profit centre. I was also a laggard because I loved Madras and walked or rickshawed in the streets all day and then explored the huge iridescent crescent beach in the moonlight (startled to find the unmarked graves of a few of the city's destitute underfoot at the dune line). Like Bombay, Madras was a far less berserk, vertiginous city than the African ones that I was familiar with. Religion and democracy were the glue. People believed in their gods and souls and had the hope of the ballot. They weren't going to crack me on the head just for a chance at my wallet. Indeed, a dead pauper in New York would fare much worse than an anonymous burial on that immortal great beach, with Ridley's sea turtles climbing out of the waves to lay their eggs next to you. I found a new hatchling scrimshawing the sand and helped it into the sea.

The train out of Madras I'd been supposed to be on derailed into a ravine. We went by its wreckage and stopped to pick up three passengers with broken arms. From Coimbatore we drove up into the Animalai Hills to a high old British logging camp called Top Slip—because the teak and rosewood had been slid downhill from there. It is now the Indira Gandhi Wildlife Sanctuary, though with the aid of elephants the hills are still being partially logged. The hushed, handsome, rising and plunging forest had a panoply of birds—golden orioles, scarlet minivets, racket-tailed drongos, pretty 'dollar birds', crow-pheasants, green barbels, blue-winged parakeets, blossom-headed parakeets, red-wattled lapwings, paradise flycatchers, whistling thrushes, golden-backed woodpeckers, mynah birds, green parrots, magpies, hoopoes, hornbills and nine-coloured pitta birds. We saw these, and also tahrs (an endangered wild goat) and sambars (a large dark form of deer), big bison and wild boars, a black-and-white porcupine, mongooses and civets, plentiful chital deer, red with white spots, and flamboyant-plumaged jungle fowl, langur monkeys, macaques and mouse-deer holes.

I was travelling with Salim, a university-educated Shi'ite Muslim from Madras. His father was a travel agent posted to Abu Dhabi; his mother was a Hindu; his early schooling Catholic. His first language had been English, because his father otherwise spoke Urdu. Our local guide, Sabrimathu, was about seventy years old, and what is called in India a 'tribal', meaning from one of the fragile indigenous tribes, in his case the Kadar. Despite a few protections the government gives them (analogous to those offered to American Indians), they tend to miss the British when you talk to them because the British praised and encouraged their tracking skills. Sabrimathu carried a little sack of tobacco leaves to chew and a bush knife; and like the British, I was delighted to listen to him communicate with another Kadar man on the opposite hillside, by means of langur barks, regarding the whereabouts of a dozen elephants we were following. We broke off hastily when the other man told us they had a baby with them.

Originally, Sabrimathu said, two peoples had inhabited these high woods. The Kadar carried spears and lived by gathering small creatures and forest plants, or scavenging from red dog (dhole) kills, if they could surround the pack and drive them off. With brands from a campfire as weapons and windfall shelters, they could coexist with the forest's tigers and also the bison (which are like the African buffalo). But there was no way to stand up to the elephants. They had to hide and run, hide again, and abandon any permanent settlement the elephants approached. The other tribe, the Kurumbas, used bows and arrows to hunt with, shooting birds out of the trees for food and skirmishing with Sabrimathu's group, whose language they didn't speak. They too fled the elephants when a playful herd or a rogue bull in 'must' rampaged through, but feared the teak loggers and British more, and so vanished north.

Sabrimathu's group numbers only a few hundred now, in ten or fifteen tiny communities of thatch huts, on this rugged borderland between the Cochin district of the state of Kerala and Tamil Nadu, where I'd come from. Sabrimathu himself had a confiding face, unkempt grey hair, a woodsman's elastic sense of time and a blurry sort of chuffing manner by which he tried to elide and conceal his feelings when supervisors and clerks condescended to him. Of course I, on the contrary, was all ears. He pointed up a forest stream to where the pythons bred, and later at a knot of crags under a cliff of the Perunkundru Hills, where a leopard mother retreated each year to bear her kits; and to a distant thicket of sidehill evergreens where a tiger generally did the same. Up on a bare saddle of scree, a bit of footpath was visible where he had met a tiger coming towards him—that situation where, he said, you 'just stand still and see whether your time has come'. It hadn't, though once a tiger jumped at him in the underbrush when he was helping a forestry official track a man-eater. It missed. He was injured another time, when he surprised a bison on a narrow trail and it charged and knocked him out and horned his arm; he showed me the scars, healed by forest medicines.

The British had naturally encouraged the Kadar people to become the mahouts here, capturing and training the local wild elephants—which they tentatively did, overcoming their age-old fears. I remember hearing, in northern Canada and Alaska, how the New World Indians at first had been unsatisfactory guides on grizzly-hunting expeditions because even though they might be wizards at tracking grizzlies, for thousands of years equipped with 'stone-age' weapons, their purpose in doing so was mainly to avoid them. They were so fearful that newcomers—white bully boys with fat-calibre rifles—still made fun of them. But here, in this other kind of devouring, homogenizing democracy, it was not the Raj or later visiting whites, but other Indians who made difficulties. And about twenty years after Independence, Sabrimathu's remnant tribe, so fragile anyway in the new India, had been ousted from their livelihood as elephant-handlers by a new people—cattle-herders, more adaptable and sophisticated, who came up from the plains—at first two families, then more. After apprenticing with the Kadar, they had finagled or bribed or genuinely convinced the authorities that they would be better at it.

We stopped at their camp, located beside a boisterous small river, the Varagaliar, in a cut between hills in the deep lovely woods, where they earn three times a labourer's wage for working a dozen elephants. We arrived in the evening as the usurpers were finishing washing the beasts, and they jeered at poor Sabrimathu's chagrin as they showed us a five-year-old they were training to blow on a harmonica, lift one of her feet with her trunk and cover one eye with her ear. She lay down in the swirling warm stream with only her trunk raised above the current to breathe, while the foreman washed her tusks, lips and eyelids. The others were not as tame, and, after being watered, washed and fed, were chained for the night, though the wild herd kept close tabs on them from nearby and sometimes came down in the night and mingled with them.

The several families of interlopers had small children, and it was idyllic, with the foaming creek and the rushing wind in the trees, miles from another human sound, yet protected from any wandering tiger by the throng of elephants, swaying on their rhythmic feet and swinging their idiosyncratic trunks to private tempos. I remembered feeling this safe in the circus, sleeping under the big cats' cages, knowing that any mugger who crept up on me would provoke a roar that would stop his heart.

Naturally I wanted to see a tiger, though there wasn't much chance of that. We drove to a few overlooks where they occasionally were sighted on a beach of the stream below, but didn't walk anywhere after dark. An old Kadar man with prostate problems had been seized in Sabrimathu's little hamlet the year before when he needed to pee in the middle of the night and left his hut. But the same villagers went out in the wood every day gathering teak seeds from the forest floor to sell, or honey and beeswax from the right clefts in cliffs and hollow trees, or sago, cardamom and ginger, or soapnuts for making shampoo, or guided the Forestry Service men on inspection tours, in order to obtain the rice which had become their new staff of life and didn't grow here. They also used to catch civets for the perfume industry, and guided tiger-rug hunters, but these latter ventures were now illegal and what poaching went on was done by gangs of in-and-out thugs with connections to outside smugglers, not by native tribal people. Sabrimathu reminded me of various aged Eskimos, American Indians and African subsistence hunters I've met over the years, who, like him, knew a thousand specifics no one will know at all when they are gone, though nobody they had any contact with seemed to care much now about what they knew. They too lived wind-scented, sunlit, star-soaked, spirit-shot lives. Humble on one level, proud on another, Sabrimathu was vulnerable to exploitation and insult partly just because he was so tactile and open to everything else. Like those millions of American Indians, he was rooted-in-place. He could be chopped like a tree or shot like a songbird.

Early on our last day at Top Slips, I woke Salim—my young travel-agent, biology-major, Muslim-Hindu-Christian escort—and told him I'd like to go on a bird walk. Amenable though sleepy, he drove me ten miles downhill through the woods to Thunnakadu

Reservoir, which is a pretty lake that was created in 1967 and looks perhaps four miles long. The valley it drowned is also lovely, set between protected bands of forest highlands of the Cardamom Hills and flowing towards the Malabar coastline on the Arabian Sea. The road we travelled gets only one bus a day, and at the lake there was no settlement at all except half a dozen wooden cabins for the road crew. They were still asleep, so we simply walked across the top of the dam to the wild side of the lake, as the fragrant, misty blues of dawn were broken by the strong-slanting yellow sun. Cormorants and kingfishers were diving, and pond herons prowling the bank, and we saw a fishing eagle. There was a bamboo raft tied ashore, of the sort the Kadar use to go angling for arm-length larder fish that they can dry.

We walked and chatted on a footpath along the lake, while red-wattled lapwings, the 'policemen of the forest', kept noisy watch over our progress, along with several 'babblers', as Salim called them, the 'seven sisters' birds, because they always move in a group. A big Brahmini kite, white-headed but otherwise a beautiful orangy brown, was being hassled by a bunch of crows above the trees, much as birds of prey are in the United States. We saw a leopard's precise tracks, and then a largish tiger's sprawling pugs, and four bear faeces, berry-filled, in different stages of drying out, as if this path were a thoroughfare. Though Salim had never seen a leopard or tiger, he wanted to turn back. There was no disputing what we were looking at—the tiger and the bear could have been nothing else—yet we could have expected that these animals would come down to drink and forage a bit at night, before climbing the bluff behind the lake again.

Overhead, a troop of langur monkeys swinging in the branches began to whoop the alarm. It had been quiet except for the bird calls at dawn and sunrise and a few magpie and lapwing minatory cries. But entering this neck of the woods provoked a monkey cacophony, a real hollering that seemed part fearful bark or howl and part self-important fun—a rather gay razzing once they were accustomed to us and had done their primary job. We continued our stroll for another quarter-mile, occasioning lots of hubbub because each marginal youngster had to prove that he knew his duty too, not just the sentinels and the leaders.

But then there was an added note, deeper in pitch, exasperated and abrupt. The langurs' hullabaloo at first had masked it, or the fact that with our presence so much advertised, we had now felt free to gab in normal tones, and therefore didn't hear the gravelly, landslide-sounding rumble a little ahead of us.

We kept walking. Then we heard it again. Not only bigger lungs and a lower pitch: the temper of the roar was totally different, like a combat colonel interrupting a bunch of excited privates. Rajah had roared horrendously at me a few times when I hosed his cage or cleaned it with the long iron rod and bumped him inadvertently. And from a distance of forty years, those capsizing blasts reverberated again for me.

'That's not a monkey!' Salim and I said simultaneously. Then, in about the time that a double-take takes, 'Isn't that a tiger?' We each nodded and smiled—then, after three or four steps, stopped in our tracks. The lake was on our left, and the woods extended to the bluff, a few hundred feet high to the right, which was one reason why a nettled tiger might feel he had been hemmed in. That he had roared at us, instead of waiting silently in the undergrowth beside the trail to simply kill us, was a good sign. On the other hand, he could have withdrawn up the valley or a hundred yards to the side without our ever knowing about him. He or she was obviously not doing that. Was he lying on a kill? Or was she a lady with some half-grown cubs? The roars, instead of ceasing when we turned around and started walking back towards the area of the dam, now redoubled in exasperation, as if the tiger, like the two caged females I'd masturbated in the circus, had flown into a sudden, unreasonable rage. Furthermore (from the volume and tone it sounded like a male), he was now paralleling us, maybe forty or fifty yards in—not visible, but roaring repeatedly, not letting us depart without a terrific chastening. He could have cut us off and mauled us, or driven us into the lake, but didn't; and eventually we met four Kadar men in dhotis who were collecting teak seeds and told them about him. Like us, they turned around immediately and fled at an inconspicuously quick scuttle.

The crew chief, when we got back to the road, said to Salim, 'Oh, you shouldn't have gone there. That side of the lake is where the tiger lives.' The estimate of the wildlife warden at headquarters was thirty-five tigers in these seven hundred square miles.

Being a fan of adages such as 'a stitch in time', 'an apple a day', 'turn about is fair play' or 'what goes around comes around', I was pleased by the symmetry of an old tiger cageboy like me being spared in India forty years later. I was glad, too, that it was still possible to experience a fright from a wilderness creature. In this Tamil Nadu region in 1993, one didn't hear talk yet of tigers being poached for the Chinese aphrodisiac market—only elephants for their tusks and sandalwood for its scented properties. But there are more than 900 million people in India, and only 2,000 tigers. And since Indira Gandhi had decided they ought to be protected, it was said that a number of generations of tigers had grown up that were less afraid of people, at the same time as the territory available for them to roam in was being constricted from every side. The point about tigers is that from our standpoint they are not predictable. They fly off the handle when pressured, and need more than just a specified number of miles to provide a food source or enough prey animals. They need space for their whims and passions and shifts of emotions. They weave more as they walk.

A few days later I was in a different part of southern India, in Hallimoyar, one of the villages along the Moyar river. This time, my guide was Murugan, a young man from the Irula tribe. The Irulas were the indigenous people here on the Moyar river—hunters and trackers, snake-catchers and soothsayers—and still have a few cohesive villages in the forest. My impression was that they were holding together marginally better than the Kadars, partly because they still had a function. Few people in modern India care whether the surviving Kadars, like Sabrimathu, could still track tigers. But the Irulas had until very recently caught cobras for snake charmers all over India—they were the ur-snake-charmers—and also as guard-figures for traditionalist temples in places where native cobras had all been killed. They caught crocodiles for the World Wildlife Fund's famous 'Crocodile Bank', near Madras, from which river breeding stock can be sent to other zoos or wildlife preserves, or anywhere crocodiles will be wanted down the road. Nevertheless, they, too, were hunkered down in hard-scrabble poverty.

Murugan was named after an ancient Tamil and Hindu god always seen with a trident. He was also known as 'Bear' because, five years before, he had been gripped and bitten by a bear—he has scars—which his father drove off by ripping a handful of thatch from the roof and setting it afire. He says his grandmother was so tough that she once killed a bear with her hands—it had attacked her on the footpath when she was coming home from the market. His father collected tamarind seeds in the forest, which was dangerous because the elephants collected them also. Other Irulas kept watch on platforms in the paddy fields for a dollar a night, throwing firecrackers or lighting piles of hay to fend off the wild pigs and elephants (three years ago, two of them had been stomped and killed). Murugan himself—wiry, cheerful and untidy like a man-of-the-woods—collected honey for a living every March, and had spotted nine bees' nests on the cliffs so far by a careful reconnaissance. The bees placed them as inaccessibly as they could, but he slipped on a bedsheet with eyeholes cut in, and worked at night, rappelling down the cliff from above, with a burning stick tied to his belt for extra protection and a big tin container to fill. Each of these nests provided him with about ten dollars' worth of honey and wax. And there were eleven Irulas, he said, who worked the ramparts of the cliffs and found more than two hundred nests, though the bears and the leopards diligently competed with them, sometimes almost alongside.

As many as forty British officers used to come to the Moyar river every year to hunt on horseback with tiger hounds, and four Irulas, including Murugan's grandfather, served as trackers, while their wives did the cooking. I asked whether Murugan had ever encountered a tiger himself. He said that, yes, four months ago, when he was doing one of his preliminary searches for honey up a tributary valley, he had seen a tiger with kittens that 'could leap sixty feet' that had killed a cow. She was crouching over it, sucking blood from its throat and, like a nervy cat, tapping the top of her head with the tuft on the end of her tail. No tiger had killed anybody recently, but five people had been killed by elephants in the past eight years (one man tusked to death in front of our rest house). But 'the elephant was the king of the jungle', he said, and shouldn't be shot, no matter what he did. During the latest frenzy of poaching, an elephant had been found in the forest, disabled and kneeling but still alive, with his trunk nailed to the ground with a sharpened crowbar and L-shaped cuts under his cheeks where his tusks had been cut out. That kind of thing, Murugan said, 'may be why they're mad'.

In India, ivory poaching has decimated only the males, because female elephants (unlike their African counterparts) do not have tusks. So what you have is herds of angry females who have witnessed a number of cruel, treacherous, lingering deaths of bulls they've known well. If chased by elephants, you run in a zigzag, hide and dash when discovered, hide again and dash if rediscovered, then turn suddenly, and turn again, because an elephant, though fast in a straight line, is less manoeuvrable than you are. It will stop and listen for you, raising its trunk to sniff the air, sometimes pawing one foot and spreading its ears like a cobra's hood. It can push down the sort of tree you might be able to climb, so you want to get up into the rocks or squeeze into a culvert under the road, if you can run that far. Though when my guide did that, a mile from here on a little jeep track, the elephant found where he was and knelt and reached as deeply as she could into the culvert with her trunk. Then she got up and stood over it and stamped her feet, trying to squash it in.

That night a leopard came into somebody's house through an unshuttered window and killed a goat, but was unable to pull it off its rope and get it back out the window, so merely crouched licking its blood at the throat. The owner of the goat, trying to save it, was so flustered that he tripped, fell and broke his arm. But his neighbours, rushing over, frightened the leopard out. This same troublesome female, with kittens to feed, had grabbed a small boy one evening a few weeks before and started to haul him away by his head. But he was heavy, and his father bravely gave chase, caught up, and rescued his son. The boy was all right now, though we saw the tooth marks.

We went on a stroll to catch some fish and look at crocodile drag-marks in the deep sand on a plump beach several miles below Hallimoyar. The river rustled by in corded currents under grandly proportioned trees. We built a driftwood fire for cooking, and napped when we weren't doing anything else. An elephant path crossed the river at this point, and we found hyena prints and dung with sambar hair in it. You could wade out in the silky water and sit on knobby rocks, or cradle yourself on the lowest branches of two or three of the trees that arced out over the river.

The water ran hip-deep near the bank, yet, though a cow was said to have been bitten on the nose upstream the day before, we trusted our guide's assurance that he knew the nature of crocodiles, and enjoyed the afternoon till sunset: whereupon we started walking back to Hallimoyar on the ox-wagon track. A brown-and-white Brahmini kite was being buzzed by a swift grey hawk. We'd seen a black buck run off in a hurry on our trip in, and expected to stumble upon other animals as dusk approached. A river temple stood along the trail, with a cobra living in a termite mound alongside that Murugan said he'd put there. I'd hoped to see the cobra, but we weren't inclined to linger, because we'd already dawdled too long at the beach. It was growing dark, and the twelve hours of night belonged to the animals.

Clouds hid the moon. Fortunately the path was composed of a whitish soil that we could fix our eyes on. But then I happened to glance up, and dimly noticed that we were about to collide with a baby elephant. How nice, I thought for just a second, a baby elephant. *A baby elephant!* Then, sure enough, the mother's shape loomed indistinctly in the gloom. Her shadowy trunk hardly moved, not yet swinging forwards and up; her tree-trunk legs looked the very pattern of patience. But as we alerted one another agitatedly in whispers, her great ears really did spread out above us like a cobra's hood. We could also make out other females at her shoulders—two, three, maybe four, waiting.

'We're trapped,' whispered our guide. 'Our luck has gone bad.'

The elephants were preparing to enter the road, so we didn't run backwards. Instead we ran upwards, up the side of a rocky ridge that fortuitously stood to our right. They could have charged uphill, but rocks are not to a pachyderm's liking. We scattered, but angled slantwise along the slope to a drop-off that seemed high enough that their trunks couldn't reach us if they followed and stood on their hind legs, trying. Looking down at the trail in a slice of moonlight, we saw more elephants in the dusk. Another group was arriving. We tried to count: thirty or forty were slowly shuffling towards the river. It was amazing, almost surreal in the dark. Fearfully, we lit a fire on a flat part of the rock—and heard a groan from some of the animals below, as though they were murmuring: *what are these crazies going to do, set the valley, too, on fire?*

After they had moved on, we yelled for a couple of hours before a gust of wind caught our voices properly and carried them to the nightwatchmen in Hallimoyar's paddy fields. Bravely, they set out to rescue us, though they didn't know who we were, and thought we might be bandits, smugglers, poachers or whatever. They said later they had been as scared of us as of the possibility that the elephants might still be on the road. The fire would have protected us for the rest of the night from cats, bears, bison, dholes or hyenas, but we were impatient, and glad of their generous spirit.

In the current happy excitement about whether we may soon discover signs of primitive life on Mars, there is a weird and tragic incongruity, because we are losing dozens of more complex but unexamined species every day right here on Earth and doing little about it. And it isn't just beetles. Creatures such as tigers and rhinos are also disappearing, creatures which from childhood have been part of the furniture of our minds. Indeed, they may have helped create our minds. When you see a tiger at the zoo you know innately that your ancestors did too. And even if children's authors have tended to create 'wild things' that are amalgams instead of simply using the real thing, these creations are surely blended from the same old veldt or jungle citizenry that shaped our imagination to begin with.

In Madras, my plane was delayed because up in New Delhi there were bomb scares at the airport. So, feeling in suspension, I persuaded a guy at the terminal to drive me up to the nearby hill where Doubting Thomas, according to some reports, was crucified. It seems natural that, in his regret, St Thomas would have been the Apostle who travelled furthest afterwards—clear to the Bay of

Bengal, there to re-enact Christ's fate. I felt a link to him, because my parents used to call me 'Doubting Thomas' when I was young and rebellious and 'doubted' their Episcopalian liturgy.

On this cathedral hill, schoolchildren were planting trees while a gang of jackdaws disputed possession of the sky with some vultures and kites, and the smell of uric acid and rotting carbohydrates drifted up from Madras's five million people below. But I also saw an egret sitting on a cow's back and a blackbird on a buffalo. A drove of white ducks on the way to market, even a drove of pigs. Brahma, Vishnu and Shiva—creator, preserver and destroyer—had topped St Thomas's appeal in this part of the world. They ride, on a swan, an eagle and a bull, among the androgynous exuberance of sculpted figures from the animal kingdom scrambling like totems up the compact temple towers. These are metaphors, of course, but with a bit of glee or mischief thrown in, and the undergirding of real elephants, cobras and tigers only a day's walk away.

Yet one does not leave wild places hopefully nowadays. Amalgams indeed are what we'll have. Virtual wilderness. 'Albino king snakes' are already in the pet stores, and 'ligers' and 'tiglons' feature in dealers' catalogues (apparently, selling a cross evades the endangered-species laws). When I remember that Siberian tiger caged in eighteen square feet in the circus, or the black-maned movie lion confined in a piano box which I cared for in California in 1953, I can't romanticize how things were at mid-century. The cruelty was abominable, but was still enclosed in a world that seemed closer to being whole. The ultimate wild things are incidentally dangerous—white sharks, harpy eagles, polar bears—and unpredictable. Even the most gorgeous tiger is less athletic, more complicated than a leopard, say, which may sometimes seem like a single, lengthy muscle. But the tiger's spirit, when ferocious, feline and imperial, can parallel ours, though without the monkeying primate qualities that have given us our berserk streak. Tigers are less heartbreaking than the beleaguered elephant, because they are not social creatures, are reactive, not innovative. But they are an apex, a kind of hook the web of nature hangs from. To know them marked my life. □

GRANTA

JAMES BUCHAN
KASHMIR

JAMES BUCHAN spent ten years as a foreign correspondent for the *Financial Times*. He has written five novels, among them *A Parish of Rich Women*, which won the Whitbread First Novel Award; *Heart's Journey in Winter*, which won the Guardian Fiction Prize; and most recently *High Latitudes*. .

If you wish to visit the valley of Kashmir without being turned back, shot or kidnapped, there are two approaches. The first is by air from New Delhi, where the valley looks orderly and comprehensible in the Himalayan sunshine: a small place of lakes and rivers, orchards, patchwork fields and tin roofs gleaming through clumps of willow, shut in by a colossal fence of mountain. The other is by a road that climbs to 7,000 feet and then through a tunnel bored, in the 1950s, through the Pir Panjal mountains. Only one tube of this tunnel is in service. Traffic flows into and out of Kashmir at alternate times; so you can crawl for several days in a fifty-mile line of trucks and army vehicles only to find the tunnel closed to your side. It is as if, after the agonies of death, you must wait in line for the formalities of hell.

In the Indian subcontinent, you do not hire a car, but a driver who sometimes has a car. A relation that would be neutral and indifferent in Europe or the United States is here personal and passionate, and cannot be annulled by payment; and anyway I have no Indian money, whereas Fayaz Ahmad Malik, my driver, has borrowed a thousand rupees for gasoline and cigarettes and for a chicken now dying in the trunk of his white Ambassador. The stopped trucks and army buses and jeeps stretch round the gorge and up the other side, and no doubt repeat themselves at ever higher elevations, round and up, as far as the Banihal Tunnel. We take it in turns to jump up on the footplates and persuade the dozy Sikh drivers to pull the chocks from their wheels and move over, so we can blunder through and gain a hundred yards. Tribespeople thread their flocks through the stationary traffic, on their way to winter pasture, so absorbed in their own calendar they don't belong in this world of violence and commerce, but with the vultures lazing in the hot sky and the squabbling monkeys.

The car has been dented by a bus of the Border Security Force, the BSF, but Fayaz is light-hearted. He dislikes every place except the valley of Kashmir and he is returning there, if at only half a mile an hour. He washed his face and brushed his teeth in the Chenab river, and his cream shirt and pantaloons are crisp and neat. I, in contrast, am coated with red mud up to my thighs from pushing him and the car through a landslip at the Nasri Nallah. I haven't slept for forty-eight hours; have been made deaf from the bellowing of Indian army one-tonners; and am choked by anxiety.

That anxiety lies on me in several layers, which I have had leisure to uncover. On the surface is the fear that we just won't get there: that we won't make it to the front of the line by nightfall or, even if we do, won't be able to persuade the Indo-Tibetan Border Police to radio to the other side and close the tunnel to the traffic from the Kashmir valley for the four minutes we need to pass through. At a deeper level, it is that we will get there but the valley will be gone: blown to pieces by the violent uprising against the Indian government that broke out at the end of the 1980s and still claims five to twenty lives a day.

In all the time I lived as a newspaper correspondent in the Muslim world, I imagined a place in Asia where, cut off by mountains or some other barrier from the bullying of the Christian West and its allies, Islam could be as peaceable, hedonistic and humane as I felt it was meant to be. Kashmir seemed to me, on my visits, to be a paradise: not in any metaphysical meaning, but in the sense of the Persian word that the Greeks transliterated into paradise: a park or garden enclosed from the desert, planted and watered, a place for pleasure, conversation and love affairs; which, as the supreme achievement of Muslim domestic culture, became a notion of timeless delight. Paddling about my cedarwood boat on Dal Lake, or fishing the high streams, my mind immersed in water, I sensed that I was missing something: that the valley had been invaded and ruined times without number, and could not remain insulated from the revolutions of the Muslim world or the sibling hatreds of India and Pakistan. Ten years later, that is my capital anxiety.

A dash past 150 trucks, and we face the gaping tunnel. Fayaz Malik combs his hair and scrubs the mud off the sides of the car: it is as if the valley is his only theatre, and outside it he and his vehicle are invisible. The senior officer is taking his nap and does not thank me for waking him. Certain decisions, whether to flatter, infuriate or bribe the man, or appeal to the urgency and dignity of the international press, the historic importance of the state elections, and the pathos of a fat Kashmiri and a dirty Englishman, I leave to Fayaz and his better judgement; and if I have a business card, Fayaz has money.

The tunnel is two and three-quarter kilometres of darkness, diesel poison and cascading water. The light at the end of it is familiar. It is not just bright, as you'd expect among high mountains, but softened by the mild colours of vegetation, by stands of pine and yellow rice fields, willows and poplars and autumnal plane trees that burst on the shining vehicle. Tumbling and curving down the steep road, floating on Fayaz's happiness—for he is, at this moment, beyond doubt, the happiest man in Kashmir—I see in an instant what has brought people to the valley for four centuries: not the weather or the handsome people or the high mountains or the lakes, but a certain formal understanding between the Kashmiris and their habitation, which for want of a better word we call harmony, and which carries the promise of a general armistice with the natural world. And also at that moment, as I check off what is against what was, I am bewildered by novelty: not just the hillsides clear-cut of trees, or the shuttered bazaar in Anantnag and the soldiers and armed police everywhere, or the filthy lake and the cruddy hotels along the Boulevard with soldiers' underclothes flapping from their balconies, or the streets full of garbage and army checkpoints; but something about the way the Kashmiris move. The men hurry along with their heads bowed, evidently on some urgent business, though the bazaar and administration have been closed by a general strike. The women are muffled in their *burqas*, as if relieved to hide their faces (and hence their identities) behind a general, harmless and degraded femininity. They look as if the Indians have knocked the stuffing out of them.

Thousands have died in the eight years since the Kashmir uprising began. Official figures put the number of dead at 14,000. Journalists in the valley say 20,000. Many of the casualties were in the army and police, victims of terrorism. Many more were Kashmiris, victims of the counter-terror.

At Butt's, I am the only guest. In the generator light, I am shown the framed testimonials of presidents and ambassadors and the guest books, where the rhapsodies of tourists give way, abruptly in January 1990, to the hand-wringings of the Delhi correspondents; but, for the moment, and until the spring comes and diplomats and reporters and tourists return, they will have only me. Mr Butt is excited, not so much by my company or custom, but because I knew his father: used to sit with the old man on an iron bedstead under the eighteenth-century plane tree in the garden. Old Mr Butt, Hajji Mohammed, had houseboats built in the war for British army and Indian Civil Service officers and their families, and is revered in the valley for having banned Indians as guests. That is untrue and would appal the younger Butt, but it is what the Kashmiris want to believe, and so the houseboats on Dal Lake are as safe a place as anywhere in the valley, if a little quiet.

On the stern of the boat, in the twenty-watt light, I drink Indian whisky from a teapot. A full moon shivers in the lake. The silence is broken, every now and then, by a single or double gunshot, the muezzin hawking into the Hazratbal mosque public-address system, or the lake belching methane from its bed of shit and silt. There are lights on the other side: the villas of war profiteers. The green bloom on the lake surface is indescribably sickly. I fear the Kashmir I knew ten years ago has no counterpart in this utterly messed-up world; or that my memory was false, just another anxious and romantic fiction of the type the British loved to spin about places on the edges of their empire, and this is reality, so that I feel my self and nationality disintegrating in the teeming darkness. At three, I wake with a bang, which is a grenade launched or tossed at an army picket at Nishat Bagh.

Srinagar, the chief town in Kashmir with about half a million inhabitants, sits at the western end of the lake. It was always a place quite unlike any other. Old British guidebooks compare it with Venice—and the valley with the southern Tyrol—but to paddle through its canals at sundown between rotten wooden buildings and sagging houseboats aground in the filthy mud is to feel far from Italy. The mosques have corrugated-iron roofs and canopied minarets that might have been designed in Iran but fabricated in Tibet; while the commercial buildings and residencies, the banks and villas of the period when the British held power beyond the mountains, were obviously supplied from the Army & Navy Stores catalogue of about 1930. This phantasmagoric city, an unimaginable mixture of Isfahan, Lhasa, Sunningdale and the

Underworld, which seemed to me on earlier visits to be suspended for ever in its particularity, has altered out of recognition. No doubt all famous cities should be imagined in their ruin.

It is not that Srinagar has been destroyed by the fighting, as Beirut was in the 1970s and Kabul in the 1980s. There is no damage from heavy weapons. The rising or 'militancy', as the Indians call it, was fought with knives, pistols, Chinese and Russian automatic rifles supplied from Pakistan and the weapons bazaars of the Afghan border, grenades and the home-made fused bombs known in the subcontinent as improvised explosive devices. It was put down with clubs, money and standard-issue carbines. The Indian Air Force never deployed an armed helicopter, and the aeroplanes from Delhi come in low over the valley as if the Stinger missile had never been invented or deployed in Afghanistan. What makes Srinagar unrecognizable is its loss of function.

The cricket pitches, houseboats, temples, Mogul gardens, shawl- and papier-mâché shops that jolt past the window of the car stand idle or have been converted to military use. The Hindu Kashmiris, known as Pandits, have had their town houses taken over by the army, machine-guns peeping out of their sandbagged upper storeys; the Pandits took fright in 1990 and fled over the mountains to Jammu on the plains. The J & K Tourism Centre, where I used to collect my fishing permits, is now a series of dormitories for low-grade civil servants whose homes are no longer safe: doors open on scenes of resourceful domesticity. And there is nobody about. You would have thought, in the week before a historic election—the first in Kashmir since 1987—the town would be dizzy with electoral cavalcades, bristling with banners and loudspeakers, candidates and their thugs. The streets and bridges are quite empty but for army patrols and Indian reporters in collapsing Ambassadors, morosely looking for trouble. It is as if the uprising has killed the entire population; or rather has sent the people burrowing into their houses, to sit all day on the floor, smoking and eating too much and trying not to think. Only the houseboat wallahs are out: so sleek and fat on my earlier visits, they have shed their weight and confidence and hang about the ghats, unshaven, poor as rats; or squabble over two European hippies, so closed off in their morphine and daily economies that they have nodded out a civil war.

Evidently, in the years since 1990, the Kashmiri Muslims and the Indian government conspired to abolish the complexities of Kashmiri civilization. The world I inhabited has vanished: the state government and the political class, the rule of law, almost all the 95,000 Hindu inhabitants of the valley, alcohol, cinemas, cricket matches, picnics by moonlight in the saffron fields, schools, universities, an independent press, tourists and—my chief problem—banks. In this reduction of civilian reality, the sights of Kashmir—the things worth seeing, in guidebook language—are redefined: not the filthy lakes and Mogul gardens with their busted fountains, or the storied triumphs of Kashmiri agriculture, handicrafts and cookery, but two entities that confront each other without intermediary: the mosque and the army camp.

The next day was Friday, the Muslim sabbath, so I attended the mosque.

A mile from Butt's, along the lake road into town, is the village of Hazratbal. Its famous mosque looks better from the houseboat than from its sandbagged courtyard. It was built, in standard white mosque marble, by the former chief minister, Sheikh Abdullah, whose tomb sits next door to Butt's, guarded by a platoon of armed police. It houses the most precious object in the valley: a quartz vial five inches long, opaque on one side and sealed at the base with silver, and in it a single strand of hair, which is known in Persian—the Latin of Kashmir—as the *Moe-e Muqaddas*, 'the Sacred Lock'. The hair is reliably reported to be from the Prophet Mohammed, and to have made its way from Medina to Hazratbal by way of Cochin 300 years ago or more.

This object attracts historical events as a magnet attracts iron filings; not because superstitious Islam is the only foundation of the Kashmiri personality, but because it can be made so. On 26 December 1963 the relic vanished, Srinagar dissolved in rioting, and the governments of India and Pakistan woke to the perils and possibilities of Muslim sensitivities in the valley. B. N. Mullik, the Indian intelligence officer who restored the relic to the shrine, called on Nehru on 9 February 1964 at his house at Teen Murti and found him in a white shawl, seated under a tree. When he heard that the relic had been found, Nehru said: 'God bless you,

Mullik, you have saved Kashmir for us.' In the autumn of 1993, a group of young men commandeered the mosque, hoping, I was told, to provoke the Indian army into storming it. In that they were unsuccessful—the Indian high command had learned something from the army's invasion of the Golden Temple in Amritsar nine years before—but even I could see that if anything was going to happen in Kashmir in the days before the election, it would be here at Hazratbal.

Waiting in the courtyard, while the worshippers scampered towards the gate, were frisked, slid off their shoes, turned west, spread their rugs and bent to their prayers, I was startled by the good nature of the police around me. Then a word burst from the mosque public address: *azadi*. It dissolved in a howl of sound, and as the police ran to the gate, their carbines jingling on their hips, it seemed to me the word had been ripped from the body of the speaker and still travelled through the air, over the lake, to beat itself against the mountain wall, over and over again. Moments later a man called Javed Mir, famous in Kashmir, was dragged past me in the courtyard by six plain-clothes coppers, his slippers catching on the stones. Javed's face had the self-absorption of a man who has been in jail a lot and is going back there, but the rest was comedy; and it occurred to me that when you want to destroy a people's will you make them and their beliefs, in this case *azadi*, comical.

Azadi is difficult to define. It is a Persian word, which has a peculiarly elegant calligraphic shape and starts off meaning freedom or leisure and then, in the nineteenth century, independence. For Javed and his friends of the Jammu and Kashmir Liberation Front, the JKLF, it means an independent state covering not just the valley but the entire princely state of Jammu and Kashmir which was ceded by its maharaja to India in 1947. It means the euphoria of 1989 and 1990, when entrenched regimes all over eastern Europe were collapsing on television every night, and when it seemed that a few petrol bombs, kidnappings and assassinations would send the Indians scampering back to Delhi. To the Indian armed forces and bureaucracy and all my Indian friends, it means the end of India as a democratic and secular commonwealth; or rather its disintegration into little ethnic or religious statelets. *Azadi* is therefore a word of tremendous power, even before it is amplified by the mosque loudspeaker.

Javed was one of a group of four young men, known as the HAJI Group from their English initials, who took to violence at the close of the 1980s. Their leader, Ishfaq Wani, was killed by the Border Security Force on 30 March 1990. There are two photographs in his family house in Maharaja Bazaar, both taken when he was on the run. The first shows a young man, burly for a Kashmiri, in a thick shawl, laughing, while he dips his right hand into something outside the picture, presumably a dish of rice. The second was taken on the morning of his death, and shows an unshaven man in a dirty jumper with a stupid, trusting look in his eyes. I am told that he is disguised as an electrician.

Ishfaq's father, Abdul Majeed Wani, a retired engineer, talked to me for hours in a debauch of tobacco in his house in Maharaja Bazaar. Mr Wani speaks slow and eloquent English, polished not so much by interviews as by his own interrogations. He said: 'I had taken Ishfaq on a tour of India, to show him that it was a composite society, but wherever he went he felt that Muslims were second-class citizens, and my persuasion was unsuccessful. I hoped that he might become engaged to a nice girl—for he was a handsome boy, strong, and a good athlete—and settle down and forget all these things, but it was not to be. The rigging of the 1987 election convinced my son and his friends that there was no alternative to armed struggle, which they felt was the only way for Kashmiris to recover their right of an honourable and peaceful existence in an independent state. They were convinced that elections and personal politics were no longer a solution. They knew it was impossible to fight India. They were doubly sure of the might of the Indian Republic and their own meagre resources, but they were also sure their sacrifices would revive the dead Kashmiri issue in international forums. I am proud that their sacrifices were not wholly in vain.'

He said that for four centuries, the Kashmiris had been under some form of oppression, were submissive, non-existent creatures. Between 1947 and 1987, armed groups had formed but never managed to operate. Ishfaq and his friends were more persistent.

On 11 February 1988 they exploded seven petrol bombs in Lal Chowk and burnt three official jeeps. All four went into hiding, but they were, in Mr Wani's words, 'the talk of the town'. In May, Ishfaq crossed to Pakistan. On the night of 31 July they advertised their return with three bombings. There was nothing very glorious about their targets then or later—four off-duty air-force officers at the bus stop in Rawanpura, a senior Hindu journalist at All India Radio, a woman doctor kidnapped outside the hospital at Maharaja Bazaar, Intelligence Bureau officers attached to local police stations—but by the following year, the state police were utterly demoralized. 'I saw Ishfaq that year, and he was very confident. He said: "We have exposed Indian power. Total control of the valley now rests with me." By September, the local administration was paralysed. All over the valley, girls and women were singing songs in praise of the boys.'

Ishfaq is buried at a place downtown called the Idgah, a wide expanse of waste ground where people gather to sacrifice their sheep or goats on the main Muslim holiday each year and which Fayaz the driver is keen to show me. The Garden of the Kashmiri Martyrs, as it is known, is a raised cemetery, planted with dwarf cypresses, gladioli, irises and roses. There are about 400 graves, with headstones to record the name, place of residence, educational achievements and place of death of the martyr or martyress. Around are the rusting pipes of a sewage scheme that never got built. The cemetery is in bad taste, not because it does not convey genuine emotion—it does—but because the language it employs is second-hand, unKashmiri: it is as if, in searching for something to express their grief, the Kashmiri Muslims could find nothing nearer than Tehran. A liberation movement gone hopelessly awry is relabelled as a history of religious persecution. In the other towns and large villages, the cemetery repeats itself on a more modest scale.

In these graves, you can read the story of the Kashmiri uprising in a quarter of an hour. Ishfaq's headstone, in the first row, is the only civilian to carry an honorific: His Excellency Ishfaq Majid Wani Sahel. Walking down the paths, you can see the JKLF unravel, and the struggle pass into the hands of groups controlled by Pakistan and then the desperadoes of Hazratbal,

69

who were given safe conduct from the mosque and quietly killed by the Indian military last spring. There are many women and children, evidence of the ham-fistedness of the Indian response. And all around you, the Muslim middle class is being thinned out, individual by individual: surgeons, lawyers, journalists. What begins as a call to arms passes through a fantasy of victory and ends in inconsolable defeat.

I called on the Indian military the next day. I was late for my appointment, but escorts were still waiting for me at every cross-roads in the barracks. As I was shown into his office, a man I'll call Colonel Ravi was seated across a neat desk, talking gently, like a father, to a Kashmiri teenage boy. I was distracted by an operations map, which had not been completely curtained off, and when I looked back from it, the boy had vanished; yet something in the way he'd occupied the space in the tiny room, how he'd tried to make himself invisible, suggested to me he'd been hard used at one time. Ravi later said, as a matter of fact, that the boy had been tortured—he used the passive voice—and provided low-grade intelligence of anecdotal character. The boy's ghostly figure haunted the room, proxy for all the thousands of Kashmiri boys beaten and killed in custody by the Indian armed forces since 1990. Colonel Ravi said: 'I would say there are some 2,200 militants still active, of which about a thousand are foreigners of some sort or other, Afghans, Sudanese and so on. Bear in mind these fellows aren't the LTTE [Tamil Tigers in northern Sri Lanka] who read the army manual, and because soldiers are trained to take cover behind a tree or culvert when fired on, put the improvised explosive device in there. I have served in the Nagaland, Mizoram and Punjab; and our experience is that these militancies last about ten years before they exhaust themselves, so this problem still has a year or two to run before the Kashmiris are tired out. The particular problem is the border with Pakistan. It is difficult terrain and has to be manned, it can't be fenced or controlled electronically. We can't totally seal it off against infiltration.'

Then he began to speak of his life and work, of the wife he never saw and the children who'd grown up without him, and how,

in the Mizo Hills, the people walked singing to their fields at dawn
and returned singing at dusk. He seemed to me to have given his
life to his country, or to an idea of it; and though he, like so many
others, might have looted timber from Kashmir and shipped it
down for a house in Manali or Dehra Dun, I doubt that he did.
He faced retirement and oblivion, and a pension that wouldn't pay
a Bombay stockbroker's sweeper, not in anger but with regret. I
felt an affinity with him that arose not from his cravat or
Camberley slang, but from the mixture of melancholy and
ruthlessness that is the lasting British bequest to its chief Asian
legatees, the Indian and Pakistani armed forces. I sensed that he
did not want to be remembered only for that freezing morning in
early January 1993, when his men burnt the bazaar in Sopore and
killed fifty-four shopkeepers and their families, or for that
phantom boy. He said: 'These people need justice. If their
government gives them justice, they will drop their guns at its feet.'

But what or rather where is justice? In the ensuing days, I had
many conversations that all seemed to begin with the word
'actually' and proceed to some combination of the words 'origin',
'roots', 'problem' or 'conflict'. That 'actually', which has such a
bourgeois ring in the English of the United Kingdom, was placed
there to show that what follows would disentangle from the chaos
of historical appearances a true narrative of Kashmiri history.
Actually, of course, it was nothing of the sort, but yet another
partisan account, the third or fourth since breakfast. For in
Kashmir, there is no fact: a Hindu government official, a Sikh army
officer and a Muslim militant in his downtown safe house will each
give an account of the past that arises in his community's share of it
and overlaps those of the others only in the common sensation of
grievance, which keeps them warm like the braziers they carry
under their shawls in the cold of January. As to those roots and
origins, on a bad day they can be geological. Qazi Ahadullah Khan,
of the Jamiat-i Islami, which seeks union with Pakistan, reminded
me that all the rivers of Kashmir flow westwards to that country.
Noor ul-Hassan, a former forester now active for human rights,
ranged over all recorded history to show that the valley had never
been ruled by Hindus from Delhi. On better days, those roots go
down only as far back as 1846, when the British sold the present

state of Jammu and Kashmir, plus some other pieces now occupied by the Pakistanis or the Chinese, to a Hindu soldier called Gulab Singh for £750,000 down, a horse, twelve goats and six pairs of shawls in tribute each year. That a Muslim people had been sold to a Hindu ruler was not at the time considered reprehensible, though the British came, for reasons of strategy and even conscience, to regret it. The British mostly left the valley to be maladministered by its maharajas, content with sport and houseboat honeymoons—non-Kashmiris weren't permitted to own land or houses in the valley—and with destroying the shawl trade through cheap Glasgow imitations.

After a while, I began to insist to my tutors that we join the story in 1947, when British authority ended. The principle accepted by the British for the princely states was that each ruler must accede to one or other of the heirs of the Raj, India or Pakistan: any sort of third way—independence, for example—was not on offer from Mountbatten, the Congress or the Muslim League. Gulab's great-grandson, Maharaja Sir Hari Singh, dithered. According to his son, Karan Singh, a sometime Congress MP now living in New Delhi, the maharaja had no taste for either of the new dominions, just wanted to pursue his pleasant existence, migrating between palaces at Jammu and Srinagar, lounging by his swimming pool, or shooting the ducks flying in at sundown on Lake Hokarsar, a loader at each shoulder, his son clicking the gold counter as each bird fell. An invasion by Pakistani irregulars on 22 October put an end to all that; the Fourth Jammu and Kashmir Infantry at Baramulla mutinied, opening the way to Srinagar; and electric power to the city was cut. The new Indian government offered military aid, but only if the kingdom joined the Union. The Instrument of Accession was signed and delivered on 26 October, and in the early hours of the next morning two Indian infantry battalions were airlifted to Srinagar. One can spend so long in 1947 that, stepping outside, you see the place transformed in the autumnal air, and think to hear the Dakotas rumbling overhead—with just twenty men in each—and see the maharaja's motorcade, he in the first car, driving, with his Russian jeweller, Victor Rosenthal, beside him, the ladies in several cars behind, winding its bumpy way up over the Banihal Pass—the tunnel wasn't yet built—towards safety and oblivion. According to Karan Singh, the maharaja was silent all the forty-eight-hour journey till, arriving at the palace at Jammu, and turning to Rosenthal, he said: 'We have lost Kashmir.'

The Indian army checked the Pakistani invasion, but could not regain the lost territory and agreed a ceasefire in January 1949. The issue was tossed into the lap of the United Nations, where it has lain ever since. The ceasefire lines were eventually stabilized, if not as frontiers at least as so-called Lines of Control. Though the accession was probably legal, Nehru—who was proud of his family's Kashmiri origins and had the softest of spots for the valley—stood by the British principle that there should be a referendum. That referendum has never been held, not least because the Pakistanis have never withdrawn from the territory they call Azad Kashmir and the territories of Baltistan, Hunza and Gilgit which have long since been absorbed into Pakistan. It is not that the valley Kashmiris would inevitably accede to Pakistan in a plebiscite, and the Ladakhis and Jammu Hindus certainly wouldn't: the plebiscite is merely the opening through which Pakistani diplomats and Kashmiri separatists, gathered in an unwieldy coalition called the Hurriyat Conference, can torment India's insecurity and bad conscience.

Power in the valley devolved on the maharaja's prime minister, Sheikh Mohammed Abdullah, who sent the maharaja into exile in 1949 and transferred without compensation the lands of Hindu landlords to their Muslim tenants; but there was no communal violence in 1947, and relations between the Kashmiri Muslims, who have a notion of caste and don't eat beef, and the Hindu Pandits were often friendly. Sheikh Abdullah promoted the notion of *kashmiriyat*: a common Kashmiri identity that arose in the place and its history and transcended allegiances of religion. The valley remained a backward place, without adequate electricity or any light industry or even the routine public works of British India, such as sewerage or railroads; but there was none of the demoralizing poverty of the Indian cities and countryside, for the land is very good, and the people owned it. When I first visited Srinagar in 1978, it looked pretty much as it does in the great map shawl in the Victoria and Albert Museum, embroidered

The Dal Lake,
1992,
photographed
by Tom Pilston

James Buchan

in the 1870s. Dal Lake was, but for a few of the maharaja's art deco whimsies, a seventeenth-century landscape.

Sheikh Abdullah himself appeared to me then as a living monument, an enduring symbol of Kashmiri particularity and bloody-mindedness, as immovable as his wedding-cake mosque at Hazratbal; but, in reality, he spent most of his political career in jail or exile. In his dealings with Nehru and the Congress, Sheikh Abdullah tried to ensure that Indian authority was restricted to the areas mentioned in the Instrument of Accession—that is, defence, foreign affairs and finance and communications—and enshrined in a notorious article in the Indian Constitution, Article 370. But in 1953, he was removed from power and was not restored until 1975. At his death in 1982, his son, Farooq Abdullah, who had trained as a doctor in London and married an Irish nurse, was installed, but ousted by the Indian government in 1984; restored in an election in 1987 that even Indian government officials accept was rigged; removed again with the collapse of public order in 1990; and was now seeking a third term in an election policed, as far as I could estimate, by a quarter of a million Indian soldiers, paramilitaries and armed police.

Thus for the Kashmiri Muslims, Jammu and Kashmir, the only state in the Indian Union where Muslims are the majority, has been cheated by successive Indian administrations of the self-determination promised by the founders and the Constitution. As the young prayer leader of the cathedral mosque in Srinagar, Mirvaiz Omar Farooq, put it to me: 'The Kashmiris felt threatened by India in their very identity. The common Kashmiri saw himself as an individual who had no identity.' *Azadi*, with its baffling mixture of religiosity, privilege and historical hair-splitting, is really just the Persian for self.

The senior officials of the Indian administration, when they are in Srinagar, live and work in fortified, guarded cottages in the district known officially as Gupkar but which the Kashmiris call the Leper Colony. These are clever and even heroic men but they suffer badly from cabin fever, and as I found in the next week, evenings on Gupkar Road can end messily. You can watch the official policy take shape before your eyes, and then disintegrate.

Azadi, say these Indian officials, is out of the question for all sorts of reasons. The Ladakhis and Jammu Hindus will no longer accept domination from the Muslims of the valley; and an independent Kashmir run by the Muslims would be bound to gravitate towards Pakistan. Eventually, India might come into conflict with China, and India cannot tolerate a disaffected valley across its supply line to Ladakh and the Chinese border. The very beauty of Kashmir is just an aspect of its backwardness, the baleful legacy of Article 370. Once integrated with mainstream India, the valley will enjoy a share of India's prosperity. The Kashmiris are already unique in an Indian context, and there's no reason to make them more so. The Indian government will restore the limited autonomy promised by Nehru and the Constitution, and deluge the valley in money. The lakes will be cleaned up somehow, and the hillsides replanted. The tourists and the Bombay film actresses, maybe even some Pandits, will return.

As the evening proceeds, and more beer is drunk, these professional statements take on emotion, become desperate or threatening: the Kashmiris are liars and cowards, even you British fellows thought so, anyway the world doesn't care, look at the fate of the British and American tourists kidnapped in 1995, the Paks are whipped, done for, and if Kashmir gets *azadi* you can kiss goodbye to the 130 million Muslims who live in the rest of India.

In truth, the government of India hasn't a policy for Kashmir, except that which was tried with success in Punjab: force on the ground shielded by ferocious diplomacy overseas, and, if that worked, a state election on however small a franchise. As it was put to me with admirable candour in Gupkar Road: the central government in Delhi must withdraw, with its unpopularity and the indiscipline of certain of its armed forces, behind a state government, and 'shoot from somebody else's shoulder'.

Kashmiri elections have never done Indian democracy proud, and those held in 1996 were unlikely to be exceptions. Since the Kashmiris of the valley weren't going to vote for the all-India parties, there was but one choice, Dr Farooq Abdullah's National Conference, and only one platform: a return to the limited autonomy within Article 370 such as his father had enjoyed up to

1953; which would ultimately, as Mohammed Shafi Uri of the National Conference explained, 'pave the way to a dialogue between India and Pakistan so they can coexist peacefully'. The *azadi* organizations gathered in the All Parties Hurriyat (or Freedom) Conference, boycotted the election and called general strikes, while the armed groups threatened (and later carried out) reprisals against people voting. To conduct an election in such conditions would be a triumph: it would install a workable government under Dr Farooq, drive the Hurriyat into the wilderness, humiliate the militants and undermine Pakistan, all in one go. As formulated to me in Gupkar Road, the plan seemed elegance itself.

In New Delhi, on my way to Kashmir, I'd made the error of calling on some foreign diplomats who had just observed, under military escort, the first two of four phases in these elections; and had said, all in all, this being India and all that, they had been quite free and fair; so I spent 21 September 1996 in a state of unnecessary surprise. By the time I arrived in Khana Pora village in Budgam district at seven a.m., an army unit in full battle gear was already encamped, and all the village men, but for one old fellow in a Persian cap, were gone. The village women, shrieking with excitement and rage, said the army had arrived at six a.m., called the men out of their houses by loudspeaker, and sent them down to the polling station. They had threatened, the women said, to cut off any hand that didn't display the indelible mark painted by Indian polling officers on the index finger. (I heard that charge often in the course of the day, but never saw such an amputation.) Later, in the Khwaja Bazaar district of Srinagar, a BSF sergeant, carrying a side arm, bawled at a group of men: 'Come to the Motherland polling booth. There is nothing to fear. The Motherland will protect you. Now come on, move along. Move!'

Among scores of Kashmiris I met that day, only two elderly men said they voted willingly. Yet once corralled into the polling stations, as far as I could see over the battered corrugated cardboard that shielded the booth, even the young men and women did vote, placing their indelible stamp against the symbol of the plough adopted by Sheikh Abdullah after his land reform. It seemed to me that the Kashmiri Muslims had squared the circle: that knowing the government of India wanted their votes, and the

Hurriyat and militants their hearts, they had satisfied both, by voting unwillingly. The exception was the Old City of Srinagar, the heart of the *azadi* movement. The streets were deserted but for army and police patrols, and the occasional sudden protest, dispersed with lathis and tear gas fired straight at the head. At one polling station, No. 47 by the Shah Hamadan mosque, just two votes had been recorded by late afternoon. Outside, a National Conference candidate and his personal security officer stood miserably by their curtained white Ambassador; and I saw where those two votes had come from. That evening, at the J & K Tourism Centre, the chief secretary held a press conference. He announced that the turnout in that Srinagar constituency had been twenty-five per cent, including postal votes—a blatant fantasy.

At that moment the process began to fall into place: smug chief secretary, fawning reporters, blind diplomats, field kitchens, convoys, bullying troops. I understood the sheer might of the Indian state. I saw that India, with its great population and almost limitless economic potential, and hardened by twenty years of fighting insurgencies such as these, would be a great power in the world, or was already; and that India's diplomatic failures— in Kashmir, for example—were not errors but the inevitable clumsiness of a state coming into its strength. And yet that transformation was far from complete. In Demina, on the outskirts of Srinagar, I photographed a BSF corporal corralling people towards the polling booth. Seeing the camera, a policeman threw his bamboo cane at the taxi. That futile and childlike gesture seemed to sum up the Indian frustration. I now saw why my Indian friends—once junior officers in Indian missions overseas and now running whole departments in India's foreign ministry—were forever changing the subject from Kashmir. K. B. Jandial, the spokesman of the Indian administration in Srinagar, patiently explained that state elections were rough affairs, and that in other Indian states you could have thirty dead by sundown. That day in Kashmir there were a hundred injured but just one fatality. When I protested that in those states the coercion came from the party wallahs, not the uniformed servants of the Indian Union, he looked at me with contempt, as if to say: Look who's just walked in, another British know-it-all.

What those attitudes had in common was a profound lack of conviction and a certain embarrassment: that India isn't Egypt or Iraq or a chaotic and insecure state such as Pakistan, but a great democracy, and what was done in Kashmir on 21 September 1996 had not added lustre to that democracy.

Indian officials like to talk of the valley as 'alienated' from Indian rule, a euphemism that does not begin to describe the mental condition of the Kashmiris. They are in shock. They simply cannot believe that between 14,000 and 20,000 people have died just to return the valley to the situation that existed before 1990: to Farooq Abdullah and the professional politicians of the National Conference. They cannot understand why the world has ignored them. They have also lost their illusions about Pakistan. They have seen that Pakistan dare not provoke an open conflict with its neighbour, which it will certainly lose; and that is why the militants have had no heavy weapons or the training to use them. I remember a young Muslim woman who was seated on the floor so still and silent that I thought she didn't understand English, suddenly speaking, crystal clear: 'Pakistan can go to hell.'

At the same time, Kashmiris nurse a hatred of India which is hard to exaggerate. What was evident in the 1970s and 1980s as mere resentment has been envenomed by the brutalities of the early 1990s, administrative corruption and the arrogance of the military in the conduct of the elections. It is evident not so much in the villages as among those educated Kashmiri Muslims who have thrown in their lot with India: bank managers, senior officers of the police with nothing to do but shuffle papers, a couple of hundred thousand government employees. They have lost whatever faith they had in Indian institutions—the bicameral legislature, the Supreme Court, the election and human rights commissions, the Central Bureau of Investigation—and see only high-caste Hindus bent on turning them into good Indians at any price. A surgeon at one of the Srinagar hospitals, having taken me round the wards, professional to his fingertips, beckoned me to the end of a corridor and, as he began to talk of the Indian administration and his own career under it, he lost all self-control, seemed suddenly no longer a skilful and conscientious doctor, but a prisoner or a mistreated pet.

Simply to govern, Dr Farooq will have to use language hostile to New Delhi, just as his father did, which will no doubt provoke the Indian government to remove him, as it did his father.

Yet something has changed; maybe all those people—Kashmiri, Indian and European—have not died without effect. For there is a solution which was first suggested to me by my driver, Fayaz Malik. He was by now quite desperate. I still had no rupees to pay him. We spoke only of my possessions, or rather the replacement value of my camera, tape recorder, binoculars and penknife, my house and car in London, and whether I'd married for love, as he had, or as some men do, for property. In other words, we talked money.

One foggy night in the government lines in Srinagar the idea took fuller shape when I talked to the most hated category of Kashmiri, the men known in the valley as renegades and in mainstream India as 'friendlies'.

In the early 1990s, the Indian military was an army of occupation, with very little knowledge of its adversary. Hampered by poor intelligence, the military had but one tactic, which was to cordon off whole villages or quarters of Srinagar and search the houses one by one, which embittered the population and usually failed to net the militants. But by the end of 1994, a group known as the Hezbul Mujahedin, well armed from Pakistan, had become the dominant militia in the valley and was seeking to bring all militant activity, including extortion and other gangsterism, under its control. There were clashes with other groups and the Indian army suddenly found itself in demand for protection or money. Over the next twelve months, whole militias defected, bringing large areas of the valley and the suburbs of Srinagar under army control. 'They turned the tide for us,' said an Indian intelligence officer, not without distaste.

Some of the renegades had decided, however implausibly, that they should stand as candidates in the elections; and that the army would manipulate the result to see them elected: pure fantasy, as it turned out. The army had put them up in one of the handsome government guest houses on Church Lane, closed off by three roadblocks: for fighting men, they seemed to be very well guarded.

In the high, verandaed rooms, they lolled on beds, reading film magazines while a romantic drama whinnied on the television. Whisky appeared from a cupboard. When I asked a young man in jeans why he'd joined the uprising, he lowered his eyes. 'Jihad,' he said, religious duty, and giggled. I asked him why he'd come over to the government side, and he looked at me startled, as if to say: That's an interesting question, I never really thought about it. Eventually, he mumbled: 'India is a powerful country.'

Another man expected to win his seat easily. I asked if he'd visited his constituency, and he said he hadn't; but the people would vote as his men told them. You see, he said, the Indian Army will need allies in the assembly, to keep the human-rights issues off the boil. After a while, the naive hopes and electronic trinkets of these men began to upset me; and I didn't want to be shot by an enthusiastic sepoy in the fog. So I took my leave. But I saw at last what had eluded me for so long: that the two basic elements of Indian political life—caste and community—had been joined by a third that could buy out these two old allegiances: money.

If that is so, both the Kashmiri uprising and its defeat were the swansong of the old India: the India of Nehru and the old Congress party, an India that strove, however unsuccessfully, for 'secularism', legality and decency. Few believe in it any more except—and this is the irony of India and its history—the officer corps and Intelligence Bureau and Colonel Ravi. In the convulsion of the 1947 order, the only block to communal disintegration is the neutral aspiration to money; and the Indian subcontinent will now pass through that revolution of culture that convulsed England in the seventeenth century, France and North America in the eighteenth, Japan and Germany in the nineteenth, Russia in the twentieth. In this new world, the old allegiances, because they will not sit on the money scale, are revealed as barbarism or folklore, and all problems become merely technical hindrances to be absolved by the application of money. Muslim militancy is simply a shortage of employment opportunities among young males. The exiled Pandits will open new businesses in mainstream India and those that don't, that sit in baking one-roomed tenements in Nagrota camp on the outskirts of Jammu, dreaming of cool weather and their fields, well, perhaps they too can share in this new money *kashmiriyat*.

And now there is nothing for me to do, except go to the bank, which will open for two hours today: discharge my debts to Fayaz and Mr Butt, distribute some presents, embrace Fayaz and leave for the airport; or rather, since the Jammu & Kashmir Bank in Rajbagh will not be open for another hour, climb, as Victorian guidebooks recommend, the extinct volcano in Srinagar known, depending on whether you are Muslim or Hindu, as Takht-e Suleiman or Shankaracharya Hill, for its prospect of the valley.

So, leaving Fayaz to work on the starter motor, I walk up two hundred steps to a granite temple guarded by a company of armed police. From its rampart, I can see the Jhelum river coiling its way between the wooden buildings, under the nine bridges, past the famous mosques of Shah Hamadan and the Jama Masjid and the fort of Hari Parbat. I feel as Bernal Diaz must have felt, as he looked down on the vale of Mexico in 1519, and saw an amphibious civilization ripe for the bone yard.

In the smoke from the lunch fires and the fog of diesel from the Boulevard, the distant landscape is transformed. This famous valley has lost its history: it is no longer the accretion of generations of Kashmiri sweat and genius, *azadi* made actual in the sensuous world, but 3,000 million rupees in future annual expenditure by Indian and foreign tourists, and high-cropping cherries and apples that have no taste, but can be transported 1,500 miles south to Bangalore. Dal Lake, though it has shrunk to half the size of when I first saw it, may just be a problem of engineering. Now that public order is more or less restored, the catchment slopes can be replanted and a sewage works built, the whole to cost five billion rupees in the money of 1987: a sum which that minor actor in this drama, the British government, has offered with conditions and contractors. The future of Kashmir is below me: Dr Farooq's beloved golf course and the international convention centre built by the government on land reclaimed from the lake. And the past is above me, the faint echo of that word I heard three weeks ago at the Hazratbal mosque, rising and rising, till it hides itself, for a while or for ever, in the indifferent snows. □

Rabindranath Tagore
the myriad-minded man

Krishna Dutta
& Andrew
Robinson

"A fascinating book about a fascinating man, a work that addresses the profound conflict between eastern spirituality and western rationality."
ILYA PRIGOGINE,
NOBEL LAUREATE

"This seems to exemplify a sort of biography little dared any more; an enquiry into the spirit and mind of a man, whom the authors trust and admire and do not presume to overinterpret."
INDEPENDENT
ON SUNDAY

"An excellent book... as an elegantly argued and subtly shaded portrait, it will be difficult to supersede."
LITERARY REVIEW

"The entire book was a revelation to me... it brings out very clearly that Tagore was intellectually more perceptive than Gandhi."
SUBRAHMANYAN
CHANDRASEKHAR,
NOBEL LAUREATE
IN PHYSICS

BLOOMSBURY
paperbacks

ANITA DESAI
FIVE HOURS TO SIMLA

ANITA DESAI's books include *Cry, The Peacock*; *Fire on the Mountain*; the children's story *The Village by the Sea*; *Journey to Ithaca*, *Baumgartner's Bombay;* and *In Custody*, which was filmed by Merchant-Ivory. She teaches in the department of Writing and Humanistic Studies at Massachusetts Institute of Technology and lives in Cambridge, Mass.

Then, miraculously, out of the pelt of yellow fur that was the dust growing across the great northern Indian plain, a wavering grey line emerged. It might have been a cloud bank looming, but it was not—the sun blazed, the earth shrivelled, the heat burnt away every trace of spring's beneficence. Yet the grey darkened, turned bluish, took on substance.

'Look—mountains!'

'Where?'

'I can't see any mountains.'

'Are you blind? Look, look up—not down, fool!'

A scuffle broke out between the boys on the sticky grime of the Rexine-covered front seat. It was quietened by a tap on their heads from their mother in the back. 'Yes, yes, mountains. The Himalayas. We'll be there soon.'

'Huh.' A sceptical grunt from the driver of the tired, dust-buried grey Ambassador car. 'At least five more hours to Simla.' He ran his hand over the back of his neck where all the dirt of the road seemed to have found its way under the wilting cotton collar.

'Sim-la! Sim-la!' the boys set up a chant, their knees bouncing up and down in unison.

Smack, the driver's left hand landed on the closest pair, bringing out an instant stain of red and sudden, sullen silence.

'Be quiet!' the mother hissed from the back unnecessarily.

The Ambassador gave a sudden lurch, throwing everyone forwards. The baby, whose mouth had been glued to the teat of a bottle like a fly to syrup, came unstuck and wailed with indignation. Even their mother let out a small involuntary cry. Her daughter, who had been asleep on the back seat, her legs across her mother's lap, now stirred.

'Accident!' howled the small boy who had been smacked, triumphantly.

But it was not. His father had stopped just short of the bicycle rickshaw ahead, which had just avoided running into the bullock cart carrying farmers' families to market. A bus, loaded with baggage and spilling over with passengers, had also ground to a halt with a shrieking of brakes. Ahead of it was a truck, wrapped and folded in canvas sheets that blocked all else from sight. The mountains had disappeared and so had the road.

After the first cacophony of screeching brakes and grinding gears, there followed the comparatively static hum of engines, and drivers waited in exasperation for the next lurch forwards. For the moment there was a lull, curious on that highway. Then the waiting very quickly began to fray at the edges. The sun was beating on the metal of the vehicles, and the road lay flattened across the parched plain, with no trees to screen it from the sun. First one car horn began to honk, then a bicycle rickshaw began to clang its bell, then a truck blared its musical horn, and then the lesser ones began to go pom-pom, pom-pom almost in harmony, and suddenly, out of the centre of all that noise, a long, piercing wail emerged.

The two boys, the girl, the baby, all sat up, shocked. More so when they saw what their father was doing. Clenching the wheel with both hands, his head was lowered on to it, and the blare of the horn seemed to issue out of his fury.

The mother exclaimed.

The father raised his head and banged on the wheel, struck it. 'How will we get to Simla before dark?' he howled.

The mother exclaimed again, shocked. 'But we'll be moving again in a minute.'

As if to contradict her, the driver of the truck stalled at the top of the line, swung himself out of the cabin into the road. He'd turned off his engine and stood in the deeply rutted dust, fumbling in his shirt pocket for cigarettes.

Other drivers got out of and down from their vehicles: the bullock-cart driver lowered himself from the creaking cart; the bicycle-rickshaw driver descended; the bus driver got out and stalked, in his sweat-drenched khakis, towards the truck driver standing at the head of the line; and they all demanded, 'What's going on? Breakdown?'

The truck driver watched them approach but was lighting his cigarette and didn't answer. Then he waved an arm—his movements were leisurely, elegant, quite unlike what his driving had been—and said, 'Stone throw. Somebody threw a stone. Hit windshield. Cracked it.'

The father in the Ambassador had also joined them in the road. Hands on his hips, he demanded, 'So?'

'So?' said the truck driver, narrowing his eyes. They were grey in a tanned face, heavily outlined and elongated with kohl, and his hair was tied up in a bandanna with a long loose end that dangled upon his shoulder. 'So we won't be moving again till the person who did it is caught, and a *faisla* is made—a settlement.'

Immediately a babble broke out. All the drivers flung out their hands and arms in angry, demanding gestures, their voices rose in questioning, in cajoling, in argument. The truck driver stood looking at them, watching them, his face inscrutable. Now and then he lifted the cigarette to his mouth and drew a deep puff. Then abruptly he swung around, clambered back into the cabin of his truck and started the engine with a roar at which the others fell back, their attitudes slackening in relief, but then he wheeled the truck around and parked it squarely across the highway so no traffic could get past in either direction. The highway at that point had narrowed to a small culvert across a dry stream-bed full of stones. Now he clambered up the bank of the culvert and sat down, his legs wide apart in their loose and not too clean pyjamas, regarding the traffic piling up in both directions as though he was watching sheep filing into a pen.

The knot of drivers in the road began to grow, joined by many of the passengers demanding to know the cause of this impasse.

'Dadd-ee! Dadd-ee!' the small boys yelled, hanging out of the door their father had left open and all but falling out into the dust. 'What's happened, Dadd-ee?'

'Shut the door!' their mother ordered sharply but too late. A yellow pye-dog came crawling out of the shallow ditch that ran alongside the road and, spying an open door, came slinking up to it, thin, hairless tail between its legs, eyes showing their whites, hoping for bread but quite prepared for a blow instead.

The boys drew back on seeing its exploring snout, its teeth bared ready for a taste of bread. 'Mad dog!' shouted one. 'Mad dog!' bellowed the other.

'Shh!' hissed their mother.

Since no one in the car dared drive away a creature so dangerous, someone else did. A stone struck its ribs, and with a yelp it ducked under the car to hide, but already the next beggar was at the door, throwing himself in with much the same mixture of leering enquiry and cringing readiness to withdraw. 'Bread,' he whined, stretching out a bandaged hand. 'Paisa, paisa. Mother, mother,' he pleaded, seeing the mother cower in her seat with the baby. The children cowered too.

They knew that if they remained thus for long enough and made no move towards purse or coin, he would leave: he couldn't afford to waste too much time on them when there were so many potential donors lined up so conveniently along the highway. The mother stared glassily ahead through the windscreen at the heat beating off the metal bonnet. The children could not tear their eyes away from the beggar—his sores, his bandages, his crippled leg, the flies gathering . . .

When he moved on, the mother raised a corner of her sari to her mouth and nose. From behind it she hissed: 'Shut-the-door!'

Unsticking their damp legs from the moist, adhesive seat, the boys scrambled to do so. As they leaned out to grab the door however, and the good feel of the blazing sun and the open air struck at their faces and arms, they turned around to plead, 'Can we get out? Can we go and see what's happening?'

So ardent was their need that they were about to fall out of the open door when they saw their father detaching himself from the knot of passengers and drivers standing in the road and making his way back to them. The boys hastily edged back until he stood leaning in at the door. The family studied his face for signs; they were all adept at this, practising it daily over the breakfast table at home, and again when he came back from work. But this situation was a new one, a baffling one: they could not read it, or his position on it.

'What's happening?' the mother asked faintly at last.

'Damn truck driver,' he swore through dark lips. 'Some boy threw a rock—probably some goatherd in the field—and cracked his windscreen. He's parked the truck across the road, won't let anyone pass till there's a *faisla*. Says he won't move till the police come and get him compensation. Stupid damn fool—what compensation is a goatherd going to pay, even if they find him?'

The mother leaned her head back. What had reason to do with men's tempers? she might have asked. Instead, she sighed, 'Is there a policeman?'

'What—here? In this forsaken desert?' her husband retorted, drawing in harsh breaths of overheated, dust-laden air as if he were breathing in all the stupidity around him. He could see passengers climbing down from the bus and the bullock cart, climbing across the ditch into the fields, and fanning out—some to lower their trousers, others to lift their saris behind the thorn bushes. If the glare was not playing tricks with his eyes, he thought he saw a puff of dust in the distance that might have been raised by goats' hooves.

'Take me to see, Dadd-ee, take me to see,' the boys had begun to clamour, and to their astonishment he stood aside and let them climb out and even led them back to the truck that stood imperviously across the culvert.

The mother opened and shut her mouth silently. Her daughter stood up and hung over the front seat to watch the disappearing figures. In despair, she cried, 'They're gone!'

'Sit down! Where can they go?'

'I want to go too, Mumm-ee, I want to go too-oo.'

'Be quiet. There's nowhere to go.'

The girl began to wail. It was usually a good strategy in a family with loud voices, but this time her grievance was genuine: her head ached from the long sleep in the car, from the heat beating on its metal top, from the lack of air, from the glare and from hunger. 'I'm hung-gree,' she wept.

'We were going to eat when we reached Solan,' her mother reminded her. 'There's such a nice-nice restaurant at the railway station in Solan. Such nice-nice omelettes they make there.'

'I want an omelette!' wailed the child.

'Wait till we get to Solan.'

'When will we reach it? *When?*'

'Oh, I don't know. Late. Sit down and open that basket at the back. You'll find something to eat there.'

But now that omelettes at Solan had been mentioned the basket packed at home with Gluco biscuits and potato chips held no attraction for the girl. She stopped wailing but sulked instead, sucking her thumb, a habit she was supposed to have given up but which resurfaced for comfort when necessary.

She did not need to draw upon her thumb juices for long.

The news of the traffic jam on the highway had spread. From somewhere—it seemed from nowhere for there was no village bazaar, market place or stall visible in that dusty dereliction— wooden barrows came trundling along towards the waiting traffic, bearing freshly cut lengths of sugar cane; bananas already more black than yellow from the sun that baked them; peanuts in their shells roasting in pans set on embers. Men, women and children were climbing over the ditch like phantoms, materializing out of the dust, with baskets on their heads filled not only with food but with amusements as well—a trayload of paper toys painted indigo and violent pink, small bamboo pipes that released rude noises and a dyed feather on a spool. Kites, puppets, clay carts, wooden toys and tin whistles. The vendors milled around the buses, cars and rickshaws, and were soon standing at their car window, both vocally and manually proffering goods for sale.

The baby let drop its narcotic rubber teat, delighted. Its eyes grew big and shone at all it saw flowering about it. The little girl was perplexed, wondering what to choose from so much till the perfect choice presented itself in a rainbow of colour: green, pink and violet, her favourites. It was a barrow of soft drinks, and nothing on this day of gritty dust, yellow sun and frustrating delay could be more enticing than those bottles filled with syrups in those dazzling floral colours which provoked in her a scream of desire.

'Are you mad?' her mother said promptly. 'You think I'll let you drink a bottle full of typhoid and cholera germs?'

The girl gasped with disbelief at being denied. Her mouth opened wide to issue a protest, but her mother went on, 'After you have your typhoid-and-cholera injection, you may. You want a nice, big typhoid-and-cholera injection first?'

The child's mouth was still open in contemplation of the impossible choice when her brothers came plodding back through the dust, each carrying a pith-and-bamboo toy—a clown that jounced upon a stick and a bird that whirled upon a pin. Behind them the father slouched morosely. He had his hands deep in his pockets, and his face was lined with a frown deeply embedded with dust.

'We'll be here for hours,' he informed his wife through the car window. 'A rickshaw driver has gone off to the nearest *thana* to

91

find a policeman who can put sense into that damn truck driver's thick head.' Despondently he threw himself into the driver's seat and sprawled there. 'Must be a hundred and twenty degrees,' he sighed.

'Pinky, where is the water bottle? Pass the water bottle to Daddy,' commanded the mother solicitously.

He drank from the plastic bottle, tilting his head back and letting the water spill into his mouth. But it was so warm it was hardly refreshing, and he spat the last mouthful out of the car window into the dust. A scavenging chicken alongside the tyre skipped away with a squawk.

All along the road, in the stationary traffic, drivers and passengers were searching for shade, for news, for some sign of release. Every now and then someone brought information on how long the line of cars and trucks now was. Two miles in each direction was the latest estimate, at least two miles.

Up on the bank of the culvert the man who had caused it all sat sprawling, his legs wide apart. He had taken off his bandanna, revealing a twist of cotton wool dipped in fragrant oil that was tucked behind his ear. He had bought himself a length of sugar cane and sat chewing it, ripping off the tough outer fibre with strong flashing teeth, then drawing the sweet syrup out of its soft white inside and spitting out, with relish, the pale fibre sucked dry. He seemed deliberately to spit in the direction of those who stood watching in growing frustration.

'Get hold of that fellow! *Force* him to move his truck,' somebody suddenly shouted out, driven to the limit of his endurance. 'If he doesn't, he'll get the thrashing of his life.'

'Calm down, Sirdarji,' another placated him with a light laugh to help put things back in perspective. 'Cool down. It's hot, but you'll get your cold beer when you get to Solan.'

'When will that be? When my beard's gone grey?'

'Grey hair is nothing to be ashamed of,' philosophized an elder who had a good deal of it to show. 'Grey hair shows patience, forbearance, a long life. That is how to live long— patiently, with forbearance.'

'And when one has work to do, what then?' the Sikh

demanded, rolling up his hands into fists. The metal bangle on his wrist glinted.

'Work goes better after a little rest,' the elder replied, and demonstrated by lowering himself on to his haunches and squatting there on the roadside like an old bird on its perch or a man waiting to be shaved by a roadside barber. And, like an answer to a call, a barber did miraculously appear, an itinerant barber who carried the tools of his trade in a tin box on his head. No one could imagine where he had emerged from, or how far he had travelled in search of custom. Now he squatted and began to unpack a mirror, scissors, soap, blades, even a small rusty cigarette tin full of water. An audience stood watching his expert moves and flourishes and the evident pleasure these gave the elder.

Suddenly the truck driver on the bank waved a hand and called, 'Hey, come up here when you've finished. I could do with a shave too—and my ears need cleaning.'

There was a gasp at his insolence, and then indignant protests.

'Are you planning to get married over there? Are we not to move till your bride arrives and the wedding is over?' shouted someone.

This had the wrong effect: it made the crowd laugh. Even the truck driver laughed. He was somehow becoming a part of the conspiracy. How had this happened?

In the road, the men stood locked in bafflement. In the vehicles, the tired passengers waited. 'Oo-oof,' sighed the mother. The baby, asleep as if stunned by the heat, felt heavy as lead in her arms. 'My head is paining, and it's time to have tea.'

'Mama wants tea, mama wants tea!' chanted her daughter, kicking at the front seat.

'Stop it!' her father snapped. 'Where is the kitchen? Where is the cook? Am I to get them out of the sky? Or is there a well filled with tea?'

The children all burst out laughing at the idea of drawing tea from a well, but while they giggled helplessly, a *chai* wallah did appear, a tray with glasses on his head, a kettle dangling from his hand, searching for the passenger who had called for tea.

There was no mention of cholera or typhoid now. He was

93

summoned, glasses were filled with milky, sweet tea and handed out, the parents slurped thirstily, and the children stared, demanding sips, then flinching from the scalding liquid.

Heartened, the father began to thrash around in the car, punch the horn, stamp ineffectually on the accelerator. 'Damn fool,' he swore. 'How can this happen? How can this be allowed? Only in this bloody country. Where else can one man hold up four miles of traffic?'

Handing back an empty glass, the mother suggested, 'Why don't you go and see if the policeman's arrived?'

'Am I to go up and down looking for a policeman? Should I walk to Solan to find one?' the man fumed. His tirade rolled on like thunder out of the white blaze of the afternoon. The children listened, watched. Was it getting darker? Was a thundercloud approaching? Was it less bright? Perhaps it was evening. Perhaps it would be night soon.

'What will we do when it grows dark?' the girl whimpered. 'Where will we sleep?'

'Here, on the road!' shouted the boys. 'Here on the road!' Their toys were long since broken and discarded. They needed some distraction. Their sister could easily be moved to tears by mentioning night, jackals, ghosts that haunt highways, robbers who carry silk handkerchiefs to strangle their victims . . .

Suddenly, one of the drivers, hitching up his pyjamas and straightening his turban, came running back towards the stalled traffic, shouting, 'They're moving! The policeman's come! They'll move now! There'll be a *faisla!*'

Instantly the picture changed from one of discouragement, despair and approaching darkness to animation, excitement, hope. All those loitering in the road leaped back into their vehicles, and in a moment the air was filled with the roar of revving engines as with applause.

The father too was pressing down on the accelerator, beating upon the steering wheel, and the children settling into position, all screaming, 'Sim-la! Sim-la!' in unison.

But not a single vehicle moved an inch. None could. The obstructing truck had not been moved out of the way. The driver still sprawled on the bank, propped up on one elbow now, demanding of the policeman who had arrived, 'So? Have you brought me compensation? NO? Why not? I told you I would not move till I received compensation. So where is it? Hah? What is the *faisla*? Hah?'

The roar of engines faltered, hiccuped, fell silent. After a while, car doors slammed as drivers and passengers climbed out again. Groups formed to discuss the latest development. What was to be done now? The elder's philosophical patience was no longer entertained. No one bandied jokes with the villain on the bank any more. Expressions turned grim.

Suddenly the mother wailed, 'We'll be here all night,' and the baby woke crying: it had had enough of being confined in the suffocating heat; it wanted air, it wanted escape. All the children began to whine. The mother drew herself up. 'We'll have to get something to eat,' she said and called over to her husband standing in the road, 'Can't you get some food for the children?'

He threw her an irritated look over his shoulder. Together with the men in the road, he was going back to the culvert to see what could be done. There was an urgency about their talk now, their suggestions. Dusk had begun to creep across the fields like a thicker, greyer layer of dust. Some of the vendors lit kerosene lamps on their barrows, so small and faint that they did nothing but accentuate the darkness. Some of them were disappearing over the fields, along paths visible only to them, having sold their goods and possibly having a long way to travel. All that could be seen in the dark were the lighted pinpricks of their cigarettes.

What the small girl had most feared did now happen—the long, mournful howl of a jackal lifted itself out of the stones and thorn bushes and unfurled through the dark towards them. While she sat mute with fear, her brothers let out howls of delight and began to imitate the invisible creature's call.

The mother was shushing them fiercely when they heard the sound they had given up hope of hearing: the sound of a moving vehicle. It came roaring up the road from behind them—not at all where they had expected—overtaking them in a cloud of choking dust. Policemen in khaki, armed with steel-tipped canes, leaned out of it, their moustaches bristling, their teeth gleaming, eyes flashing and ferocious as tigers. And the huddled crowd stranded on the roadside fell aside like sheep; it might have been they who were at fault.

But the police truck overtook them all, sending them hurriedly into the ditch for safety, and drew up at the culvert. Here the police jumped out, landing with great thuds on the asphalt, and striking their canes hard upon it for good measure. The truck's headlights lit up the bank with its pallid wash.

Caught in that illumination, the truck driver rose calmly to his feet, dusted the seat of his pyjamas, wound up the bandanna round his head, all in one fluid movement, and without a word leaped lightly back into the driver's seat of his truck. He turned the key, started the engine, manoeuvred into an onward position and, while his audience held its disbelieving breath, set off towards the north.

After a moment they saw that he had switched on his lights. He had also turned on his radio, and a song could be heard.

Father, I am leaving your roof,
To my bridegroom's home I go . . .

His tail lights could be seen dwindling in the dark. The police swung around, flourishing their canes. 'Get on! *Chalo!*' they bellowed. '*Chalo, chalo*, get on, all of you,' and they did.   □

Don't miss out on major issues

Whether it's reportage from troubled places, quests for the beautiful and the outrageous, revealing memoirs and intense confessions, stunning photography or compelling fiction, every quarterly issue of *Granta* features the best of it.

Why not become a subscriber and get all this, delivered to your home, at a discount of up to 30%? Or give a gift subscription to a friend?

'An oasis of good writing.' *New Statesman*

'The pinnacle of literary and political writing.' *Vogue*

'A cover-to-cover bargain.' *Time Out*

'The most impressive literary magazine of its time.' *Daily Telegraph*

Save up to 30% with a Granta subscription

YES I would like to subscribe for

❑ 1 year (4 issues) at £24.95 *(saving 22%)*
❑ 2 years (8 issues) at £46.50 *(saving 27%)*
❑ 3 years (12 issues) at £67.00 *(saving 30%)*

(*Granta* sells for £7.99 in bookshops.)

Subscribe for yourself

Please start my subscription with issue no _____

NAME & ADDRESS *(please complete even if ordering a gift subscription)*

_____

_____

_____

POSTCODE _____

97C5S57B

Total* £ _____

❑ Cheque (to 'Granta') ❑ Visa, Mastercard/Access, AmEx

Card no:

/__/__/__/__/__/__/__/__/__/__/__/__/__/__/__/__/

Expire date /__/__/__/__/ Signature_____

* POSTAGE: NO ADDITIONAL POSTAGE REQUIRED FOR UK SUBSCRIPTIONS. FOR EUROPE
PLEASE ADD £8 PER YEAR. FOR OVERSEAS SUBSCRIPTIONS, PLEASE ADD £15 PER YEAR.

❑ Please tick this box if you would prefer *not* to receive promotional offers from compatible organizations

or for a friend.

I would like to give a subscription to the following. My name, address and payment details are above.

NAME AND ADDRESS: Mr/Mrs/Ms/Miss

_____

_____

_____

Return, free of charge if posted in the UK, to:
Granta, Freepost,
2-3 Hanover Yard, Noel
Road, London N1 8BR

Postcode _____

NAME AND ADDRESS: Mr/Mrs/Ms/Miss

_____

_____

Or use our

UK (free phone and fax):
FreeCall 0500 004 033
OUTSIDE THE UK:
Tel: 44 171 704 0470
Fax: 44 171 704 0474

Postcode _____

GRANTA

SUKETU MEHTA
MUMBAI

PHOTOGRAPHS BY
SEBASTIÃO SALGADO

SUKETU MEHTA was born in Calcutta in 1963, grew up in Bombay and now lives in New York.

SEBASTIÃO SALGADO's books include *The Other Americas* (1983) and *Workers* (1995). In 1995 he spent a month photographing Mumbai as part of a larger project on modern urban life. 'The huge concentration of people and the explosive growth and migration,' he says, 'make Mumbai a model for the future of urban civilization.' An exhibition of his work in India, sponsored by Christian Aid, will tour the UK in the autumn.

Bombay (now officially Mumbai) is a city with an identity crisis; a city experiencing both a boom and a civic emergency. It's the biggest, fastest, richest city in India. It held twelve million people at the last count—more than Greece—and thirty-eight per cent of the nation's taxes are paid by its citizens. Yet half the population is homeless. In the Bayview Bar of the Oberoi Hotel you can order Dom Perignon champagne for 20,250 rupees, more than one-and-a-half times the average annual income; this in a city where forty per cent of the houses are without safe drinking water. In a country where a number of people still die of starvation, Bombay boasts 150 diet clinics. *Urbs prima in Indis*, says the plaque outside the Gateway of India. By the year 2020, it is predicted, Bombay will be the largest city in the world.

Four years ago this divided metropolis went to war with itself. On 6 December 1992 the Babri Masjid, a mosque in Ayodhya, was destroyed by a fanatical Hindu mob. Ayodhya is many hundreds of miles away in Uttar Pradesh, but the rubble from its mosque swiftly provided the foundations for the walls that shot up between Hindus and Muslims in Bombay. A series of riots left 1,400 people dead. Four years later, at the end of 1996, I was back in Bombay and was planning a trip with a group of slum women. When I suggested the following Friday, 6 December, there was a silence. The women laughed uneasily, looked at each other. Finally, one said: 'No one will leave the house on that date.'

The riots were a tragedy in three acts. First, there was a spontaneous upheaval involving the police and Muslims. This was followed, in January, by a second wave of more serious rioting, instigated by the Hindu political movement Shiv Sena, in which Muslims were systematically identified and massacred, their houses and shops burnt and looted. The third stage was the revenge of the Muslims: on 12 March ten powerful bombs went off all over the city. One exploded in the Stock Exchange, another in the Air India building. There were bombs in cars and scooters. Three hundred and seventeen people died, many of them Muslims.

Yet many Muslims cheered the perpetrators. It was the old story: the powerful wish of minorities all over the world to be the oppressor rather than the oppressed. Almost every Muslim I spoke to in Bombay agreed that the riots had devastated their sense of

self-worth; they were forced to stand by helplessly as they watched their sons slaughtered, their possessions burnt before their eyes. There are 1.6 million Muslims in Bombay: more than ten per cent of the city's total population. When they rode the commuter trains, they stood with their heads bent down. How could they meet the eyes of the victorious Hindus? Then the bombs went off, and the Hindus were reminded that the Muslims weren't helpless. On the trains, they could hold their heads high again.

Last December I was taken on a tour of the battlegrounds by a group of Shiv Sena men and Raghav, a private taxi operator, a short, stocky man wearing jeans labelled 'Saviour'. He was not officially a member of Shiv Sena, but he was called upon by the leader of the local branch whenever there was party work to be done. He led me through Jogeshwari, the slum where, on 8 January 1993, the second wave of trouble began. A Hindu family of mill workers had been sleeping in a room in Radhabai Chawl, in the Muslim area. Someone locked their door from the outside and threw a petrol bomb in through the window. The family died screaming, clawing at the door. One of them was a handicapped teenage girl.

Raghav and a couple of the others took me into the slums through passages so narrow that two people cannot walk abreast. They were cautious, at first. But as we passed a mosque, Raghav laughed. 'This is where we shat in the Masjid,' he said. One of his companions shot him a warning look. Only later did I learn what he meant. The Sena zealots had burnt down this mosque; it was one of the high points of the war for them, and they recalled it with glee. One man had taken a cylinder of cooking gas, opened the valve, lit a match and rolled it inside. He then joined the police force, where he remains to this day.

We were discussing all this not in some back room, in whispers, but in the middle of the street, in the morning, with hundreds of people coming and going. Raghav was completely open, neither bragging nor playing down what he had done; just telling it as it happened. The Sena men—the *sainiks*—were comfortable; this was their turf. They pointed out the sole remaining shop owned by a Muslim: a textile shop that used to be called Ghafoor's. During the riots some of the boys wanted to kill him, but others who had grown up with him protected him, and he got away with merely having his stock burnt. Now it has reopened, under the name Maharashtra Mattress. Raghav pointed to the store next to it. 'I looted that battery shop,' he said.

He led me to an open patch of ground by the train sheds. There was a vast garbage dump on one side, with groups of people hacking at the ground with picks, a crowd of boys playing cricket, sewers running at our feet, train tracks in sheds in the middle distance, and a series of concrete tower blocks beyond. A week ago I had been standing on the far side with a Muslim man, who pointed towards where I now stood, saying, 'That is where the Hindus came from.'

Raghav remembered. This was where he and his friends had caught two Muslims. 'We burnt them,' he said. 'We poured kerosene over them and set them on fire.'

'Did they scream?'

'No, because we beat them a lot before burning them. Their bodies lay here in the ditch, rotting, for ten days. Crows were eating them. Dogs were eating them. The police wouldn't take the bodies away because the Jogeshwari police said it was in the Goregaon police's jurisdiction, and the Goregaon police said it was the railway police's jurisdiction.'

Raghav also recalled an old Muslim man who was throwing hot water on the Sena boys. They broke down his door, dragged him out, took a neighbour's blanket, wrapped him in it and set him alight. 'It was like a movie,' he said. 'Silent, empty, someone burning somewhere, and us hiding, and the army. Sometimes I couldn't sleep, thinking that just as I had burnt someone, so somebody could burn me.'

I asked him, as we looked over the waste land, if the Muslims they burnt had begged for their lives.

'Yes. They would say, "Have mercy on us!" But we were filled with such hate, and we had Radhabai Chawl on our minds. And even if there was one of us who said, let him go, there would be ten others saying no, kill him. And so we had to kill him.'

'But what if he was innocent?'

Raghav looked at me. 'He was Muslim,' he said.

A few days later I met Sunil, deputy leader of the Jogeshwari *shakha,* or branch, of the Shiv Sena. He came with two other Sena boys to drink with me in my friend's apartment. They all looked around appreciatively. We were on the sixth floor, on a hill, and the highway throbbed with traffic below us. Sunil looked out of the window. 'It's a good place to shoot people from,' he said, making the rat-tat-tat motion of firing a sub-machine gun. I had not thought of the apartment this way.

Sunil was one of the favourites to be *pramukh,* the leader, of the entire *shakha* one day. He first joined the Shiv Sena when he needed a blood transfusion, and the Sena boys gave their blood, an act which touched him deeply—his political comrades were, literally, his blood brothers. He was in his twenties now, helpful, generous and likeable. He has a wide range of contacts with Muslims, from taking his daughter to a Muslim holy man to be exorcised, to buying chickens in Mohammedali Road during the riots, for resale to Hindus at a good profit. But what preyed on his mind now was the conviction that the handicapped girl who died in the fire in Radhabai Chawl had been raped by her Muslim assailants. There was no evidence for this; the police report did not mention it. But that didn't matter. It was a powerful, catalytic image: a disabled girl on the ground with a line of leering Muslim men waiting their turn to abuse her, while her parents matched her screams with their own as their bodies caught the flames.

Sunil insisted on referring to the riots as a 'war'. Certainly, at the J. J. Hospital, he had witnessed scenes typical of wartime: corpses identifiable only by numbered tags. And at Cooper Hospital, where Hindus and Muslims were placed next to each other in the same ward, fights would break out; wounded men would rip saline drips out of their arms and hurl them at their enemies. During the riots, the government sent tankers of milk to the Muslim areas. Sunil, with three of his fellow *sainiks* dressed as Muslims, put a deadly insecticide in one of the containers: the Muslims smelt it and refused all the milk. Sunil's men also shut off the water supply to the Muslim quarter. After six days, he said, the Muslims were forced to come out to the big *chowk* in the centre of the quarter. 'That's when we got them,' he recalled.

I asked him: 'What does a man look like when he's on fire?'

The other Shiv Sena men looked at each other. They didn't trust me yet. 'We weren't there,' they said. 'The Sena didn't have anything to do with the rioting.'

But Sunil would have none of this. 'I'll tell you. I was there,' he said. He looked directly at me. 'A man on fire gets up, falls, runs for his life, falls, gets up, runs. It is horror. Oil drips from his body, his eyes become huge, huge, the white shows, white, white, you touch his arm like this'—he flicked his arm—'the white shows, it shows especially on the nose.' He rubbed his nose with two fingers, as if scraping off the skin. 'Oil drips from him, water drips from him, white, white all over.

'Those were not days for thought,' he continued. 'We five people burnt one Mussulman. At four in the morning, after we heard about the Radhabai Chawl massacre, a mob assembled, the like of which I'd never seen. Ladies, gents. They picked up any weapon they could. Then we marched to the Muslim side. We met a *pau* wallah [bread-seller] on the highway, on a bicycle. I knew him, he used to sell me bread every day. I set him on fire. We poured petrol over him and set light to him. All I thought was that he was a Muslim. He was shaking. He was crying, "I have children, I have children." I said: "When your Muslims were killing the Radhabai Chawl people, did you think of your children?" That day we showed them what Hindu dharma is.'

Island dwellers

'We used to roller skate down Teen Batti,' an architect said to me. He used the past imperfect tense; he meant that he used to *be able* to roller skate down Teen Batti. Teen Batti is at the top of the road that winds up from the sea; the Ridge Road leads from there up Malabar Hill. The area is now a shabby high-rise ghetto where the cars leave no room for the juvenile traffic of roller skates and bicycles. What he said stuck with me because I used to roller skate down Teen Batti and cycle around there too. I cannot imagine a twelve-year-old boy doing so now.

The sounds, colours and moods of the sea lent heft and weight to my childhood. From my uncle's apartment I can still see

The fish dock

Laundry

Unloading fish

The fruit market

Office life

*The highest
office rents
in the world*

the rocks where the boys from our building would catch little fish trapped in the hollows when the tide went out. We sat down there and watched the whole progress of the sunset, from light to dark, and planned our lives—who would become the police inspector, who the astronaut. Gradually, a colony of hutments took over those rocks, and when we walked on them we would sometimes slip and fall on shit. The rocks are now a public latrine, full of strange smells. There are two million people in Bombay who have to defecate in any space they can find. The sea air sometimes wafts the stench over the skyscrapers of the rich, nudging them, reminding them.

We lived in Bombay and never had much to do with Mumbai. Mumbai was what Maharashtrans called the city; and Bombay was the capital of Maharashtra. But so far as we Gujaratis—migrants, like so many in Bombay—were concerned, Mumbai meant the people who came to wash our clothes or look at our electricity meters. We had a term for them—*ghatis*: people from the ghats— meaning someone coarse, poor. There were whole worlds in the city which were as foreign to me as the ice fields of the Arctic or the deserts of Arabia. I was eight years old when Marathi, the language of Maharashtra, became compulsory in our school. How we groaned. It was a servants' language, we said.

I moved to New York when I was fourteen. When I went back I found that the city had grown in wild and strange ways. In front of my uncle's building, for instance, was a monstrous skyscraper, its skeleton completed more than a decade before, lying vacant. Several such buildings dot the city. The flats have been bought for huge sums but are empty because they violate municipal height limits. The builders knew they would not get planning consent but went ahead anyway. The first priority was to put up the concrete reality; they could deal with the extraneous issues—municipal clearances, legal papers, bribes—later. But the city corporation put its foot down, and the fate of the buildings entered the courts. While the most expensive, most desirable real estate in Bombay lies vacant, half the population sleeps on the pavement.

Land is to Bombay what politics is to Delhi: the reigning obsession, the fetish, the *raison d'être* and the topic around which conversations, business, newspapers and dreams revolve. Property is the mania of island dwellers all over the world, and Bombay is washed by water on three sides. It regards the rest of India much as Manhattan looks on the rest of America: as a place distant, unfamiliar and inferior. The lament I kept hearing—from both Hindus and Muslims—was that the riots were an ungentle reminder that Bombay was part of India.

In 1994 a survey revealed that real-estate prices in Bombay were the highest in the world. There was general jubilation in the city. It confirmed something that Bombayites had long felt: that this was where the action was, not New York or London. Here, if you wanted a flat in a new building shooting up from the narrow strip of land behind the National Centre for the Performing Arts in Nariman Point, you would need three million dollars.

My uncle

My father's brother is a diamond merchant. He came to Bombay in 1966, against the will of my grandfather, who saw no reason why anyone should leave the family jewellery business in Calcutta. But my uncle was a young man, and the economic twilight of Calcutta had begun. In Bombay he built up a diamond-exporting business and is now rich. He owns a large four-bedroom flat on Nepean Sea Road with a fine view of the ocean. He travels to New York and Antwerp as often as if he were going to Ahmedabad or Delhi.

I am very fond of him. When I was a child he bought me fireworks. And now whenever I come back, he arranges everything, from airline tickets to meetings with influential people.

During the riots he sheltered two small Muslim boys in his flat. They were friends of his son who were scared of the Hindu wrath in their own neighbourhood. They had to be smuggled into my uncle's building because the neighbours would have objected if they had known he was sheltering Muslims; it might even have attracted the attention of the rampaging mobs outside. My family remembers the boys, then seven and twelve years old, as being very quiet, not fully understanding what was going on, but aware that their family was in great danger.

My uncle also cooked food in a Jain temple and went, at great risk, to the Muslim areas, to distribute it to people trapped

117

by the curfew: 5,000 packets of rice, bread and potatoes a day.

The man who did these things could also say: 'The riots taught the Muslims a lesson. Even educated people like me think that with such *junooni* [wild] people we need the Shiv Sena to give them *takkar* [counterforce]. The Shiv Sena are fanatics, but we need fanatics to fight fanatics.'

He looked past me, out of the window, and told me a story.

He had a good Muslim friend in Calcutta, a friend who was at school with him in the tenth standard; they would have been about fifteen. He went with this friend to see a movie, and before the main show a newsreel came on. There was a scene with many Muslims bowing in prayer, doing their *namaaz*. Without thinking, my uncle said out loud in the darkened theatre, perhaps to his friend, perhaps to himself, 'One bomb would take care of them.'

Then he realized what he had said, and that the friend beside him was Muslim. But the friend said nothing, pretending he had not heard. 'But I know he heard,' said my uncle, the pain still evident on his face, sitting in this flat in Bombay thirty-five years later. 'I was so ashamed,' he said. 'I have been ashamed of that all my life. I began to think, how did I have this hatred in me? And I realized I had been taught this since childhood. Maybe it was Partition, maybe it was their food habits—they kill animals—but our parents taught us that we couldn't trust them. The events of Partition washed away the teachings of Gandhiji. Dadaji [my grandfather] and Bapuji [his brother] were staunch Gandhians except when it came to Muslims. I could never bring a Muslim friend home and I couldn't go to their home.'

The next day my uncle sat in the room with the little temple, doing his morning puja. 'Don't write what I told you,' he said.

I asked him why.

'I've never told anyone that before.'

I have written it anyway. He had something to explain to himself and he's not through sorting it out in his mind—he's a long way away from it, as most of us are—but he's begun.

In the Bombay I grew up in, being Muslim or Hindu or Catholic was merely a personal eccentricity, like a hairstyle. We had a boy in our class—Arif—who, I realize now, must have been Muslim. He was an expert in scatology and taught us an obscene version of a patriotic song in which the heroic exploits of the country's leaders were replaced by the sexual escapades of Bombay's movie stars. He didn't do this because he was Muslim, but because he was a twelve-year-old boy.

In Bombay, back then, it didn't matter. In Mumbai, now, it matters very much.

Powertoni

Sunil, the deputy leader of the Shiv Sena's Jogeshwari branch, could afford to be relaxed. 'The ministers are ours,' he said. 'The police are in our hands. They cooperated during the riots. If anything happens to me, the minister calls.' He nods. 'We have *powertoni*.'

He repeated the word a few times before I realized what it meant. It was a contraction of 'power of attorney', the ability to act on someone else's behalf, or to have others do your bidding, sign documents, release criminals, cure illnesses, get people killed. In Mumbai, the Shiv Sena is the one organization that has *powertoni*. So far, the only people punished for their involvement in the riots have been fourteen Muslims. And the man with the greatest *powertoni* is the leader of Sena, Balasaheb Thackeray—the Saheb.

Sunil and the Sena boys described him to me. He did not actually hold any office of state, but it was impossible to talk directly to him, they said; even the most eloquent, fearless man like their branch leader became tongue-tied, and the Saheb would berate him, 'Stand up! What's the matter, why are you dumb?' It was impossible to meet his eyes. Nevertheless, he liked people to be direct. 'You should have the daring to ask direct questions. He doesn't like a man who says, er . . . er . . .'

They told me what to say if I met the Saheb. 'Tell him: "Even today, in Jogeshwari, we are ready to die for you." But ask him: "Those people who fought for you in the riots, for Hindutva, what do you think of them? What can your Shiv Sena do for them? Those who laid their lives down on a word from you? What should their mothers do? What can the old parents of the Pednekar brothers, who have no other children, do?"'

I felt like a go-between carrying messages from the lover to

119

the loved one: 'Tell her I am ready to die for her!' But there was also a hint of reproach in their questions, as if they felt that their Saheb had been neglecting them, these people who had died for his love; and that somehow the blood sacrifice their comrades had made had gone unacknowledged.

Bal Thackeray's monstrous ego was nurtured from birth. His mother had five daughters and no sons. She prayed ardently for a boy and was blessed with Bal, whom she believed was a *navasputra,* a gift from God.

He worked for most of his life as a cartoonist. Then, in 1966, he formed a new political party of the people we called *ghatis.* He named it the Shiv Sena, Shivaji's Army, after the seventeenth-century Maharashtran warrior-king, who organized a ragtag band of guerrillas into a fighting force that defeated the Mogul emperor Aurangzeb and held sway over most of central India.

The Shiv Sena branch in Jogeshwari is a long hall filled with pictures of Thackeray and his late wife, a bust of Shivaji and pictures of a body-building competition. Every evening, Raghunath Kadam, the branch leader, sits behind a table and listens to a line of supplicants. A handicapped man is looking for work as a typist. Another wants electricity in his slum. Warring couples come to him for mediation. An ambulance is parked outside, part of a network of ambulances all around Bombay that the Sena operates at nominal charges. In a city where municipal services are in a state of crisis, going through the Sena ensures access to such services. The Sena also acts as a parallel government, like the party machines in American cities that helped immigrants find jobs and fixed street lights.

Thackeray, now seventy, is a cross between Louis Farrakhan and Vladimir Zhirinovsky. He appears in Salman Rushdie's *The Moor's Last Sigh* as Raman Fielding, leader of a thuggish political movement called Mumbai Axis. Thackeray has the cartoonist's art of being outrageous and loves to bait foreign journalists with his professed admiration for Adolf Hitler. In an interview with *Time* magazine at the height of the riots, he was asked if Indian Muslims were beginning to feel like Jews in Nazi Germany. 'Have they behaved like the Jews in Nazi Germany? If so, there is nothing

Balasaheb Thackeray OUTLOOK

wrong if they are treated as Jews were in Nazi Germany,' he said.

His party has an uncomplicated way of dealing with its opponents. Its newspaper, *Saamna* (the word means confrontation), has waged a fierce campaign against M. F. Hussain, India's best-known painter, for painting a nude portrait of the goddess Saraswati, twenty years ago. *Saamna* suggested that by painting the Hindu goddess naked, Hussain had 'displayed his innate Muslim fanaticism'. Hussain had for a long time had an inkling that he would be targeted eventually. In October 1996 he went to London and dared not return. In his absence, the police filed multiple criminal cases against him for insulting religious beliefs and inciting communal disharmony.

121

Saamna's editor, Sanjay Nirupam (a Member of Parliament), put the case clearly: 'Hindus,' he wrote, 'do not forget Hussain's crime! He is not to be forgiven at any cost. When he returns to Mumbai he must be taken to Hutatma Chowk and be publicly flogged until he himself becomes a piece of modern art. The same fingers that have painted our Mother naked will have to be cut off.'

What's striking about the writer's notions of punishment is that they seem to be derived straight from the shari'a.

'Thackeray is more Muslim than I am,' said Shabana Sheikh, a woman in the Jogeshwari slums. He is a man obsessed by Muslims: 'He watches us: how we eat, how we pray. If his paper doesn't have the word Muslims in its headline, it won't sell a single copy.'

In March 1995 the Shiv Sena, as the majority partner in a coalition government, came to power in Maharashtra state (the city government had already belonged to them for a decade). It examined the awesome urban problems plaguing the city, the infestation of corruption at all levels of the bureaucracy, the abysmal state of Hindu–Muslim relations, and took decisive action. It changed the name of the capital city to Mumbai; the station, Victoria Terminus, became Chhatrapati Shivaji Terminus. Ironically, Thackeray himself has an English name: his father anglicized the spelling to chime with the novelist he most admired.

I was never able to carry the Sena boys' message to the Saheb. He had grown wary of journalists. His words were being pored over by the Srikrishna Commission, an official inquiry into the riots. Instead, I went to meet the man who will lead the Sena after Thackeray's death: his nephew, Raj.

I was nervous as I entered the *Saamna* office. It has a reputation. Ramesh Kini, for instance, was a supervisor in an eyeliner factory, a middle-class Maharashtran resident of Matunga, such as form the core of Sena support. He was also the victim of a campaign of harassment by his landlord, who was trying to get his family evicted from his rent-controlled flat. His landlord also had connections in the Sena. One morning Kini came here to this office; by midnight he was dead. The police found his body in a theatre in Pune, several hours away, and registered a case of suicide. Then his widow went public and named Raj Thackeray, the man I was about to meet, the Saheb's twenty-eight-year-old nephew, as one of the murderers.

Before entering his office, I was asked to take off my shoes. When I went in, I found out why. Behind where the short, slim, intense man sits is a shrine decorated with images of gods; there is also the usual photograph of the Saheb. The whole office looked rather like a film set, so replete was it with iconography, and after a while I realized that Raj's mannerisms—the way he held his hand to his mouth, his glare, were also taken directly from the movies. There was an air of unconvincing menace about him. A policeman with an automatic rifle follows him everywhere; when he visits the bathroom, the policeman stands outside.

I asked him about the city. He glared at me. 'You're calling it Bombay.' I realized my transgression and referred to it as Mumbai for the rest of our meeting.

Raj has been groomed to fill the older Thackeray's place to the extent of following in his career path—he is also a cartoonist; prominent on his desk is a calligraphy set and a book, *WWII in Cartoons*. I asked him about his favourite cartoonists. 'Balasaheb Thackeray,' he said without thinking.

'All Balasaheb is saying,' he said, with the air of a man advancing a perfectly reasonable proposition, some civic improvement scheme, perhaps, 'is that whoever is against this nation should be shot and killed.' He paused. 'And if the Muslims are more this way, then we are not guilty.'

He told me about the Shiv Sena's answer to Bombay's problems. 'There should be a permit system to enter Mumbai, just like a visa. This would be checked at the railway stations, airports, highways. The constitution should be changed, if you want to save the city. Those people who have work should come and do it and go away. Outsiders should be stopped from immigrating. Who are they? They are not Maharashtrans.'

Almost as we spoke, a group of Sena members, including a former mayor of the city, was visiting the offices of a Marathi newspaper that had dared to print a speech critical of the Saheb. A former deputy municipal commissioner in Bombay, G. R. Khairnar, who has a reputation for fighting corrupt politicians, had lashed out at Thackeray in a hysterical speech, calling him, among other things, the Devil. The Sena duly broke the windows in Khairnar's house and beat up journalists, blackening one editor's face with coal tar. The police filed a case against the newspaper, 'for wantonly creating provocation with intent to spread discontent and cause riot'.

Thackeray loves big business, and big business loves him. The Sena cut its teeth fighting communists in the factories, so the Sena-controlled unions are much more dependable than the Left-controlled ones. The party's money comes not from the rank and file but from the city's leading businessmen. The main opposition comes from rural areas and from Marathi writers.

The Sena also shows a distinct bias towards kitsch. Last November, for instance, Thackeray allowed Michael Jackson to perform in India for the first time. This may or may not have had to do with the fact that the singer had promised to donate the profits from his concert (more than a million dollars) to a Sena-run youth-employment project. The planned concert offended a number of people in the city, including Thackeray's own brother, who asked: 'Who is Michael Jackson, and how on earth is he linked to Hindu culture which the Shiv Sena and its boss Thackeray talk about so proudly?'

But the Shiv Sena supremo (as he sometimes signs his letters), responded, 'Jackson is a great artist, and we must accept him as an artist. His movements are terrific. Not many people can move that way. You will end up breaking your bones.' Then he got to the heart of the matter. 'And well, what is culture? Jackson represents certain values in America which India should not have any qualms in accepting.' The pop star acknowledged Thackeray's praise by stopping off at the leader's residence on the way to his hotel from the airport and pissing in his toilet, a fact which Thackeray brought with pride to the attention of the city's media.

Sunil and his friends talked with equal pride about the time every year on the Saheb's birthday when they go to his bungalow, and watch a long line of the city's richest, most eminent people line up to pay homage to their Saheb. 'We watch all the big people bow and touch his feet.' Another *sainik* added: 'Michael Jackson only meets presidents of countries; he came to meet Saheb.' The movie industry, especially, is in thrall to the Saheb, seeking his favour in everything from exempting a movie from entertainment tax, to getting an errant actor released from jail. In August 1996 the prime minister himself, Deve Gowda, flew to Bombay to meet the Saheb at a dinner organized at the residence of the movie star and entertainment magnate Amitabh Bachhan. Every time one of the corporate or screen gods, or a foreigner, or the prime minister, kowtows before him, the foot soldiers of the Sena get a thrill of pride, and their image of the Saheb as a powerful man, a man with *powertoni,* is reinforced.

A lover's embrace

The manager of Bombay's suburban railway system was recently asked when the system would improve to a point where it could carry its five million daily passengers in comfort. 'Not in my lifetime,' he answered. Certainly, if you commute into Bombay, you are made aware of the precise temperature of the human body as it curls around you on all sides, adjusting itself to every curve of your own. A lover's embrace was never so close.

One morning I took the rush hour train to Jogeshwari. There was a crush of passengers, and I could only get halfway into the carriage. As the train gathered speed, I hung on to the top of the open door. I feared I would be pushed out, but someone reassured me: 'Don't worry, if they push you out they also pull you in.'

Asad Bin Saif is a scholar of the slums, moving tirelessly among the sewers, cataloguing numberless communal flare-ups and riots, seeing first-hand the slow destruction of the social fabric of the city. He is from Bhagalpur, in Bihar, site not only of some of the worst rioting in the nation, but also of a famous incident in 1980, in which the police blinded a group of criminals with knitting needles and acid. Asad, of all people, has seen humanity at its worst. I asked him if he felt pessimistic about the human race.

'Not at all,' he replied. 'Look at the hands from the trains.'

If you are late for work in Bombay, and reach the station just as the train is leaving the platform, you can run up to the packed compartments and you will find many hands stretching out to grab you on board, unfolding outward from the train like petals. As you run alongside you will be picked up, and some tiny space

125

SEBASTIÃO SALGADO

will be made for your feet on the edge of the open doorway. The rest is up to you; you will probably have to hang on to the door frame with your fingertips, being careful not to lean out too far lest you get decapitated by a pole placed close to the tracks. But consider what has happened: your fellow passengers, already packed tighter than cattle are legally allowed to be, their shirts drenched with sweat in the badly ventilated compartment, having stood like this for hours, retain an empathy for you, know that your boss might yell at you or cut your pay if you miss this train and will make space where none exists to take one more person with them. And at the moment of contact, they do not know if the hand that is reaching for theirs belongs to a Hindu or Muslim or Christian or Brahmin or untouchable or whether you were born in this city or arrived only this morning or whether you live in Malabar Hill or Jogeshwari; whether you're from Bombay or Mumbai or New York. All they know is that you're trying to get to the city of gold, and that's enough. Come on board, they say. We'll adjust. □

GRANTA

R. K. NARAYAN
KABIR STREET

R. K. NARAYAN was born in Madras in 1906. With the help of Graham Greene, he published the first of his twenty-nine books (*Swami and Friends*) in 1935. Subsequent novels, such as *Waiting for the Mahatma, The Painter of Signs* and *The English Teacher*, made him the most widely read Indian writer in the English language. Many of his stories were set in the fictional town of Malgudi. 'Kabir Street' is an extract from the sequel to *The World of Nagaraj* (1990), which he is still writing. He lives in Madras.

R. K. Narayan with his wife, Rajam, in 1935

Nagaraj had begun to have doubts about his standing in his ancestral home, 14 Kabir Street. He was the titular head of the family, his wife, Sita, being the real ruler of the empire extending from the street to the lichen-covered backyard wall with a door opening on to the sands of the River Sarayu.

The river had provided water for their domestic needs, till a well was dug, when the traffic towards the river ceased, and the back door, through disuse, got welded to the frame with ancient rust and dust. Otherwise the backyard remained unchanged with its tin-roofed bathroom and toilet beside the well. Four tall coconut trees loomed challengingly, in addition to guava, jackfruit, pomelo and a spreading tamarind, shedding leaves which remained unswept amid a jungle of wild vegetation.

Nagaraj's nephew Tim commented on the wild state of the backyard whenever he saw it: 'Too bad! Uncle, you must get a couple of men to clear the jungle.'

'Yes, yes,' Nagaraj would say. 'I have asked them to come,' inwardly wondering who 'they' were.

Sita was more emphatic. 'If they can't get anyone, tell me plainly, I will do something. Cobras may be living under the fallen leaves. What a lot of trouble your father used to take to keep the place clean! You are indifferent.'

'Naturally, not being my father,' he retorted silently, but aloud, 'Sita, leave it to me.'

'Cobras,' she began again, but he cut her short. 'Nonsense! Cobras have better business than counting dead leaves.'

'Not only your father, but your mother was cleaning and clearing.'

'She was a busybody—all the time sweeping and dusting . . . '

'That was why everything was so tidy.'

'Why don't you follow her example?'

This could only be a brief exchange while he passed from the puja room into the kitchen.

After lunch Nagaraj dressed in a silk jibba, white dhoti and an upper cloth dyed in ochre (as ordered by a swami he had met in the park long ago), surveyed himself in their ancient oval mirror and set off with a brief, 'I'm off. Shut the door.'

Sita moved into the kitchen, muttering. 'No use talking to

him. He doesn't care. Must find someone to clear the jungle.'

Nagaraj went down Kabir Street, paused for a second at the archway to the market to greet his friend Jayaraj the photo-framer, who was hunched over some coloured prints of gods and nailing gilt frames around them. His next stop was the corner stall, where he held out his palm while his friend Kanni placed on it a couple of betel leaves and a pinch of scented areca nut, which he popped into his mouth and chewed contentedly, saying, 'Put it on my account.'

'No need to say it,' muttered Kanni as a routine formula.

Crossing Market Road, Nagaraj reached Margosa Avenue and then Coomar's Boeing Sari Emporium. Coomar had not come yet. A couple of attendants were stacking up saris in showcases. Nagaraj settled in his usual corner, took out the ledgers and scanned the columns.

He asked loudly, addressing no one in particular, 'Where is the proprietor?'

'Sent word he will be late.'

'Thank God,' Nagaraj said to himself, feeling relieved. He glanced through the columns on a page or two and put away the ledger, got up on an impulse and while passing the manager murmured, 'I'll be back,' whispering under his breath, 'no need to count Coomar's profits today.'

He stepped out and went down the street without any plan. He paused at the junction. If he went straight ahead, his steps would lead him home. 'I don't need to go home and face Sita's endless questioning. I want to be a free man at least for a couple of hours. Home is not the best place at the moment.' Tim and his wife Saroja had moved in permanently. Saroja was always playing her harmonium, and Tim had taken up amateur dramatics. Now he and his gang would be there—as usual—rehearsing *Harischandra*. If the moral of the famous story affected the unwashed, unshaven ruffians even slightly, things would not be so bad. But they were an untidy lot whose touch would contaminate. How dare they usurp his seat on the *pyol*.

Sita should be advised to scrub the place and wash it with phenol. But it was unlikely she would take it in the right spirit, since she constituted herself champion of Tim in every misdeed. She was a good wife but a muddle-headed aunt. Last evening the lounging fellows ignored him as he stood there glaring at them to convey his distaste for the whole lot.

They were chattering away while another set was singing to the accompaniment of Saroja's harmonium. He wondered for a while, 'Why not push them off the *pyol* on to the street?' but retreated to Sita's room with the intention of shouting at her. She was lying on the bare, cool cement floor reading a magazine.

He felt tongue-tied in her presence. Plucking up courage, he said, 'I can hardly hear my own voice in this house.' She lowered the magazine, looked at him over the frame of her spectacles and asked, 'What is it that you want to say?'

Nagaraj muttered within himself, 'She looks owlish with the spectacles over her nose,' but said aloud, 'Nothing really . . . I don't even know where I can sit.'

She pulled off her spectacles, obviously getting ready for a duel, and said: 'With so many rooms built by your worthy forefathers! You don't even know who built this house!'

'I could tell you a lot when we have a little silence.'

'You always have a grudge against Tim and his friends. After all, you were the one to pamper him, separating him from his parents.'

This angered Nagaraj, but he could only say, 'Well, if you are going on that line . . . I don't know . . . I don't know how to live in this house!'

'As we have always done. What is special now?'

'I have no place to sit quietly and watch . . . '

'Watch what? The street? To watch mongrels fighting in the dust or the drunken engineer tottering homeward? You lose nothing by not watching. You speak as if you were missing a royal procession.'

'I don't know where to sit.'

She laughed at his complaint. 'Second time you are complaining. Could it be that you have suddenly assumed giant proportions, like the Vamana avatar of Vishnu who appeared like a pygmy at first?'

'I know the story; you don't have to repeat it.'

She was adamant and continued her narrative. 'He appeared as a pygmy and asked Bali, the demon king who had to be destroyed, for three paces of the Earth as a gift. King Bali, who never refused an appeal, readily granted it. Vamana assumed a giant stature . . . '

'I know the story,' repeated Nagaraj weakly.

'Vamana's first stride spanned the whole Earth, the second spanned all Heaven. "Where is the space for my third?" asked Vamana, and the King bowed down and offered his head, and the God placed one foot on it and pressed him down to extinction.'

'Why?' asked Nagaraj.

'You said you knew the story. Why don't you conclude it?' teased Sita. 'Why don't you throw away all those notebooks in which you have scribbled notes about Narada and sit down to write the story of Vamana?'

'Excellent advice,' Nagaraj cried in joy, and hugged her after making sure no one was watching.

After this she said, 'Follow me,' and led him to the veranda *pyol* where the rehearsal group had fallen asleep, leaning on each other. She clapped her hands, and when they woke up, she ordered them out. 'You may all go. Tim won't be back.' They scrambled to their feet and made their exit.

She turned to Nagaraj and said, 'There, I have found space for your first step . . . for your second and third we will also find space.'

At this point Saroja's harmonium ceased. She appeared at the door to declare with some heat, 'Tim said they should wait for him.'

'At the street corner, I believe,' Nagaraj said with a chuckle. Saroja retreated to her room grumbling.

Nagaraj sat on the *pyol* watching the street. The vendor of sweets with a tray-load on his head passed down the street, crying sonorously, 'Bombay *mittai*, Delhi Durbar *mittai*.' He made his appearance at the same hour in the evening to reach the school gate at closing time.

Nagaraj reflected on the sweet vendor, who probably made the sweets in one of those huts in a slum at the end of Kabir Street on what was once open ground. Where was the need for slums in Malgudi? He was not able to find an answer. He must ask Zachariah (the only creature on earth apart from the zebra using a 'Z', an otherwise neglected and useless letter of the alphabet) who taught at St Joseph's and who read many newspapers and was well informed.

Why go so far? There was the Talkative Man living in the first house in their row. He saw him emerge from his home pushing out his bicycle. Nagaraj was about to hail him but changed his mind. If T.M. was asked one question he would invent ten other questions and grab his attention for hours.

Nagaraj looked away from T.M. and tried to resume his reflections on the sweet vendor but lost the thread of his thoughts. Sita brought him a tumbler of coffee.

'Oh, I'd have come in myself,' he said.

'The boys are rehearsing, and I thought . . . ' she said.

He paused to listen to the players. A gruff voice was saying, 'Summon the executioner.'

'No, Your Majesty . . . the woman must be spared . . . '

At this a female voice pleaded, 'I am a helpless woman . . . '

Nagaraj drank his coffee in one gulp and, wiping his lips with the towel on his shoulder, cried, 'A female voice! Is it mimicry or a eunuch in their midst?'

'They must have a real girl—Saroja's friend. Tim brought her in two days ago for a role. She is talented and will go far.'

Nagaraj returned the brass tumbler. He felt disturbed. A girl in the midst of this riff-raff! He must tell Tim bluntly to put an end to this nonsense. He rehearsed his speech: 'Tim, kick out your friends. I did not bring you here for this sort of thing. When I am provoked, you will find me a different man and tremble. Take care! Don't push me too far. I don't want to speak bitter words which I may regret later . . . '

If Tim should turn round and ask, 'What is wrong with us?' he must have a ready answer. Burning words that would prove a turning point in his career. It was, however, difficult to corner Tim who was always going out or coming in with his gang. But if he was available, Sita must be out of earshot. She was a contradicting type. Hence he must compose his talk suitably.

Probably the best course for him would be to say, 'Sita, don't you think Tim is developing marvellously? He reminds me of Shakespeare, who brought home actors and displeased his father.

I've heard about it all from Zachariah who has visited Shakespeare's birthplace.'

This sentence ought to draw out a contradiction. She should say, 'I don't know. Only thing I want is that Tim should be handled properly. He must do useful things or go back to his father with Saroja and her harmonium. I won't have him here.'

'What about the girl who has come with the group?'

'She must be thrown out along with the rest.'

This imaginary conversation ended abruptly when Sita moved in softly and asked, 'Are you talking to yourself?'

Nagaraj simpered and explained, 'I was repeating, *"Om Namasivaya,"* as I always do when alone.'

'Excellent habit. But I did not notice it all these days.'

'How could you? I repeat the mantra mentally and meditate.'

'It will do you good,' she said and left him.

He continued his meditation on the subject of Tim. 'It is better I put it all down in writing. Talk to him and also hand him a document, that'll work.'

He got up, went in to pick up pen and paper, and resumed his seat on the *pyol* with a notebook on his lap. 'Hey Tim,' he wrote. 'This won't do. I didn't bring you down here to make our home a retreat for loafers and now a girl in addition! What sort of girl is she? You are a married man with a wife and her harmonium, which I have tolerated long enough. Now this is too much. If you don't kick out that girl and the gang immediately, I'll talk to your father.'

At this point he paused to speculate on what his brother, Tim's father, would say. Was he likely to respond with: 'I'm happy you have brought it to my notice. Thrash him and throw him out. I'll also give him the same treatment when he comes here. God bless you for your forethought'?

Sita came out, threw a brief glance at him and his notebook and went down the steps. The girl's voice rang out again, 'I'm a woman. Have mercy.' And another voice over it, 'Say "I am a woman" louder. Don't swallow the last words.'

Nagaraj resumed his letter to Tim: 'If I see your friends again, I'll call the police. I'll tell Coomar, who is chummy with the police chief, who will send policemen with batons to beat up your gang and lock them in a cell . . . and if they include you, I won't come to your rescue. Poor Saroja. Her father must come down and take her away.'

The last proved prophetic. The following week a letter arrived from Trichy. Saroja's father had written, 'Is it true? Saroja is complaining that her fingers ache playing the harmonium to a set of rowdies Tim brings home. He has become indifferent to her welfare and is paying attention to some adventuress. What are you doing about it? You must check him. Otherwise I am preparing to bring Saroja home, which is better than tolerating a vagabond of a son-in-law. What are you going to do about it? I must know immediately. I am sending a copy of this letter to Tim's father, Gopu. As a father, he must show some responsibility . . . '

Luckily, Sita had gone out to meet her friend as usual. She was not the sort to stay at home in the afternoon. Nagaraj felt thankful for this habit of hers. He was home when the letter came and he would hide it from her. Why? No. Better that she understood Tim, her great favourite. But the prospect of Saroja going away saddened him. He liked her to be around, but without her harmonium. It was a good sign that she was complaining of aching fingers. She probably needed some outlet for her artistic aspirations, but why not take to painting or writing poetry, activities performed in dead silence and never a nuisance to others?

Saroja's father would expect a reply. He dare not write one without discussing the subject with Sita. But she need not be told. He quietly carried the letter to the backyard, tore it to bits and dropped them into the well, then walked to the post office at the market gate and sent off a telegram to the gentleman in Trichy. It was more expensive than a postcard, but then you didn't have to go through the pains of composition. 'Am watchful. Pray let's not force the pace.' He had come across the phrase in a news-sheet the Talkative Man had shown him a couple of days earlier. He had no idea what it meant, but it sounded profound, and also sounded like 'forceps'—he was reminded of a cousin in Kumbam who was known as 'Forceps Kuppu' since he was a forceps-delivery case. But that family was out of touch. He felt sad for a moment over how one's kith and kin could become scattered and vanish like a spray of water.

135

While Nagaraj was going to his seat on the *pyol*, Tim arrived with four of his mob, all talking loudly. Their dress was offensive—coloured pants, flowery shorts, lungis, long hair, shaven pates, beards, quite an assortment.

Tim himself was unshaven, crowned with an untended, wild crop. He came in like an invader, and his mob rushed in and blocked the kitchen doorway, chattering away simultaneously:

'The story of *Harischandra* is popular . . . '

'We must start with a popular subject . . . '

'What about costumes?'

'I know a fellow who will give us costumes on hire . . . '

At this moment, Tim shouted, 'Auntie, can you give us coffee?'

Before she could answer, another demanded, 'Tea for me.'

'Lemonade for me,' said a third.

Sita explained over the babble, 'Tim has started a theatre group.'

Nagaraj ignored her information, shut his eyes and ruminated, 'Am I or am I not the head of this family? Nobody cares for me.' He felt an aversion to this crowd and self-pity for being isolated.

His wife tolerated and admired the scamp with his harmonium-playing wife and drama crowd. Sita's smugness angered Nagaraj. It seemed as if he had no place in the scheme of things. Best thing for him would be to get away—like the Buddha, without a word to anyone, carrying nothing except his soul.

The next day he went through his daily routine quietly. Ate and dressed in his usual manner, took leave of Sita while she was still in the kitchen, 'I am off; bolt the door.' He went through the daily exercises with precision, but only up to a point—till he reached Market Road. There, instead of going straight on to Margosa Avenue to his seat at Coomar's to write accounts, he turned to his right and found himself in the Town Hall park, where he sought a bench away from the habitual loungers to brood in peace over his life.

Looking round he found a hermit-like figure under a banyan tree, with beads around his neck, clad in ochre and vermilion with sacred ash splashed across his forehead. Wondering if it could be the same swami he had met long ago, Nagaraj got up and paced up and down, throwing quick side glances at the swami to make out whether he was the old one or another.

Difficult job distinguishing one swami from another—they looked alike, like soldiers in an army. 'A swami lost in meditation will not notice me,' he said to himself.

But on his tenth trip, the swami called out, 'Hey, what makes you perambulate in this manner? Have you no better business?'

Nagaraj felt overwhelmed and suppressed the question, 'Are you the old swamiji or a different one?', but he halted his steps and made a deep obeisance.

The ascetic commanded, 'Be bold, come here and sit down.' Nagaraj sat down immediately facing the swami. The swami roared out a second command, 'Move to the side! Have you not noticed the worshippers line up on two sides? Never stand plumb straight in front of God. Do you know why?'

Nagaraj remained dumb, reflecting, 'It is my fate to blink like a schoolboy wherever I go,' as he hurried out of the straight line. He wanted to have his say in the matter, 'The rule applies only to the God in a shrine. You are only a swami,' but left it unsaid, debating within himself whether he should not get up and run away.

The swami explained, 'If you sit in the direct vision of God, you will get scorched.' Then he said, 'Ask any question that may be troubling your mind.'

While Nagaraj was considering this offer, the swami suddenly asked, 'Do you know who you are?' While Nagaraj was trying to frame a proper answer, wondering if his name and address would be sufficient and regretting that he had been postponing the printing of a visiting card, the swami said, 'Don't answer now. Brush aside all other thoughts and concentrate on, "Who am I?" and see me again in fifteen days with whatever answer you get. Now go.'

'Will your holiness still be here?'

'No.'

Nagaraj felt bewildered but relieved, prostrated hurriedly, scrambled to his feet and left in a state of confusion. ☐

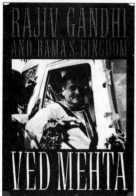

GRANTA

MARK TULLY
MY FATHER'S RAJ

DAVID JONES/P A NEWS

MARK TULLY is a journalist and broadcaster. He spent twenty years as chief of the BBC's Delhi bureau, before becoming its South Asia correspondent. His books include *Amritsar: Mrs Gandhi's Last Battle*, *From Raj to Rajiv*, *No Full Stops in India* and a collection of short stories, *The Heart of India*. He lives in Delhi.

Mark Tully

Iwas born in Calcutta in October 1935 and grew up on the southern outskirts of the city, in one of the areas where the British lived. Our first address was number six, Regent's Park, Tollygunge, but as the family grew—eventually I had five brothers and sisters—we moved to number seven in the same road. This was similar to number six, a two-storey house hidden in its grounds behind high yellow walls, but even larger. The lawn could double as a tennis court. The rear compound was so big that it could house quarters for our dozen and more servants, and those quarters could seem hidden, tucked away.

My father, William Scarth Carlisle Tully, was a businessman, or what Calcuttans knew as a 'box wallah'. In those days, Calcutta was still the commercial capital of the Raj, more important even than Bombay, though by this time the viceroy and the British administration had moved to Lutyens's new capital, New Delhi. My father arrived in Calcutta from London, via a posting in Rangoon, in 1925. He worked for the firm of Gillanders Arbuthnot, which sounds like a character from P. G. Wodehouse but was in fact the oldest of India's major 'managing agencies'. In our house the name had no comic resonance at all. In British India, managing agencies meant power, influence and profit. They existed because, though plenty of companies in Britain wanted to make money in India, they had neither the expertise nor inclination to manage businesses there. Managing agencies did that for them, and behind their names—often with a Scottish inflection: Shaw Wallace, Mackinnon Mackenzie—sheltered wide portfolios of interests. Gillanders, for example, had been founded in the early nineteenth century by the Gladstone family—the same family as the great Victorian prime minister's—to ship textiles to India and indigo back to Britain. By the time my father began to work for them, they managed sixty companies. Gillanders ran tea gardens and the picturesque little railway, the Darjeeling Himalayan, which carried the tea down the mountains. They represented insurance companies and banks. They managed the mining of diamonds, gold, tin, copper and coal.

They were moral and they were mean. They prized their reputation for the former, forbidding their staff to trade privately or play the Calcutta stock exchange, and insisting that they

140

banked their money in the company bank, so that the firm's senior partners could keep an eye on the finances of their young assistants, who might be running up debts or making money on the side. My father approved. He would warn young employees just out from London: 'Gillanders has got a reputation second to none which has taken more than one hundred years to build up, so you have to be on your best behaviour because you could muck the whole thing up in one afternoon.'

He did not approve, however, of the London office, which was dominated by Gladstones and which officially controlled the partners (who made the company's money) in Calcutta. He felt that they were out of touch—understandably so when letters, the main means of communication, took three weeks on their sea voyage between Britain and India—and also incompetent and ridiculously parsimonious. On one important mission to London my father was asked to explain the intricate finances behind the building of the Howrah bridge, the first permanent bridge across the Hooghly river in Calcutta, to the Prudential Assurance company, which Gillanders hoped would provide some of the money. Nobody in the London office was able to do this, and my father was summoned from his home leave in Winchester. Gillanders did not offer to pay his train fare, and when he suggested a taxi might take him between Gillanders and the Prudential, he was told that there was a perfectly good direct bus, a partner adding that he hoped my father had the tuppence for the ticket.

He also remembered, in a similar spirit, events in Rangoon, where his first job had been to 'check steamers', which meant visiting ships riding at anchor which had cargo to be handled by Gillanders. A small steam launch was the way other agents made these trips, but Gillanders insisted that a sampan was quite good enough for their men. My father and his small boat would toss around like a cork in the wake of launches and tugs. Still, he would say, 'I managed to smoke my Burma cheroot without being sick.'

These were the stories my father told; this was the world he came from.

We did not get on. I sometimes look back on my childhood in Calcutta and wonder how the seeds of our tempestuous relationship came to be sown. My father was a stern man and a moralist, ideal Gillanders material, but he was certainly not brutal. His bright brown eyes could freeze anyone who aroused his anger, which was easy to do. There were sometimes terrifying outbursts of temper. Once he dragged me screaming with fear up to the high diving board of the Tollygunge Club swimming pool, shouting, 'I'll teach you to be a coward,' though that is the only physical clash I can remember. My resentment of him came more, I think, from his constant criticism of me. His life was filled with correctness—the right way to hold a knife and fork, the right way to sit (and stand, and ride a bicycle), the right way to talk to servants—and I managed to get most things wrong. He was particularly keen on the right way to speak and the right way to spell. Any hint of what was known as a 'chi-chi' or Eurasian accent was pounced on; the letters I sent him from my boarding school came back to me with the spelling mistakes underlined in red.

Of course, he accepted without question the convention that the British in India must remain above India and not become part of it. He employed Nanny Oxborrow from England to make sure that we kept our distance to avoid social contamination—to 'go native' was still a meaningful phrase then, and a pejorative one. Nanny did no work herself; there were children's maids and Jaffa, the nursery boy, to do that. Her responsibility was to see that we did not get too close to these Indian servants. When, for example, we went for our morning pony ride, Nanny would come too— walking alongside and slowing our progress—in case we were tempted to talk to the groom, or syce, in his own language. Once I got a sharp slap from her when she found our driver teaching me to count to ten in Hindustani.

We met our parents by regular appointment twice a day. After our pony ride, nanny would take us to their bedroom to watch them having *chota hazri*, or small breakfast—tea and delicious green bananas. Then in the evening, after Nanny had supervised our baths, she would accompany us to the drawing room, where my parents would be drinking sherry. On Sundays we saw more of our parents—Nanny had the day off and the special privilege of a glass of sherry when she returned from evensong at the Anglican cathedral (I can still remember the sweet

Mark Tully as a child in India

smell of it on her breath). It was a formal childhood, but perhaps not quite so formal as it now sounds. We weren't a social family—my father despised cocktail parties and receptions—but we had our share of birthday parties, with roundabouts, conjurors and snake charmers on the lawn and trips to the swimming pools and fancy-dress carnivals of Calcutta's several clubs. Over the past few decades, Calcutta has become a byword for poverty, but in those days the only time poverty impinged on our white lives was (paradoxically) when my mother took us to the fashionable shops near the Maidan, the city's equivalent of Hyde Park or Central Park. There we would see lepers squatting on the pavement begging, fingers reduced to stumps, toes eaten away. I was fascinated. My mother would drag me away.

My fifth birthday should have been the signal to ship me off as a boarder to pre-preparatory school in England—that was the normal practice, so that children could be spared the Indian climate and the risk of disease. But no passenger liners ran during the war, and I was sent instead to a school in the hills at Darjeeling which had been founded to cater for children like me, cut off from their rightful English education by Hitler. I wept bitterly as I said goodbye to my parents on the station platform at the start of each term, though I now look back fondly on the school itself. It gave us freedom. We were allowed to roam the bazaars, to climb up to the army camp where American troops gave us sweets, and sometimes to visit the cinema. I learned enough Hindustani and Nepali to amuse the rickshaw pullers and porters who carried people and freight up the steep streets and lanes. My father would not have approved if he'd known.

He came to see me at the school only once. Then, early in 1945, before the war with Germany was over, he booked his wife, six children, nanny and father-in-law on a cargo liner, the *Chinese Prince*, which was the first available ship to Britain. I was nine, and relieved to be leaving him behind. He joined us eighteen months later. After that, unshielded by nannies and nurseries, the seeds of our antagonism ripened into wheat and tares.

I often think of him now. Who can explain the dynamics that work between father and son? What made him as he was? I certainly don't think of him as a bigot and a racist. He respected his Bengali clerks, his babus, and made friends of a few Indians he met in the Calcutta Musical Society (he had a magnificent bass voice). He was typical of his time; he had the best as well as the harshest of an older set of values. He was loyal and attracted loyalty. He was absolutely honest. He was generous to relatives who fell on hard times. He wanted (I now see) the best for his children. But he would never have broken the rules that governed the British relationship with India, nor the rules that governed how the British in India behaved among themselves. Indians were a separate and different people, the divide was to be observed and never crossed. As for our fellow Britons, they fell into a hierarchy as rigid as Indian caste. Among the business community, the managing agents were the élite, and retailers were at the bottom of the pile. Barriers could be crossed, but of one upwardly mobile Calcutta friend of our family my father would always observe darkly: 'He has a chip on his shoulder. He can never forget that he came out to Calcutta with Bathgate the chemists.'

My father had a chip on his own. His origins were towards the lower end of the English middle class. His father owned a garage, he'd gone to a minor public school—Weymouth, long since closed. Calcutta society contained much grander people, with more glorious educations and lineages. My father felt they looked down on him. He wanted to be accepted—he was a member of Calcutta's premier club, the Bengal, and was mortified when he was blackballed for the Royal Calcutta Turf—and the fact that my mother's grandfather had been a housemaster at Winchester school, ancient and proud, only made him more prickly and difficult.

He determined that his children would go to 'good schools', and I was sent to Marlborough, where I began my long rebellion against everything my father wanted me to be. When my turn came for National Service, I infuriated my fellow officers by suggesting that the differences between them and their men should be abolished, and by courting the popularity of the men I commanded. My father took work home every evening to his study. I wasted my time at school and university. At the end of every school term he would insist that I submit a receipt for the ten shillings he had sent me for my train fare home. I have never kept any accounts since.

And yet I not only owe my life to him, but also the shape and the satisfaction of it. In my late twenties I got a job in the personnel department of the BBC. A posting in junior management came up—assistant representative of the BBC in Delhi—and I was interviewed for it. I was asked by a member of the appointments board if I could speak Hindi. 'Not well at all,' I replied, 'but I can recite "Humpty Dumpty" and "Little Miss Muffet" in Hindustani.' They were not amused, but I got the job. At the age of thirty, after twenty years, I went back to India.

That was more than thirty years ago. India is where I have lived almost constantly since. My zeal for it began as a reaction to my father's insistence that England was my home, the place I belonged to, the country that made me. For me, it turned out to be India that supplied those feelings, that anchorage.

My father never visited me in Delhi, though we softened to each other in the years before he died, but I owe the one enthusiasm in my life, which became a passion, to him. □

ESSENTIAL READING FROM GREENWOOD

HANDBOOK OF TWENTIETH-CENTURY LITERATURES OF INDIA

Edited by Nalini Natarajan

October 1996 472pp 0-313-28778-3 Hardback £67.95

India has a very rich literary heritage resulting from its many different regional traditions, religious faiths, ethnic subcultures and linguistic groups. Nalina Natarajan's new handbook takes the reader on a fascinating literary tour of India, to reveal how the country's diversity and heterogeneity have influenced its contemporary writings.

CONTENTS: Regional Literature of India: Paradigms and Contexts, *Nalini Natarajan*; 20th-Century Assamese Literature, *Mahaseta Barua*; 20th-Century Bengali Literature, *Sudipton Chatterjee and Hasan Ferdous*; 20th-Century Indian Literature in English, *Alpana Sharma Knippling*; 20th-Century Gujarati Literature, *Sarala Jag Mohan*; 20th-Century Hindi Literature, *Nandi Bhatia*; 20th-Century Kannada Literature, *Ramachandra Deva*; 20th-Century Malayam Literature, *Thomas Palakeel*; 20th-Century Marathi Literature, *Shripad Deo*; 20th-Century Punjabi Literature, *Atamjit Singh*; 20th-Century Punjabi Literature, *Atamjit Singh*; 20th-Century Tamil Literature, *P.S. Siri*; 20th-Century Telegu Literature, *G.K. Subbarayudu and C. Vijayasree*; 20th-Century Urdu Literature, *Omar Qureshi*. Special Topics - Dalit Literature in Maranthi, *Veena Deo*; Parsi Literature in English, *C. Vijayasree*; Sanskrit Poetics, *Arasu Balan*; Perspectives on Bengali Literature and Film, *Mitali Pati and Suranjan Ganguly*.

- -

ORDER FORM

Please send me _____ copies of **HANDBOOK OF TWENTIETH-CENTURY LITERATURES OF INDIA** by Natarajan
0-313-28778-3 Hardback £67.95

❏ Payment enclosed (please make cheques payable to EDS)

❏ VISA ❏ MASTERCARD

Card No.:

Expiry date: _____

Name: _____

Address: _____

_____

_____

VAT No.: _____

GREENWOOD PUBLISHING GROUP

3 Henrietta Street, London, WC2E 8LU Tel: 0171 240 0856 Fax: 0171 379 0609

VED MEHTA
COMING DOWN

Jawaharlal Nehru, 1950

VED MEHTA was born in Lahore in 1934. His first book, *Face to Face* was published in 1957. Since then he has written many autobiographical works, including *Vedi*, *The Ledge Between the Streams* and *Sound Shadows of the New World*. 'Coming Down' is an extract from *The Halcyon Days of the New Yorker*.

I had just graduated from Oxford—the year was 1959—and strapped to a seat in an aeroplane taking me from London to New Delhi, I was besieged by family memories. I recalled my father's favourite song, a sort of patriotic hymn for all Indians, whether Hindu, Muslim, Sikh or Christian. I remembered from my earliest childhood how he would sing it as he was doing ordinary things, like tying his shoelaces. It began:

> In the whole world, India is the best, India is ours,
> We are her nightingales; this is our garden.

The author of these lyrics was Muhammad Iqbal, a Muslim born in 1877 whom my father regarded as one of the greatest poets east of Suez. Iqbal's couplets were still always on my father's lips, even though he could never get over the fact that sometime in the 1930s Iqbal, originally an Indian patriot, had become a Muslim fanatic. He had altered his lyrics, so that they now went:

> Muslims are we, the country is ours, the whole world is ours.
> China and Arabia are ours, India is ours.
> Under the shadow of swords we have grown up.
> The crescent scabbard is our national emblem.

These rousing words had turned the song into the anthem of the Muslims who wanted to divide British India and create a country for themselves. This shift from patriotism to separatism was also the history of many of my father's Muslim friends: once comrades of the nationalists against the British, they had become the nationalists' mortal enemies. And because of this Muslim fanaticism, our family lost practically everything we owned when, in 1947, Lahore, where we lived, ended up as part of Pakistan, and we found ourselves refugees in the newly partitioned, independent India. I lost then the country of my childhood.

Two years later, aged fifteen, I set out on my own for America in quest of a formal education—something that was unavailable in India because of my blindness. After seven years in America, immediately followed by three years in England (while there, in 1957, I published my first book, a youthful autobiography entitled *Face to Face*) I was returning to India, but to a new, unfamiliar India—to the wounds of Partition, which, it seemed, would never heal. How would I find my bearings in the country that my family now called home, and how would I adapt to the bigotry and intolerance aroused by Partition after those years at Oxford?

The whole family would be at Palam Airport to receive me, I now reflected. They would be there in full force—my father and mother, my sisters and brothers and cousin-sisters and cousin-brothers, my aunts and uncles, and even many college friends of my sisters. That was the Indian way—to seize upon any excuse for a get-together. But I had become an outsider during my decade in the West. What could they know about who I was—who I had become? And what did I know about them?

I wanted to recognize everyone, to greet everyone by name, to be viewed as a good Punjabi son who had not been spoilt or corrupted by western ways. I wanted to do nothing less than dazzle them with my feats of memory, even as I realized that my memory was a hopelessly tangled skein of associated impressions.

Certainly there was no way I was going to recognize my younger brother Ashok, who was born when I was ten. Although I felt very close to him in my mind, my most vivid memory of him was of a five-year-old boy who, in learning how to ride a bicycle, had reminded me of my own dogged determination to ride one. He would now be fifteen, and his voice would have changed.

As we touched down at the airport and taxied along a bumpy runway, I wondered what I would say to my family—what they and I would make of each other. I felt terribly alone. As the plane came to a halt, the passengers clapped, as if it had accomplished a human feat. Then, even as my heart started beating fast, I heard a thunderous thump-thump on the side of the plane. While I was still wondering what was happening, my mother came running up the aisle. 'Your daddy and all your brothers and sisters are beating on the plane to greet you,' she said, out of breath. My first thought was one of amazement at how they had all evaded the customs, immigration, and security authorities to come right out on to the runway, but in a moment I realized that this was India, where a little string-pulling here and there could work miracles. My mother was jerking at my arm. 'Come, youngster, come,' she said. 'They are all waiting for you.'

I picked up my hand luggage, laden with Cadbury's chocolates and bottles of Scotch whisky—treats almost impossible to come by in India then—and followed her, marvelling as the crew held back the other passengers to let me disembark.

My ears felt funny, but I recognized the voices of all those except Ashok who were gathered on the runway and crowding around me. It was early morning, and yet, as I knew from the pilot's announcement, the temperature was almost 110 degrees. Delhi's July heat had the pressure of a physical force; the blazing sun seemed to push me down and crush me. We were rushed into a couple of waiting airport cars for the short ride to the terminal.

People around me were chattering in Punjabi among themselves, as if they did not know what to say to me. Now and again, one of them would turn to me with some casual remark like, 'It must feel great to be back home,' but more often I heard, 'He hasn't changed at all,' or 'He looks just like Vedi—a little filled out, but just the same.' It was unnerving to hear myself spoken of in the third person, and, although on the plane I had longed for people to speak Punjabi to me, now that they began doing it I felt, perversely, that they were not acknowledging my western education. I felt I had been dropped into a strange country where I would never feel at home. The lobby of the terminal seemed full, yet it contained a very small segment of the clan. Eventually we completed the formalities, and I found myself ushered—almost swept along—into my father's car, a 1948 Vauxhall, which he had bought second-hand a couple of years earlier.

Not only was driving in the heat a little like going through a bank of fire, but the hellishly loud engines of buses and lorries idled almost at our ears, and the motors of rickety scooters pulling rickshaws exploded in the hot air like erratic gunshots—all this amid petrol fumes and the stench of dirty open drains, dung and ordure. The car, weaving in and out of the mêlée of traffic and pedestrians, was constantly starting and stopping. Dust, almost as gritty as sand, bombarded us through the open windows. I missed the well-regulated and orderly—almost predictable—traffic in the West. I could barely hear, much less answer, my father's and sisters' constant questions about Oxford, the trip and my feelings at finally reaching home.

At the house, everyone smelt of sweat, soap and coconut hair oil, and the air smelt of garlic, onion and mint chutney: everything seemed musty and close. The house had an attached kitchen so it lacked the airy feeling I remembered from the houses of my childhood, where the kitchen was usually in a separate building. Even in this diminished house, however, my family had a room called the drawing room. The little furniture it contained was built in, and there was a lot of jostling, nudging and joking as people tried to find places on seats along the walls or on the carpet. No doubt partly because Indians' speech tends to be higher-pitched than westerners', all the voices sounded light and thin, like the chattering of the birds outside. Also, possibly because my hearing had still not adjusted to my being on the ground, or perhaps because I was straining to recognize every last voice around me, all the talk sounded unreal, as if I were hearing it through a filmy curtain. Suddenly people on the carpet were shifting to clear a path. 'Here is your Masterji,' my mother said, ushering in a short, bouncy Sikh, one of many singing masters who had taught me when I was a child. Masterji had always been attended by a boy disciple, carrying a harmonium on his head, and he had such a disciple with him now. 'This way, Masterji.'

'Sit yourself down here, Sirdarji, and the boy can put the harmonium in this corner.'

'Your brain must be roasting under your great hair and turban.'

I almost jumped as I heard all this. Whose idea was it to have that clown here, at what should be one of the most intimate moments of my life? I felt he embodied the wretched childhood I had been trying to escape from by going to America and England for my education, since my supposed musical talent was what had caused my father to delay making arrangements for any formal education for me earlier.

Years had passed since I had even given a thought to Masterji, but he now greeted me as if I'd had a lesson from him yesterday. 'Oh, my special chela,' he said. 'How are you coming along with practising your singing?'

I could not help smiling. I had scarcely sung a note of a raga since I saw him last. But, intent on rising to the occasion like a good Oxford man who is able to handle any situation, I said in Punjabi, 'As you know, I was never good at practising. Still, what a surprise to see you on my first day home, Masterji.'

Without further ado, Masterji sat down cross-legged. The boy set the harmonium in front of him and began to massage Masterji's shoulders and back as he picked out a melody.

'*Pug ghunghuru bandh Meera nautchire*,' he sang, as if he were a one-man band welcoming me home. I knew the melody from childhood and had come to think of it as Masterji's signature tune.

'Masterji, stop and sweeten your mouth,' my mother said. Carrying a platter of sweetmeats, she was somehow threading her way towards him through the crowd of relatives.

'Not yet, thank you,' Masterji sang out, incorporating the reply into his refrain.

Masterji's melody had neither a beginning nor an end, so at one point he arbitrarily left off playing the harmonium and burped loudly, as if to say that he had digested his breakfast and was now ready for applause and sweetmeats.

'*Wahwah!*'

'*Bohut acche!*'

'Encore!'

I joined in the cheering, but only half-heartedly. Since I had learned to enjoy western operas, Indian singing sounded to me a little like the whine of a mosquito.

'I told you to bring some buttermilk for Masterji to wash down the sweetmeats, Ramu—what's keeping you?' my mother called out. I was amused to hear that my mother had renamed her servant after a Hindu god, as if to invoke the god every time she called the servant.

Ramu ran in with a pitcher of buttermilk for Masterji and lemonade for his listeners. Masterji applied himself to eating and drinking, and so did everyone else, if a little less diligently.

From outside came sounds of new arrivals, their sandals shuffling along the veranda.

'Who's coming? Where will you put them all?' I asked.

'They're my friends from Nizam-ud-din Colony,' my mother said. 'Come out and meet them. They have brought *sagan* for you.'

Sagan was a ritualistic offering made by well-wishers on special occasions. My soul rebelled at the primitive custom. Besides, these people were friends my mother had made since coming to Delhi. I didn't know them and didn't want to meet them.

'I don't want their *sagan*,' I said. 'I'll have nothing to do with them. They're just here because they see me as a novelty.'

'Come out and just say *namaste* to them—for my sake,' my mother pleaded.

'Send them away, get them away—I want no part of their *sagan*,' I said, my voice growing louder.

I was a child again, a tyrant ordering my mother around.

She went out, sniffling, to deal with her friends as best she could.

'*Pug ghunghuru bandh Meera nautchire*,' Masterji resumed.

I felt like crying. 'What can it cost you just to go out and greet them?' I asked myself, answering, 'But it's the principle of it.' The Indian in me, the good son, was at war with the western self, and I felt that as long as I lived the two would always be at war.

When I was growing up, my father was fond of repeating the statement: 'Children are their parents' continued growth.' That was his way of saying that parents lived through their children—that children fulfilled the unfulfilled ambitions of their parents. Certainly in my father's day Indian families were close in a way that families in the West have not been since the advent of industrialized society. Indeed, my father and I were so close that when we talked it seemed as if two halves of me were conversing: one, like my father, was clear; the other, like my usual self, was confused.

In 1958, when I was in my second year at Oxford, my father stopped to see me on his way to America.

He said, 'It's not too soon to lay the groundwork for your return home and begin planning your future.'

'I don't know what I want to do,' I said. 'Whenever I think about my future, I get very gloomy.'

'Would you like to stay on at Oxford?'

'I don't think that's on the cards. Even if I got a teaching job here, I don't think I would enjoy being an Indian in England.'

'I thought that you had never encountered any prejudice here—that the English found you exotic, just as they did me when I was a student here in the good old days.'

I tried to explain that things were different back then. Gandhi and Nehru had not begun their long struggle for independence. I would feel like a traitor to the national struggle if I ended up in England, even though I couldn't rule it out—I sometimes felt that only at Oxford had I ever been happy. I wanted to be a scholar and a teacher and pass my life at a university, and to teach at a university in England, a First from Oxford was all I needed—that's all my tutors had. In India or America I would also need a Ph.D so I had applied for admission and financial aid to graduate schools at Harvard, Yale and Princeton. But I couldn't help wondering whether it wasn't time instead for me to try something like the Indian Foreign Service, to start making use of my Indian upbringing and western education.

'That's exactly what I wanted to talk to you about,' my father said. He added that the public praise of my book by the former prime minister of Britain, Clement Attlee, had come to the notice of Prime Minister Nehru. (My English editor, Mark Bonham-Carter, was a friend of Attlee's and had sent him a copy of the book. Attlee had written back a warm letter of appreciation, which had been quoted widely in the publisher's advertisements.) Nehru thought that the country should make use of me and had therefore asked Sir Raghaven Pillai, the secretary general of external affairs, who was the highest-ranking civil servant, if there might be a job in the government for me.

I was stunned. It was one thing for Attlee to be quoted on my book, apparently as a favour to a friend; quite another thing for the prime minister of India to try to find a job for me in the government. I couldn't have imagined such a turn of events in my wildest dreams. I asked, 'But how do you know all this?'

'I met Sir Raghaven at a party, and he told me about it at great length. You should lose no time in following up this lead.'

A month or so after my father's visit, I got off a letter to Sir Raghaven. He wrote back, saying that he had to consult his colleagues and make some enquiries, after which he would send me the government's considered reply. During the following six months I heard nothing from him except for one reassuring message through my father—that I should concentrate on getting a First, and that something would be worked out. Then, in March 1959, when finals were at hand, and the anxiety of possibly stopping my formal education and being on the move once again was building up to fever pitch—when I felt I simply had to decide what to do in life—I received a long letter from Sir Raghaven in which he said that he had not been 'inactive' on my behalf, but that entry into the Foreign Service, as in all Indian regular services, was by a national examination administered by the Union Public Service Commission. He said that the Commission required that a candidate write all the papers in his own hand and pass an eye test, and that, even if it were possible to induct me somehow into the Service through a special dispensation, he and his colleagues felt that I would not be able to discharge many of the duties and responsibilities of a government officer. He therefore offered to create for a year a special post with restricted duties and responsibilities but with pay and allowances not less than those for a Foreign Service officer of my age—a position that would give me a chance to get reacquainted with India, and give both the government and me an opportunity to assess what my future course should be.

The letter, for all its palpable goodwill and friendliness, struck me as bureaucratic and unimaginative. To throw up the obvious obstacles of handwriting and eyesight at this late stage seemed absurd, and the creation of a special post discriminatory. But my father was enthusiastic. 'You are being considered in deference to the wishes and interest in you of the prime minister himself, with whom you will come in contact from the very beginning,' he wrote. 'It will be a great experience . . . In any case, let the correspondence lead on to a definite offer, which we shall consider from all angles.'

Around the time I received Sir Raghaven's letter, the Harvard fellowship in history came through. (Yale and Princeton had turned me down for financial assistance, apparently because I had been honest and told them that I couldn't decide between history and English.) I provisionally accepted it, thinking I would spend the summer of 1959 in India with my family and look into Sir

Raghaven's offer. If I liked being in India, and the government job offered true promise, I could renounce, or possibly defer, the Harvard fellowship.

During this stay in India, after spending some time with my family, I met up with my Oxford friend Dom Moraes, and while we travelled together to Nepal and Calcutta, I made it a point to see professors, students, writers, journalists, government officers and politicians, in the hope of rediscovering the country of my birth. Wherever I went, my impressions of the independent India were solicited as if I were an illustrious man of the world rather than a twenty-five-year-old recent graduate. I began to have the feeling that all India was one small village of movers and shakers, and that I was a part of that village—in America I would be nobody but in India I was somebody. Yet, even as I enjoyed a certain celebrity, I hated it. I longed to be anonymous, the way I was in the West. In any event, I suspended judgement about my future. Before I left India, however, I visited Sir Raghaven and called on Foreign Secretary Dutt. I also had Sunday lunch with Prime Minister Nehru.

As my car pulled up, he greeted me from the veranda—a veranda on which my brother Om had taken a couple of pictures of my father and me with Nehru ten years earlier, when I was a boy of fifteen. That meeting had been at the request of my father, who wanted to show me off as a wunderkind going to America for my education. At that meeting, I typed a few sentences that he had dictated and read a passage in Braille to him in order to impress him with my accomplishments and independence. That meeting had been pro forma. Now Nehru had invited me to Sunday lunch.

He ushered me into the house, and soon I was sitting at the lunch table with him, his daughter, Indira, and his two grandsons, Rajiv, fifteen, and Sanjay, thirteen. The occasion was intimate. The talk was about, among other things, a visit to a doctor by Rajiv and Sanjay to have warts removed from their faces. On my earlier visit, I had been preoccupied with what Nehru thought of me, but now I tried to evaluate him as my friends at Oxford would, even thinking what I might write to them about this meeting. I noticed he spoke to his family like an indulgent Hindu

patriarch, treated the bearers who served us like an impatient
Mogul emperor, and conversed with me like an eager English
undergraduate—as if he embodied in his person the Hindu, Mogul
and British Indias.

When I was leaving, Nehru invited me to visit him again,
making me think that he did not often get a chance to speak
freely with young people. And, indeed, a few weeks later I was
there again, talking to him almost like a friend. He reminisced
about his Cambridge days, and I about my Oxford days.

Then he suddenly asked me, 'Did you get your First?' I
caught my breath, as if he'd punched me in the stomach. I had
just recently received the shocking news that I had missed getting
a First by one place—I had been judged eighteenth in a year in
which the examiners awarded seventeen Firsts in history. To be so
near and yet so far was all but intolerable. When the shock had
worn off a little, I rationalized that I might have got a First if I
hadn't packed up my notes and books and sent them off to
America immediately after my written examination, unaware that
I might be called for a viva, or oral examination, on my written
papers (as it turned out, I had a viva lasting forty minutes); or if,
once I had been called for the viva, I hadn't set the date early, so
that I could spend more time in India. If this and if that—the
'what ifs' of parlour games. I had such a deep sense of failure and
shame that I felt I could never again set foot in England. I could
never go back to Oxford, never face the porters and scouts who
had viewed me as a First, never see again my friends who had all
got their Firsts as a matter of course. I felt that because I'd got a
Second I was second-rate and never felt it more than I did now in
the prime minister's presence.

'No, sir, I didn't get my First,' I told him, almost choking
with tears. I waited for him to say, 'Never mind. I got a Second
too, (which would be the truth)—but Nehru said nothing, denying
me a chance even to mention extenuating circumstances. That was
just as well, because to have mentioned them would have been
tantamount to challenging the examiners' verdict. It was just as
well to be manly and bear the wound silently, I thought.

Later, both Nehru and Sir Raghaven assured me, in
conversations, that the offer of the special post would be kept open

as long as they were in government, thereby making me fancy that if I was not happy at Harvard I could drop out of the Ph.D program, perhaps after a year, and try out the government's post. So before leaving India for America I typed out a formal response to Sir Raghaven. One purpose of my letter was to ask the government to clarify and define its offer, so that I could make an intelligent decision in due course. But I never received a reply, and this silence made me wonder if there had ever been a serious possibility of my making a career in the Indian government. Perhaps the government's silence was a sign to me to leave the little circle of India for the big circle of the world. □

TREVOR FISHLOCK
AFTER GANDHI

TREVOR FISHLOCK has been Delhi and New York correspondent for the London *Times,* and Moscow correspondent for the *Daily Telegraph.* He is the author of *India File, The State of America* and *Out of Red Darkness.* His most recent book, *My Foreign Country*, about Britain, has just been published.

Trevor Fishlock

The western state of Gujarat, where Mahatma Gandhi's life began, has a prohibition law in deference to the great man's memory. 'The sentiment that attaches to Gandhi's name in Gujarat makes it impossible to repeal the law,' I was told one warm evening. 'The outcry would be tremendous.' This was said over a beer under a vast sky of swarming stars. Gujarat's liquor consumption is as high as in any state in India, and bootlegging, with the connivance of certain police and officials, is big business. 'One for the road,' said my Gujarati companion, pouring another beer. 'One for the family planning,' another man chimed in; and they laughed.

I landed at Bhuj, the chief town of Kutch. The airfield is on a military base, and on the way out I passed a notice bearing a miniature Services homily: 'The more you sweat in peace, the less you bleed in war.' Kutch is a peninsula between the Sind and Thar deserts, close to the Pakistan border, a region of black mudflats and tawny salt-crust desert. Camel herds float on the haze, strings of donkeys jingle by, sheep and goats worry at meagre scrub under the eyes of turbaned boys, and mongooses scuttle over dusty roads. Alleviating the harshness of the land the people embrace an art alive with vivid colour and design. They paint their spotless thatched mud houses with brilliant patterns. The women, as bright as parakeets, weave and embroider gorgeous blouses, skirts and cloaks.

I hired a car, and a driver who made a temple of it every morning by burning incense sticks on the dashboard beside the picture of his protecting goddess. We drove south, fairly fast because the roads in Gujarat are better than in most of India. Our horn trumpeted as we passed work gangs resurfacing the highway, sweating women and girls bearing dishes of tar and stones on their heads for the steamrollers to flatten. Their tar-baby children played at the roadside.

We crossed the marshes and salt pans of the Little Rann of Kutch. Although the causeway was not old, its balustrades were already crumbling in parts like biscuit—it often seems in India that building materials are pre-aged. On the mudflats stood the shacks where salt workers live for eight months a year. I was told that because they spend so much time up to their knees in salt,

160

their legs do not burn on their cremation pyres, such a curious story that I thought I would not check it with a pathologist in case he declared it nonsense.

We entered what might be called Gandhi country. Gandhi was born at Porbandar on the coast in 1869, and his family moved to Rajkot when he was seven. He was of the *banya* caste of shopkeepers, *gandhi* being a Gujarati word for grocer, and although he was no businessman he was a meticulous book-keeper. His parents were devout Hindus, and Gandhi also imbibed Gujarat's Jain tradition. Pious and austere, Jains prohibit hunting, military pursuits and animal slaughter, and do not farm, because ploughing kills insects. Some monks used to walk on stilts to lessen the chance of squashing beetles underfoot, and a number of ascetics go naked or wear very little. Gandhi himself took to the *dhoti,* for its homespun simplicity, in 1921 and never wore anything else. Jains strive to be self-reliant, and self-reliance lay at the heart of Gandhi's teaching.

The unfolding landscape was studded with small temples and shrines, marked with flags on tall, thin sticks, where numerous deities are acknowledged and guardian gods invoked. We followed famous pilgrim roads and paused at sacred mounts and holy boulders. On the road to Rajkot I glimpsed a man in a loincloth prone on the roadside, his right arm outstretched, a brown coconut at the end of his fingers. I asked the driver to stop and watched how this glistening figure propelled himself. He placed a thin cushion on the hot asphalt, beside the coconut, prostrated himself with his middle on the cushion, reached for the coconut with his right hand and stretched his arm in an arc to put it at his fingertips' end, as a rugby player holds the ball for a goal kicker. He rose, moved the cushion beside the coconut and repeated the process. Trucks roared inches from his head, horns shrieking, rocking his body. Every fifty yards or so, he left the coconut, walked back and retrieved his mobile temple. This was a four-wheeled cart, painted orange, decorated with pictures of gods and fitted with a cassette player and a battered red conical loudspeaker, a lamp and stove, a torch, umbrella and containers of sugar, milk and tea. He pulled the temple up to the coconut and restarted his punishing progress.

He had a ragged beard, grey hair secured in a topknot, a

161

sacred thread across his chest. Grit and tar were embedded in his skin. Two trucks drew up, and their drivers climbed down to talk to him and receive his blessing. He made tea for us all on his stove, boiling up milk and sugar and stirring in a handful of tea leaves.

He said he was sixty years old and was fulfilling a vow. He wanted to see a new temple built at Dwarka, one of the seven sacred cities in India and one of the four Holy Abodes of Vishnu, the preserver of order. So that God would take notice of his prayers he had vowed to spend his life moving a coconut in this painstaking manner from Dwarka to Bhuj and back again. In Bhuj he would break the coconut at a temple, as an offering, and after two days' rest would set off with a new coconut back to Dwarka. The round trip takes one and a half years. He had been doing this for six years and would do six more. 'People give me food and shelter because this is holy work. As you can see, truck drivers sound their horns in salute and stop for tea and a blessing. They respect my pilgrimage.'

When Gandhi was seven, his father was appointed finance minister to the ruler of Rajkot. Gandhi went to the Alfred High School in the city from 1880 to '87. It is a grey stone building with towers. A marble plaque records its distinguished old boy as 'Mahatma in the Making'. Gandhi was born Mohandas Karamchand Gandhi, and only later became known as the Mahatma—the Great Soul. Youths were playing cricket in the dusty forecourt. In the school's gloomy main hall there was a dog-eared display of attendance registers and reports showing that Gandhi was an indifferent pupil. I wanted to visit the city museum nearby, but it was closed because of a holiday. 'You must be knowing,' said the exasperated man who had promised to show it to me, 'that everyone wants a job in government because it is a life of holidays and idle chat and going for tea and not caring about the wants of the people.'

Some of the sons and grandsons of the former princely rulers of India have turned their palaces into hotels. Portraits of tubby forebears look down on the visitors who come to wonder at these relics of power and wealth. One evening I had a palace in Gondal to myself, eating dinner in solitary splendour at the head of a long table built for thirty, a waiter on my left standing throughout the meal to serve, and another on my right to clear the dishes, the manager sitting opposite me, not eating but watching.

As I lay in my grand brass bed next morning, I heard film music and the high-pitched singing of a passionate heroine. It was just before five o'clock. Closer at hand, tambourines and bells struck up, playing an accompaniment to a chant in praise of a god. This roused the lion in the travelling circus camped across the road and he gave vent not to a roar, but to a deep groaning originating in his gut. This caused the silly peacocks in the palace grounds to utter sharp 'miaow, miaow' calls, like children imitating cats. Soon, a muezzin switched on the loudspeakers in the nearby mosque, cleared his throat and launched a penetrating call to prayer; and then came the earwax-cracking whistle of a train. There is no need for an alarm clock in India.

Heading along the Gulf of Cambay, in the reddening light of late afternoon, I came upon a spectacle that for Gandhi would have been the worst of all his nightmares of industrialized people and places. It suggested to me the florid and melodramatic prose of Victorian travellers: O Horror! O terrible Vision! O Fires of Hell!

This was Alang. On a four-mile stretch of beach, about a hundred ships—cruise liners, huge container vessels, freighters and gigantic supertankers—had been driven ashore to be torn to pieces. It is the largest ship-breaking business in the world, and more than a hundred thousand men work round the clock, falling upon each vessel like columns of soldier ants. They strip its furnishings—crockery, woodwork, instruments, cables and machinery—and then dismantle the hulls, slice the decks into pieces and chop up the frames and keel so that after a few weeks or months not an ounce of steel, brass or copper, not even a rivet, is left. Within a short time the space is filled by another ship, run ashore on the spring tide into this amazing knacker's yard.

The rough and narrow roads into Alang are crammed with scores of yards and stores filled with sofas, doors, refrigerators, water closets, capstans, lifeboats, pumps, cranes, dinner plates, life jackets, winches, baths, mirrors. But it is on the foreshore and on the ships, drawn up side by side and towering above the workers,

163

that the spectacle of Alang is awesome and Vulcanic. When I saw it the air was filled with the deafening clangour of hammers and chisels on steel, the roar of crane engines, the hiss of oxyacetylene cutters, the throb of trucks hauling chunks of steel to the rolling mills, the shouts of men.

And these men, in their close-packed thousands, swarmed over piles of steel, cable, piping, machines, their faces illuminated by spark showers and the unwatchable incandescent light of the cutters. Theirs were helot-faces, shiny with sweat, piratical under bandannas, unshaven, raw, lupine, the whites of the eyes stark in the smoky, dirty gloom. The scene brought to my mind pictures of gun decks at Trafalgar and ironworks in Wales in the 1830s. The ships were dismembered by hand, the only tools being chisels and hammers and gas cutters. It is too dangerous for men to be on the ships after dark, and they work on the foreshore when the sun goes down. Even so, an engineer told me, four men are killed every month, ten are badly injured, and a hundred suffer small wounds like the loss of a finger. Exhausted after their shifts they flop into huts in the shanty colonies that have sprung up to house them.

Alang is a boom town, a man's town. Young, risk-taking workers flock here to earn twice the wages they could get anywhere else. Thirteen years ago it was a hamlet, too small for most maps. A man set up as a breaker, with one ship, and the business took off. As labour costs grew in the ship-breaking industries in Taiwan, China and elsewhere, Alang expanded phenomenally. Mr Prakash, a marine engineer, told me that Alang will be in business as long as there are ships on the ocean. 'In the first place, India has a huge and growing appetite for steel. At any one time there are four or five hundred ships in the world that are worn out and have to be broken up. If you could sell the air it would be worth money: it is full of metal dust.'

After dinner in a hotel that evening Mr Prakash talked about Gandhi. 'I saw him many times—he put his hand on my shoulder, and I remember his voice, low and meek, but inspiring. He was our liberator, but he will be forgotten in time. You only have to look around to see that there is much he would hate: the pollution, people pouring into the cities from the countryside, the decline in the art of reading literature and history. Meanwhile, the

Shipbreakers at Alang

165

relationship between Muslims and Hindus will grow worse before it gets better, and I'm very sorry because I don't like the fundamentalists. They hated Gandhi's guts. For all the corruption, India just goes on. I feel proud of my country, its history and culture. We are growing. People want to work and learn. We are taxiing on the runway. We will leave America behind. Nothing will stop us becoming the greatest economic power in the world.'

Around midday, nine men sat themselves side by side on a veranda in the village of Utelia. They were grey-haired elders, prosperous cotton and wheat farmers, wearing loose white shirts and trousers and turbans of poppy red, white and powder blue. They joked and puffed *bidis*, small cheap cigarettes tied with a thread. One of them drew from his pocket a glistening black pellet of opium, the size of a sugar cube.

He put it into a steel saucer, poured on some water and rubbed it with his forefinger to dissolve it, as you might an Oxo cube. He took out a wad of cotton, shaped it into a cone, and dripped the opium solution through it like filtering coffee. He repeated this process several times and was left with a clear brown liquid. After rinsing his right palm with water, he poured a small puddle of opium into it, and offered it to the first man in the line, who bent forward and licked it up like a cat. The palm was washed, charged with opium and offered to the next man. The last in line washed his own palm and performed the same service for the dispenser. This was a twice-a-month social ritual, it was explained to me, a matter of fellowship, something that men mature into. 'It is better for a man than wine or whisky.'

I asked them about Gandhi, and they talked for a while and one of them came up with a consensus answer. 'Gandhi gained us our freedom, but instead of the British Raj we were saddled with politicians interested only in filling their bellies and their wallets. Gandhi has practically been forgotten, and his legacy squandered.'

Utelia is a village of about three thousand people, in the heart of which stands the palace where I stayed. It is not one of those shining marble palaces, more a country mansion. The *thakor*, or raja, showed me a portrait of his grandfather, wearing the two medals he was given at the Delhi Durbar in 1911. Grandfather was the last *thakor* to rule this district before the princes gave up their power and their lands were absorbed into the new Indian state.

'My family ruled for three hundred and fifty years,' the *thakor* said. 'We used to take half the crops and in return we looked after the people, protected them, provided doctors, sorted out disputes, took action in times of calamity. We were judge and jury. We had responsibility. Now we are farmers with five hundred acres and although we have no power, and our relationship with the people has changed, I think we are respected. An affection and a sentiment persist. People complain about the difficulty in getting bureaucrats to act. They say: "You used to own us, but now nobody is our owner." By that they mean they could knock at our door and get things done.'

In the early morning I went to the ashram near the ancient city of Ahmedabad, by the Sabarmati river, where Gandhi lived for twelve years from 1918. 'Sir,' cried the rickshaw driver, dropping me off, 'I am a Christian—you must give me extra money.'

A museum now, the ashram remains a sanctuary, a quiet, shaded place of low, pale-red buildings. Sunlight filters through the cover of neem and mango trees. A notice at the prayer ground overlooking the river suggests that Gandhi's 'hallowed voice' still lingers. Gandhi, I thought, would have been pleased to see the women swabbing the stone floors and bending like gleaners to sweep the sandy ground with swishing brooms. He worked for a total revolution, an India not only free but also hygienic.

Some elderly people were dozing on the veranda of the old ashram guest house, and pigs foraged at the back of it. A man slept under the tree where Gandhi and seventy-eight followers had gathered to begin their Salt March south to the coast. With his astute eye for symbolism, the politically cunning Gandhi picked up salt on the shore in defiance of the salt monopoly law and made plain to the world India's discontent with colonial rule.

Gandhi's red-tiled house faces the river. A picture on the veranda shows him meditating, his head haloed by the moon. His room has pale blue walls, straw mats on the flagstones, a spinning wheel, a low desk painted black. Mr Desai, one of the ashram guides, remembered: 'Everything was in Gandhi's eyes—big eyes with a steady gaze. His body was thin, yet he could walk very fast; and he had a quiet voice which he never raised. I was behind him when he was shot. He was walking quickly because he was late. I saw Nathuram Godse bow, and one of the girls said: "We are in a hurry." Everyone knew something was going to happen.'

Wasn't Gandhi half-forgotten? 'No. He set ideals which are hard to live up to, but Jesus Christ hasn't been forgotten, has he? Gandhi offered a new way, but the nation has become corrupt; the leaders have forgotten the people. My faith is that God will send another Gandhi to get us out of the crisis.'

The caption to the photograph of Gandhi at the entrance to the museum says, 'My life has been so public that there is hardly anything about it that people do not know.' It is true. Gandhi's was a life laid bare in a candid autobiography, remarkably copious correspondence, discourses and confessions. He told in his autobiography of the anguish he felt because, aged sixteen, he was making love to his wife at the moment his father died. He forswore sex when he was thirty-six, a renunciation intended to help him find transcending spiritual strength. He defended his later practice of sleeping with naked girls, like his great-nieces Manu and Abha, saying he was testing his resolve and purity. He confessed to the practice because he felt concealment of it was dishonest. He was right in thinking it would cause controversy: some of his followers were deeply shaken. But then nothing was ever easy with Gandhi. He posed difficult questions and even to those devoted to him he often seemed radical, quirky and harsh. He was sometimes very hard on Kasturbai, his wife. In the ashram Gandhi worked on his beliefs, his 'whole India' approach to politics, spiritual socialism, non-violent resistance, self-denial, the power of truth, spinning-wheel economics, sanitation, nature cures, strict diet, religion. His insistence on bringing untouchables into the ashram community almost destroyed it, so much did it offend deeply held beliefs and prejudices. His wife was one of the protesting rebels.

When he founded the Sabarmati ashram it was on the quiet edge of the city. Now it has been enveloped. The river bridge into Ahmedabad is crammed with buses, trucks, scooter rickshaws and undulating camels. Once outside the ashram gates you are on a busy, stinking highway, near a petrol station and opposite a car showroom and motorcycle emporium. Look at the traffic and you can see that no vehicle encapsulates the burgeoning of the ambitious middle class as well as the motor scooter. The husband drives, his son stands in front of him, his wife perches side-saddle behind him in her fluttering sari, clutching a baby, and behind her sits her daughter. The scooter horn squawks like a duck, and the family weaves in and out of the anarchic traffic; and my heart is in my mouth just to see them.

I walked along the rubbish-strewn path beside the road. A child was defecating on the footway. Gandhi never made any progress in his battle against excreta. Turning down a lane, I came to a factory which works by Gandhian principles. It recycles waste paper and manufactures dark green soap and every year builds two thousand spinning wheels in three sizes, the kind of wheel that symbolized Gandhi's economic beliefs and brought him solace. The director said, 'It is all inspired by Gandhiji. There are four thousand workers here and in villages, spinning, weaving, making furniture and paper. Wages are low, and wages and selling prices are geared so that there is no profit and no loss.' I was shown around in the company of a young bearded man with messianic eyes and a happy smile. 'Gandhi had the answer to every problem,' he said. 'I am going to start an ashram and lead a life like his.'

In city and village I asked children who Gandhi was, and they unfailingly answered, 'Father of the nation.' It remains a matter of wonder that, in its struggle for freedom, India poured its mass of contradictions, prejudices, divided loyalties and hopes not into some swaggering warrior, some thundering orator, some budding dictator, but into a stick-like ascetic in a loincloth, neither saint nor soldier, sometimes cranky, difficult and wrong, who travelled third class, believed himself to be God's instrument and, as a reformer, took on India, its traditions and divisions, as well as the British. The forces of history would have ensured independence without him, but Gandhi gave the mass of people an identity and dignity, a part in the play, an idea of India.

At the same time, he seems a distant parent now, a fading photograph on the wall.

The few dozen steps that Gandhi took in the minutes before he died are marked as red stone footprints on a path beside the terrace lawn at Birla House in Delhi. They are a poignant memorial; and a fitting one too, for Gandhi was a strong, brisk and purposeful walker all his life. He knew India through his feet.

On a bright morning, I followed the footsteps, past shrubs and blossomy trees. Kites, the constant witnesses in the Indian sky, circled high overhead. I heard a man shout, 'No, no,' and saw him run towards a European woman walking on the lawn. He waved his arms. 'No shoes, no shoes.' For a while I tagged along with a party of schoolchildren. Every child learns that Gandhi was the father of the nation, and the primary-school books that chronicle his life remind me of Sunday-school Bible stories. Birla House is both a museum and a shrine.

Gandhi spent the last five months of his life in this house, praying and trying to extinguish the violence between Hindu and Muslim mobs. In all the turmoil this colonnaded white mansion was an oasis of sorts. It stood among the leafy avenues, spacious bungalows and majestic red buildings of the New Delhi created in the 1920s as a new Rome for India's British overlords.

He lived here at the expense of Ghanshyam Das Birla, a banker and industrialist, his admirer for more than thirty years, one of a handful of rich benefactors. Gandhi had, long before, reduced his personal life to a skeletal simplicity but his work needed money and organization. Someone, for example, had to arrange for a goat always to be on hand to supply his milk, since he wouldn't drink from the sacred cow. It was an old joke that it cost a fortune to keep Gandhi in poverty.

His room is as he left it, furnished with a carpet, a spinning wheel, a low white table, a mattress and cushion. Walking to the garden on the evening of 30 January, he knew that his life was in great danger. During a prayer meeting a few days before, a Hindu who detested his preaching of peace between Hindus and Muslims threw a bomb at Birla House. Gandhi refused protection. 'If I am to die by the bullet of a madman, I must do so smiling. There must be no anger within me. God must be in my heart and on my lips.'

He set out for his regular evening prayer meeting just after five o'clock on 30 January 1948. He wore the sandals and homespun white *dhoti* and shawl that had been his invariable dress for nearly thirty years. His arms, as always, rested on the shoulders of his two great-nieces, whom he called his walking sticks. People on the lawn jostled forward as they saw the familiar figure, the nut-brown skull, wire-framed spectacles and cup-handle ears. Mickey Mouse, one of his disciples once called him.

The red footprints on the path turn to the left and ascend five steps to the lawn. The last footprint is a left one. People crowded around Gandhi, to touch him and receive his blessing. Nathuram Godse, the thirty-seven-year-old editor of two Hindu extremist tabloids, who believed Gandhi's creed would destroy Hindu India, emerged from the throng.

Gandhi put his palms together in the *namaskar* greeting which means, 'I acknowledge the Divine in you.' Godse shot him three times in the chest. It is said that with his dying breath Gandhi murmured, 'Ram', the name of God. The photograph of the dead Gandhi in Birla House is captioned, 'The assassin of the ages came with unholy design and lodged hot lead in the flesh of the man who had known no enemy.' Gandhi's followers saved Godse from being lynched in the mêlée. Later, they petitioned unsuccessfully to save him from the gallows.

The place where Gandhi fell is marked by an obelisk, four feet high, in a small pink stone square. Not far away is a stone bearing the words of Gandhi's dream of an India in which all communities live in harmony, without the curses of untouchability, drink and drugs, in which women enjoy the same rights as men and 'since we shall be at peace with the rest of the world . . . the smallest army imaginable'.

I returned to my taxi. The driver had not known where Birla House was, nor of its significance as the place of Gandhi's death. Soon I was back in the city's swirl. When I went to live in India in 1980, Delhi still had a fairly easy pace, with bearable traffic and modest commerce. Cinemas showed a short black-and-white official film asking people, please, to improve their behaviour in public, not to spit, pick their noses, urinate or scratch their groins. I am sure that Gandhi, the social reformer, lifelong campaigner for cleanliness, would have approved. The change in Delhi is astonishing, and its growth explosive. It now contains all the evidence of an ebullient society with the commercial instinct on a free rein: roads packed with cars and fringed with advertising hoardings, tower blocks, air pollution. Gandhi's preaching about the blessings of simplicity seems a long distance away, though his portrait still hangs in many offices and homes, and adorns the 500-rupee banknote, the largest denomination note, which millions of Indians will not even have seen, let alone held in their hands. The reverse shows Gandhi, pilgrim's staff in hand, striding at the head of the eighty-day Salt March in 1930, in the central act of his struggle against British rule.

Near India Gate, the memorial to thousands of Indian soldiers killed fighting for king and Empire in the First World War, I saw the *chhatri*, the domed plinth, which once housed a statue of George V. The statue was removed after Independence, and it was thought that it would be replaced by a figure of Gandhi. When I enquired, years ago, why the plinth was empty I was told that no agreement could be reached on whether the greatest Indian since Buddha should be depicted standing or sitting. Another opinion was that it would be incongruous for Gandhi to look out over what he would have deplored, the display of military might which occurs every year on India's Republic Day, 26 January. The *chhatri* remains uninhabited and enigmatic. □

WILLIAM DALRYMPLE
CASTE WARS

WILLIAM DALRYMPLE's book on Delhi, *The City of Djinns*, won the
Thomas Cook Travel Award and the *Sunday Times* Young British
Writer of the Year prize. His new book, *From the Holy Mountain:
Travels in the Shadow of Byzantium*, has just been published.

Laloo Prasad Yadav, chief minister of Bihar

On the night of 13 February 1992 two hundred armed untouchables surrounded the high-caste village of Barra in the northern Indian state of Bihar. By the light of burning splints, the raiders roused all the men from their beds and marched them out into the fields. Then they slit their throats with rusty harvesting sickles.

Few of my Delhi friends were surprised when I pointed out the brief press report of this massacre, buried somewhere in the middle pages of the *Indian Express*. It was the sort of thing that was always happening in Bihar, they said. It was a commonplace that the state was wracked by violence, corruption and endemic caste warfare. Things were so bad, indeed, that the criminals and the politicians of the state were said to be virtually interchangeable: no fewer than thirty-three members of Bihar's State Assembly had criminal records.

One morning last October, for instance, the overnight train from New Delhi to Calcutta made an unscheduled stop at Gomoh, in southern Bihar. Mumtaz Ansari, the local Member of Parliament, stepped into a first-class compartment, along with three security guards. Neither Ansari nor his henchmen had tickets; they began to turf other passengers out of their seats. One of these passengers, a retired government official, was rash enough to protest. Ansari answered that it was he who made the laws, so he had the right to break them. When the old man continued to protest, the MP waved his hand and ordered the guards to beat him up. At the next stop, Mr Ansari was received by a crowd of supporters including a fellow MP and ten armed retainers. The retainers dragged the retired official on to the platform to finish off the work begun by Mr Ansari's guards. As the train pulled out, the old man was left bleeding on the platform.

In Patna, it was said, no one bothered buying cars any more; armed citizens had taken to stopping them in broad daylight, asking the drivers to get out and forcing them to sign sale deeds. Building contractors on the trail of unpaid bills had started kidnapping government engineers for ransom. In some upper-caste areas, the burning of untouchables had become so common that it was almost an organized sport. In reaction, various lower-caste self-defence forces had been formed and were said to be busily

175

preparing for war in villages they had rechristened Lenin-nagar or Stalinpur. There were estimated to be ten private armies at work in different parts of Bihar; in some areas violence had spun out of control, and they were approaching a situation of civil war.

Bad things went on in Bihar, my friends told me; that was just the way it was. But the Barra massacre stuck in my mind, and a year later, when I found myself in Patna, I decided to hire a car and visit the village. The road was the worst I had travelled on in India: although the route was one of the principal highways of Bihar, holes the size of small bomb craters dented the surface. On either side, the rusting skeletons of dead trucks lined the route like a succession of memento mori. We seemed to be travelling back in time. The electricity pylons came to a halt. Then cars and trucks disappeared from the road. Wells began to replace handpumps. We passed the odd pony trap and four men carrying a palanquin. They flagged us down and warned us about highwaymen. They told us to be off the roads by dark.

Eventually, we came to Barra. It was a small, ancient village raised above the surrounding fields on an old earthen tell. I was shown around by Ashok Singh, one of two male survivors of the massacre. He walked me over to an embankment where a small white monument had been erected to the memory of the forty-two murdered villagers. A hot wind blew in from the fields, dust devils swirled in the dried-out paddy.

I asked: 'How did you escape?'

'I didn't,' he said. He pulled off a scarf and showed me the lurid gash on his neck. 'They cut me, then left me for dead.'

He began to describe in detail what had happened. He had gone to bed after eating his supper, as usual. He, his brothers, father and uncle were all asleep on their charpoys when they were woken by the sound of explosions at ten-thirty. They were frightened and went to the women's part of the house to alert their wives and mothers. The explosions and the sound of gunfire came closer. Then a burning splint was thrown on to the thatch of their roof, and there was a shout from outside that everyone should come out and give themselves up.

'As soon as the roof caught fire, my uncle and I began trying to put out the blaze. We didn't take any notice of what was being shouted, so eventually these low people had to break down the door and drag us all out. There were hundreds of them, armed with guns, spears, bows, lathis and sickles. They left the women by our house, but they tied the men up with lengths of cloth.'

'Did they say where they were from?'

'No, but they were local men. We could tell from their accents. At first they left us lying where we were as they destroyed all the village houses with fire and dynamite. Then they dragged us men to the edge of the village. They made us sit. Then, one by one, they started killing us, right there where we were sitting. A great crowd was watching, but only two people were doing the killing so it took a long time. I was very frightened. My mind went blank.

'They killed all my brothers. They killed my father, my uncle and my cousins. Eventually my turn came. One of the men pushed me forwards, and the other got his sickle and took three swipes. It made deep cuts on the back of my neck and head. I was senseless. The next thing I knew I woke up in hospital in Gaya. It was three weeks before I could get out of bed.'

'You were very lucky.'

'How can you say that? I lost eight of my kin.'

Ashok's face crumpled, and he looked down. 'I would like to take revenge,' he said quietly, 'but I don't have the capacity.'

Ashok showed me the houses he and the widows of the village had erected with the money they had received from the government in compensation. They were miniature castles: tall and square, with no windows except for thin arrow slits on the third storey. Unwittingly, they were almost exact miniature copies of the Peel towers erected in the Scottish borders in medieval times, when central authority had completely broken down. There could be no better illustration of Bihar's regression into the Dark Ages.

'When the Harijans pass us on the road,' Ashok continued, 'they make threats: "we have not finished with you yet" or "you will meet the same fate as your brothers". Every night we are frightened. Every night I have nightmares. They may come again. The police and the state government of Laloo Prasad Yadav are on their side. This massacre was his handiwork.'

'In what sense?'

'Laloo is from a low caste,' Ashok said. 'He is always

encouraging these oiks to rise up against us. When he came here after the massacre, we threw stones at him. Every day we pray for his downfall.'

Cowherds were leading the buffalo back to the village for milking. Women were lighting dung fires and beginning to cook supper. The afternoon was drawing in. I thought of the warnings we had received to be off the roads by the fall of darkness.

'The lower castes are rising up, and the government will not protect us,' said Ashok, as we walked back to the car. 'We are left to the mercy of God.'

In 1991, when he came to power as chief minister of Bihar, Laloo was an unlikely figure in North Indian politics. The Indian establishment was then still firmly dominated by the higher castes: Nehru, Mrs Gandhi and Rajiv were all Brahmins, as was the last prime minister, Narasimha Rao. Brahmins have ruled India for forty-four out of the fifty years since the British left.

But Laloo was the son of a low-caste village cowherd, and his political views were formed by a childhood in which he was persecuted by the high castes of his village. From the beginning of his career he spoke out bitterly against the Brahmins and the Hindu revival that in many areas was bringing about a new hardening in the caste system: 'Our fight is against the wearers of the Sacred Thread [the Brahmins],' he told his audiences. 'For centuries the priests have made fortunes by fooling villagers. Now I tell them they should learn to milk cattle and graze them; otherwise they will starve.'

This was a radical new message, but to many people's surprise, it worked. In the 1991 general election Laloo—supported by the combined votes of the poor, the lower castes and the Muslim community—won an unprecedented majority. Since then a quiet social revolution has taken place in India. In the recent general election, lower-caste politicians won power in state after state. Ten years ago every second person at Delhi drinks parties was an old school friend of various cabinet members, if not the prime minister. Now, quite suddenly, these people don't know anyone in power.

Laloo himself has managed to remain chief minister of Bihar

despite evidence that his government—his own family, indeed—is deeply corrupt and presiding over the looting of the state treasury. The alleged embezzlement of vast sums of agricultural subsidies has cast a particular shadow over his reign, a scandal referred to in the Indian newspapers as 'the multi-crore fodder scam'. But politics in Bihar is a rough game. One MP went on record to declare that 'without a hundred men armed with guns, you cannot hope to contest an election'.

I booked a flight to Patna in the hope of arranging an interview with Laloo. The flight was delayed, and we sat on the tarmac for half an hour. Then Laloo himself turned up, striding on board like a conquering hero. He had been speaking in Delhi, it turned out, and had brought half his cabinet with him.

He was small, broad-shouldered and thickset, and his grey hair was cut in a boyish early-Beatles mop. He had reserved the whole of the first row of the plane for himself and his aides; MPs and bodyguards filled up the next seven tiers of seats. They were all big, sinister-looking men. All—including Laloo—were dressed in the white homespun cotton pyjamas that have become the unmistakable badge of political power.

The delay, the block booking and the extravagant manner in which Laloo lolled lengthwise along the front row of seats, like some degenerate Roman emperor, seemed to confirm all I had heard. Certainly, the entourage at the front of the plane seemed bewitched by their leader. They circled the chief minister, leaning over the plane seats, squatting in front of him on their haunches and laughing at his jokes. When I eventually persuaded one of the MPs to introduce me to his leader, he knelt down in front of Laloo while he explained who I was.

Laloo took it all in his stride. He indicated that I should sit down on the seat beside him—leaving the MP on his knees to one side—and asked how he could help. I asked for an appointment to see him. With a nonchalant wave of his hand he called over a secretary who fixed the interview for five-thirty p.m.

'But,' he said, 'we could begin the interview now.'

'Here? In the plane?'

'Why not? We have ten minutes before we arrive.'

179

So we began. I asked Laloo about his childhood. He proved only too willing to talk about it.

'My father was a small farmer,' began Laloo, scratching his groin. 'He looked after the cows and buffalo belonging to the upper castes; he also had three acres of his own land. He was illiterate, wore a dhoti and never possessed a pair of shoes. My mother sold curds and milk. She was also illiterate. We lived in a mud-thatch cottage with no windows or door; it was open to the dog and the jackal.'

Laloo leaned back against the side of the plane, his legs stretched over two seats. 'I had five brothers and one sister. There was never enough money. When we were old enough we were all sent out to graze the buffalo. Then my two elder brothers went to the city [Patna] and found jobs working on a cattle farm near the airport. They earned ninety-four *paise* [then the equivalent of five pence] a day. When they had saved enough money, my brothers called me to Patna and sent me to school. I was twelve. Until that time I did not know even ABC.'

I asked: 'How were you treated by the upper castes?'

Laloo laughed. The other MPs—who had gathered around to listen—joined in with a great roar of well-practised laughter.

'All my childhood I was beaten and insulted by the landlords,' said Laloo. 'They would punish me for no reason. Because we were from the Yadav caste we were not entitled even to sit on a chair; they would make us sit on the ground. I remember all that. Now I am in the chair and I want those people to sit on the ground. It is in my mind to teach them a lesson.

'I don't hate them,' he continued. 'But their minds have to be changed. We have been an independent country for fifty years, but there has been no alteration in the caste system, no social justice. I want to end caste. I want intercaste marriages. But these Brahmin priests will not allow it.'

'But caste has been around for three and a half thousand years,' I said. 'Isn't it the foundation of Hinduism?'

'It is an evil system,' said Laloo. 'It must go.'

The plane was circling above Patna. Below, you could see the grey width of the Ganges on the edge of the city, flowing past the ghats and out into the fertile flood plains of Bihar.

'Go back to your seat now,' said Laloo curtly. 'I will talk to you again this afternoon.'

No one has ever called Patna a beautiful city, but I found I had forgotten how bad things were. As you drive in through the outskirts, the treeless pavements begin to fill with sackcloth shacks. The shacks expand into slums. The slums are surrounded by garbage heaps. Goats, pigs, dogs and children compete for scraps of food. Open sewers line the road. Sewer rats the size of cats scamper among the rickshaws.

Bihar is one of the last areas of the subcontinent which really conforms to the image of India promoted by well-meaning Oxfam advertisements, all beggars, cripples and overpopulated leper hospitals: 'Send £10 and help Sita regain her sight . . . ' The reality, on the threshold of what is already being called the Asian Century, is that India is the sixteenth biggest economy in the world, and in a population of 950 million has a class, according to the more excitable estimates, of around 150 million people with spending power greater than that of the average Briton. There is talk—again, in the more optimistic metropolitan circles—of the country gearing up to follow Taiwan and South Korea as the next site of the Asian Economic Miracle. Certainly there has recently been a rush of western bankers opening offices in Delhi and Bombay; even Sotheby's has moved east.

Yet while much of India seems to be surging purposefully towards a future of prosperity, health and full literacy, Bihar and its ninety million people have begun to act as a kind of leaden counterweight. The economy is stagnant, and crime is out of control: 64,085 violent offences (armed robbery, looting, rioting and murder) took place between January and June 1996 alone. These figures include 2,625 murders, 1,116 kidnappings and 127 abductions for ransom. This means that Bihar witnesses fourteen murders every day and one kidnapping every four hours. Whatever index of Indian prosperity and development you choose—literacy, deaths in custody, quality of roads, number of cinemas—Bihar comes triumphantly at the bottom.

The day I flew back to Patna there were four stories vying for attention on the front page of the newspaper; each in its own way seemed to confirm the collapse of government in the state. A group of tribals, demanding an independent state in the hills of southern Bihar, had carried out a raid on a mine, making off with 600 kilograms of gelignite and more than a thousand detonators. The Patna police had killed 'a notorious criminal' wanted in several cases of *dacoity*—banditry—including the kidnapping of the Gupta Biscuit Company's proprietor. A Congress politician had accused the Bihar government of 'ignoring the famine-like situation prevailing in the state'. And new figures showed that in the previous three months '1,437 criminals' had been taken into custody, during the '116 riots' that Patna had suffered so far that year.

I went to see Uttam Sengupta, editor of the Patna edition of the *Times of India*, to find out whether these reports were exaggerated. It had been a somewhat upsetting week, he said. Two days earlier an assassin had taken a pot-shot at him with a sawn-off shotgun. The pellets had lodged themselves in the back door of his old Fiat. Sengupta had escaped unscathed but shaken.

He said that what was happening in Bihar was nothing less than the death of the state. The government was broke and unable to provide the most basic amenities. The National Thermal Power Corporation, the Indian national grid, had recently threatened to cut off Bihar's electricity supply until its dues were paid. In the main Patna hospital there were no drugs, no bandages and no bedlinen. Its only X-ray machine had been out of order for a year; the hospital could not afford to buy the spare parts. Patna went unlit at night as there were no light bulbs for the street lamps. Apparently the city required 6,000 bulbs. On one occasion during Diwali, the Hindu festival of light, the administration managed to muster as many as 2,200; but normally only a fraction of that number were available. Occasionally businesses clubbed together to light a single street; otherwise, every day at sunset, much of Patna, a city of more than a million people, was plunged into medieval darkness. Outside the capital, electricity was irregular, despite the fact that Bihari mines produced almost all of India's coal for power generation. The result was an unofficial wave of privatisation. Middle-class residents in blocks of flats had begun to pool their resources and buy their own generators.

When Delhi newspapers publish articles on Bihar's disorders

and atrocities, they tend to make a point of emphasizing the state's 'backwardness'. What is needed in Bihar, they say, is development: more roads, more schools, more family-planning centres. But as the ripples of political and caste violence spread from Patna out into the rest of the country, it seems equally likely that Bihar could be not so much backward as forward: a trendsetter for the rest of India. The first ballot-rigging recorded in India took place in Bihar in the 1962 general election. Thirty years later such rigging is common across the country. Again, the first example of major criminals being awarded parliamentary seats took place in Bihar in the 1980 election. Today many senior Indian politicians have at various times had serious charges—ranging from murder to kidnapping—pending against them.

So infectious is the Bihar disease that it throws into question the whole notion of an Indian economic miracle. Few doubt that if the 'Bihar effect'—corruption, lawlessness, marauding caste armies and the breakdown of government—does prevail then, as Uttam Sengupta put it: 'India will make what happened in Yugoslavia look like a picnic.'

Later that afternoon I went to the chief minister's residence. I found Laloo sitting outside—his legs raised on a table—surrounded by the now familiar circle of toughs and sycophants. I remembered the incident on the train when a civil servant had been beaten up by Laloo's supporters, led by Ansari the MP, and asked him if the press reports had been accurate.

'Why don't you ask the man responsible?' replied Laloo. He waved his hand at a man to his left. 'This is Mumtaz Ansari.'

Ansari, a slight, mustachioed figure in white pyjamas, giggled. 'It is a fabricated story,' he said, a broad grin on his face. 'A baseless story, the propaganda of my enemies.'

'It was only his party workers who beat the man up,' explained Laloo. 'Ansari had nothing to do with it.'

'So the man *was* beaten up?'

'A few slaps only,' said Ansari. 'The fellow was misbehaving.'

'What action have you taken?' I asked Laloo.

'I told my MP: "You must not behave like this. A citizen is the owner of the country. We are just servants."'

'That's all you did?'

'I have condemned what happened,' said Laloo, smiling from ear to ear. 'I have condemned Mr Ansari.'

Both Laloo and Ansari burst out laughing. Laloo finished the cup of tea he was drinking, threw the dregs over his shoulder and dropped the cup on the grass, calling for a turbaned bearer to pick it up. 'Come,' he said, standing up. 'This was a small incident only. Let me show you my farm.'

He took my arm and led me around what had once been the neat rose garden of the British governor's residence. Apart from a small patch of lawn at the back of the house, the whole plot had been ploughed up and turned into a series of fields. In one corner stood Laloo's fish pond and beehives; in another, his dairy farm, rabbit hutches, cattle and buffalo sheds. In between were acres of neat furrows planted with chillies, spinach and potatoes. 'This is *satthu*,' he said. 'Very good for wind.'

'Who eats all this?' I asked.

'I do, along with my wife and family. We villagers like fresh produce. The rest we distribute to the poor.'

While we examined a new threshing machine (manned by a cousin) Laloo talked again of the Brahmin political establishment.

'The BJP and the Congress are both Brahminical parties,' he said. 'The backward castes have no reason to vote for them. Already they have realized this in Bihar. In time they will realize this everywhere. The support of these parties will dry up like a dirty puddle on a summer's day.

'The backward castes will rise up,' he said as he led me to my car. 'Even now they are waking up and raising their voices. You will see: our revolution will break the power of these people . . . '

In the darkness, Laloo punched the air like a demagogue on a rostrum: 'We will have a flood of votes,' he said. 'Nobody will be able to check us.'

The driver was itching to be off: it would soon be dark, and he wanted to be back at the hotel before sunset. Even in Patna, he said, it was madness to be on the roads after dark. □

GRANTA

VIRAMMA
PARIAH

VIRAMMA is an agricultural worker and midwife in Karani, a village
near Pondicherry in south-east India. She told her life story, over ten
years, to Josiane and Jean-Luc Racine. It was published in France as
Une vie paria, and will be published in the UK by Verso.

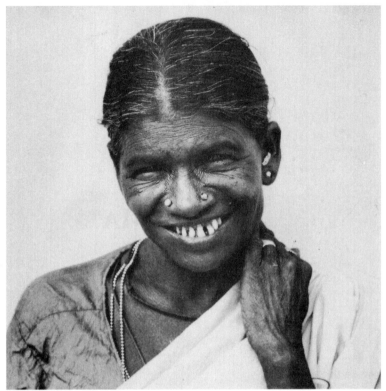

Viramma   J. C. RACINE

186

I am the midwife here. I was born in the village of Velpakkam in Tamil Nadu, and when I married, I came to Karani, my husband's village. I was still a child then. I am a farm worker and, like all my family, I am a serf, bonded to Karani's richest landowner. We are Pariahs. We live apart from the other castes; we eat beef, we play the drums at funerals and weddings because only we can touch cow hide; we work the land. My son Anbin corrects me when I say 'Pariah'; he says we should use the word 'Harijan'. Every day people from the political parties come to the village and tell us to demand higher wages, to fight the caste system. And they mean well. But how would we survive? We have no land, not even a field.

We midwives help women during labour and are paid twenty rupees a month by the state. When a woman goes into labour, her relatives come and find me: 'Eldest sister-in-law! The woman's in pain at home!' So I drop everything; I go and see her, examine her, turn her round one way, then the other; I pester her a bit and then tell her more or less when the child is going to be born. And it always turns out as I said it would. When the child is born, I cut the cord with a knife and tell one of the other women attending to find a hoe and a crowbar and to dig a hole in the channel near the house. I wait for the placenta to come out and go and bury it immediately. Then I take care of the mother. I stretch her out on a mat, propped up with pillows, wash the baby with soap and hot water and lay it down next to its mother. Then I put a sickle and some margosa leaves at the head of the mat, so spirits don't come near them—those rogue spirits love to prowl around the lanes in the evening or at night, eating any food left lying on the ground and trying to possess people.

It's well known that they follow us everywhere we go, when we're hoeing or planting out; when we're changing our sanitary towels; when we're washing our hair. They sense that we're going to visit a woman in labour and then they possess us. That's why we put down the sickle and the margosa leaves. After the birth I'll visit the mother quite often, to make sure everything's going all right. If impurities have stayed in the womb, I'll cook the leaves of the 'cow's itch' plant, extract the juice and make the mother drink it three times.

187

That's how a birth happens here. We Pariahs prefer to have babies at home. I tell the nurse if the newborns are boys or girls, and she goes and enters them in the registers at Pondicherry hospital. In the past, we'd take women to hospital only in emergencies. We went there in an ox-cart or a rickshaw, and often the woman died on the way. Nowadays doctors visit the villages and give medicines and tonics to women when they become pregnant. In the sixth or seventh month they're meant to go to the dispensary for a check-up. A nurse also comes to the village. Yes, everything has changed now.

I had my twelve children alone; I didn't let anyone near me. 'Leave me in peace,' I always said to the nurses. 'It will come out on its own! Why do you want to rummage around in there?' I always give birth very gently—like stroking a rose. It never lasts long: I'm not one of those women whose labours drag on all night, for days even.

When I'm giving birth I first make a point of preparing a tray for Ettiyan—the god of death's assistant—and his huge men, with their thick moustaches and muscly shoulders. On the tray I put green mangoes, coconuts and other fruit as well as some tools: a hoe, a crowbar, a basket, so that they can set to work as soon as the child comes out of the sack in our womb. Yes! I've seen enough to know what I'm talking about. I've had a full bushel of children! Everything we eat goes into that sack: that's how the child grows. Just think what a mystery it is. With the blood he collects over ten months, Isvaran [the god Siva] moulds a baby in our womb. Only he can do that. Otherwise how could a sperm become a child?

I've always had plenty of milk. It used to flow so much that the front of my sari was all stiff. It's well known that we breastfeed our children for a long time. That prevents us from having another child immediately. If we were always pregnant, how could we work and eat? Rich women can stretch their legs and take a rest. But to get my rice, I have to work: planting out, hoeing, grazing the cows, collecting wood. When we've got a little one in our arms, it's the same: we take it everywhere, and we worry, because while we're working we don't really know what it's doing, where it is. That's why we try to wait at least three years, until the child grows up, walks and can say, 'Dad', 'Mum', 'That's our cow'. That's what we take as a sign. Then we can start 'talking' again, 'doing it'. If we time it like this, the child will be strong and chubby.

But Isvaran has given me a baby a year. Luckily my blood has stayed the same; it hasn't turned, and my children have never been really emaciated. Of course that also depends on the way you look after them. For me, that used to be my great worry! I managed to feed them well. As soon as I had a little money, I'd buy them sweets. I'd make them rice whenever I could, some *dosai*, some *idli*. I'd put a little sugar in cow's milk . . . That's how I took care of them. There are some women who just let their children be without giving them regular meals. Human beings can only live if you put at least a little milk in their mouths when they're hungry! It happens with us that some women skip their children's mealtimes when they're working. But how do you expect them to grow that way?

Isvaran has done his work well; he's put plenty of children in my womb: beautiful children, born in perfect health. It's only afterwards that some have died. One of diarrhoea, another of apoplexy. All of them have walked! Two of my children even came to the peanut harvest. I pierced their noses to put a jewel in. I plaited their hair and put flowers in it and pretty *potteu* on their foreheads, made with paste. I took good care of my little ones. I never neglected them. I dressed them neatly. If high-caste people saw them running in the street, they'd talk to them kindly, thinking that they were high-caste children.

How many children have I had? Wait . . . I've had twelve. The first was a girl, Muttamma. Then a boy, Ganesan. After that, a girl, Arayi. *Ayo!* After that I don't remember any more. But I've definitely had twelve: we registered them at the registry office. Yes, when there's a birth, you have to go there and declare it. 'Here sir, I've had a boy or a girl and I name it Manivelu, Nataraja or Perambata.' Down there they enter all that into a big ledger. *Ayo!* If we went to that office, perhaps they could tell us how many children I've had and their names as well. *Ayo!* Look at that, I don't remember any more. They're born; they die. I've haven't got all my children's names in my head: all I have left are Miniyamma, my fourth child; Anbin, my eighth; and Sundari, my eleventh.

189

A pregnant woman is prey to everything that roams around her: ghosts, ghouls, demons, the evil spirits of people who have committed suicide or died violent deaths. She has to be very careful, especially if she is a Pariah. We Pariah women have to go all over the place, grazing the cattle, collecting wood. We're outside the whole time, even when the sun's at its height. Those spirits take advantage of this: they grab us and possess us so we fall ill, or have miscarriages. Something like that happened to me when I was pregnant with my second child.

One of my nephews died suddenly, the day after his engagement. One night when I was asleep I saw him sitting on me—I felt him! My husband told me that I had squeezed him very tight in my arms, that I'd been delirious and mumbling something. The following day we decided that the boy needed something, and that's why he'd come. My husband went to get bottles of arrack and palm wine. I arranged the offerings in the middle of the house: betel, areca nuts, lime, a big banana leaf with a mountain of rice, some salt fish, some toast, a cigar, bottles of alcohol, a jar of water and a beautiful oil lamp. In the meantime my husband went to find the priest from the temple of Perumal [Vishnu]—he's the one responsible for funerals. The priest asked us to spread river sand next to the offerings. He called on Yama, the god of death, and drew the sign of Yama in the sand. We ate that evening as usual and went to sleep in a corner. You must never sleep opposite the door, because a spirit might slap you when it comes in if it finds you in its way. You have to be brave when a spirit arrives! In fact you won't see it; you only hear its footsteps, like the sound of little bells, *djang, djang*, when an ox-cart goes by. It goes *han! han! han!* as if it's craving something. It always comes with its messengers, all tied to each other with big ropes. You hear them walking with rhythmic, heavy steps: *ahum! ahum! ahum!*

We were very afraid. As soon as the spirit came in, the lamp went out in a flash, even though it was full of oil. We heard it walking about and eating its fill and then suddenly it fled. We heard it running away very fast. When day broke soon after it had gone, we rushed to see what had happened. The rice was scattered everywhere. On the sand we found a cat's paw-print, and part of Yama's sign had been rubbed out. The spirit had come in the form of a cat! While we were waiting for the priest to come, we collected the offerings in a big wicker basket. The priest himself was very satisfied and said that the spirit wouldn't come back. But I fell ill soon after and had a miscarriage.

There are worse spirits, though: the *katteri,* for example, who spy on women when they are pregnant. You have to be very careful with them. There are several sorts of *katteri*: Rana Katteri, who has bleeding wounds and drinks blood; or Irsi Katteri, the foetus eater—she's the one who causes miscarriages. As soon as she catches the smell of a foetus in a woman's womb, she's there, spying, waiting for her chance. We can tell immediately that it's that bitch at work if there are black clots when a baby aborts: she sucks up the good blood and leaves only the bad.

My first three children were born at my mother's house. Their births went well, and they died in good shape. It was the spirit living in that house who devoured them. My grandfather knew about sorcery. People came to see him; they used to say that he called up the spirit, talked to it and asked it to go along with him when he went out. It lived with him, basically. When my grandfather died, we tried to drive it away but it was no use; it used to come back in the form of my grandfather; it joined in conversations, calling my grandmother by her name like her dead husband used to. And my grandmother used to answer back, 'Ah! The only answer I'll give you is with my broom, you dog! I recognize you! I know who you are! Get out of here!' It would just throw tamarind seeds at her face. When a sorcerer came from Ossur to try and get rid of it, it turned vicious. The sorcerer told us he couldn't do anything against it. The spirit had taken root in that ground. It was old and cunning: we were the ones who had to go. It destroyed everything! Everything! A garlic clove couldn't even grow! My father had to sell his paddy field. I gave birth three times there: none of those children survived. The spirit ate them as and when they were born. Nothing prospered. That's how it is with the spirits.

All my children have been buried where they died: the first ones at Velpakkam, the others at Karani. My mother insisted we burn the first-born and throw her ashes in the river so a sorcerer didn't come and get them. The ashes or bones of first-borns are coveted by magicians. A tiny bit of ash or hair is enough for them. You see them with a hoe on their shoulder prowling around where a first-born has been burnt or buried. We made sure that everything disappeared. We have a saying that if you dissolve the ashes completely in water, you'll immediately have another child.

Until they grow up, we mothers always have a fire in our belly for our children: we must feed them, keep them from sickness, raise them to become men or women who can work. One of my three sisters died of a kind of tuberculosis. She had been married and she left a son. I brought him up after her death, but like his mother, he was often ill. Before she died, my sister had prayed that he would become strong, so I took up her prayers. I went into three houses and in each one I asked for a cubit of fabric. I put the three bits of fabric on the ground and laid the child on them. Then I went into three other houses and exchanged the child for three measures of barley, saying, 'The child is yours; the barley is mine.' Of course afterwards I would get the child back. Then I went to three other houses to collect handfuls of dirt. I mixed the three handfuls, spread them out and rolled the baby in them, saying, 'Your name will be Kuppa! You are Kuppa! You have been born of dirt!' Then I pierced his nostril with a silver thread which I twisted into a ring. That worked very well for him! He's still alive and he still wears that ring in his nose today.

What is more important for us women than children? If we don't draw anything out of our womb, what's the use of being a woman? A woman who has no son to put a handful of rice in her mouth, no daughter to close her eyes, is an unhappy woman. She or her parents must have failed in their dharma. I have been blessed in that way: Isvaran has filled my womb. Ah, if all my children were alive, they'd do all the trades in the world! One would be a labourer, another a carpenter. I would have made one of them study. We could have given two daughters away in marriage and enjoyed our grandchildren. I would be able to go and rest for a month with each of my sons. Yes, we would have been proud of our children. □

Translated by WILL HOBSON

V. S. NAIPAUL
NOTEBOOKS

No other writer has equalled V. S. Naipaul as a delineator of modern India. From his first visit in 1962 he produced *An Area of Darkness*, an account which caused controversy in India (then a country more sensitive to external criticisms of itself) and ranks alongside the fiction of Kipling, Forster and Rushdie and the films of Satyajit Ray as a key influence on the way we imagine India. Naipaul returned in 1975 to write *A Wounded Civilization*. Two months before he landed in Bombay, Mrs Indira Gandhi, then prime minister, had declared her Emergency in an experiment with dictatorship which lasted eighteen months.

The first page of *A Wounded Civilization* is reproduced opposite. The early pages of Naipaul's private Bombay diary, reproduced on succeeding pages, show how those published words came to be written; how Naipaul works.

Foreword

THE lights of Bombay airport showed that it had been raining; and the aeroplane, as it taxied in, an hour or two after midnight, blew the monsoon puddles over the concrete. This was in mid-August; and officially (though this monsoon was to be prolonged) the monsoon still had two weeks to go. In the small, damp terminal building there were passengers from an earlier flight, by Gulf Air. The Gulf was the Persian Gulf, with the oil states. And among the passengers were Indian businessmen in suits, awaiting especially careful search by the customs men; some Japanese; a few Arabs in the desert costumes which now, when seen in airports and foreign cities, are like the white gowns of a new and suddenly universal priesthood of pure money; and two turbaned and sunburnt Sikhs, artisans, returning to India after their work in an oil state, with cardboard suitcases and similar new shoes in yellow suede.

There is a new kind of coming and going in the world these days. Arabia, lucky again, has spread beyond its deserts. And India is again at the periphery of this new Arabian world, as much as it had been in the eighth century, when the new religion of Islam spread in all directions and the Arabs—led, it is said, by a seventeen-year-old boy—overran the Indian kingdom of Sind. That was only an episode, the historians say. But Sind is not a part of India today; India has shrunk since that Arab incursion. No civilization was so little equipped to cope with the outside world; no country was so easily raided

August 20.   The monsoon rain was blown on the concrete by the aeroplane as it landed. I had once been in Bombay during the monsoon and begun to pine for the plastic mackintosh I had left behind at London airport. I remember the dread with which I had arrived at Bombay in 1962; the excitement of my long rainy arrival, by aeroplane, in 1967. With each successive arrival in India my dismay and apprehension lessen. It may be that I have learned a new way of seeing or know better now what to expect, it may also be that one's sense of dissolution has now spread, that there are no longer places where one can retreat; that I am now aware of a more general uncertainty and am, perhaps importantly, less of a colonial.

The taxi shuttered past the sleeping city, the slums, the blackened concrete tenements, the bright cinema posters. Yet even on this night drive the vitality of Bombay was something that could be sensed; the setting for the muddle of dereliction and decay, so that perhaps dereliction & decay can no longer be opposed to creation, that all is in a state of decay & remaking. Buildings I had seen only as or as architects' drawings models/pieces in full grown. At the Inter-continental it was all light and glitter, the glitter that suggests movement, township. But there was noise in the galleries of the Taj Mahal, each among each dim lay ushers, gully among gully dawn a-up. The sun in dull and cool, his cool. In the monsoon in an air-conditioned room the bed feels damp.

The East is strange indeed now. Burned in the cul of a new world. Arabs, Japanese, Indians. The Indian press therefore to the Middle East or West Asia has the next emphasis.

August 20

The monsoon rain was blown on the concrete by the
aeroplane as it landed. I had never been in Bombay during
the monsoon and began to grieve for the plastic
mackintosh I had left behind at London airport. I
remember the dread with which I had arrived at Bombay
[by ship] in 1962; the excitement of my early morning
arrival, by aeroplane, in 1967. With each successive arrival
in India my dismay and apprehension lessen. It may be
that I have learned a new way of seeing or know better
now what to expect; it may also be that one's sense of
dissolution has now spread; that there are no longer places
where one can retreat; that I am now aware of a more
general insecurity and am, perhaps importantly, less of a
colonial.

The taxi stuttered through the sleeping city, the flats, the
blackened concrete tenements, the bright cinema posters.
Yet even on this night drive the vitality of Bombay was
something that could be sensed: the creativity in the midst
of dereliction & decay, so that perhaps dereliction & decay
can no longer be opposed to creation, that all is in a state
of decay & making. Buildings I had seen only as models
or as architect's elevations were now full grown. At the
Intercontinental it was all light and glitter, the glitter that
suggests imminent tarnishing. But there was order in the
galleries of the Taj Mahal [hotel], arch answering arch
down long vistas, gallery answering gallery down & up.
The room was white and cool, too cool. In the monsoon in
an air-conditioned room the bed feels damp.

The East is strange indeed now. Beirut is the centre of a
new world: Arabs, Japanese, Indians. The Indian press that
refers to the Middle East as West Asia has the right
emphasis.

So now to other wings of the day: the Sikh workers, sunburned, returning on new clothes by Gulf Air. Indians are and go to these places in numbers now as clerks, accountants, vegetable sellers. So I was told by the girl — an Anglo-Indian as I learnt, and a former model — whom I met at the flat of the photographer, with Richard Simpson. She herself has been working in Sharjah for two years and is back on a holiday. The rats playing at night around the filling of India. At first they had seemed to be scuttling; to me I realised that they were playing like baby rabbits; they were not looking for shelter.

It is Kansas in Delhi, they say. Here people still talk freely. But the newspapers are to be read in a special way. They are full of stories of raids on grain merchants who have been hoarding grain, cinema managers who have been holding back on entertainment taxes, hotel-keepers who have been arrested, and several who have been dismissed. The journalists are demoralised. The Illustrated Weekly which sold 260,000 (they was 1969 from 50,000) is now gone to decline.

The photographer & the model: the Picasso theme.

—

August 21 The Congress this morning; more cryptic paragraphs about arrests & raids. But the people arrested seem small fry: A dull paper. There is a quality about Censored newspapers; one can be amusing to decipher them. But there is no fun in the news on AIR. In between the news, high, there are items that are more interesting: agri-machinery export last year up to 375 crores of rupees; the steel plant at Rourkela made a profit for the first time.

It was a holiday Rakhi Bandan, when brothers are given

So now to other images of the day: the Sikh workers, sunburned, returning in new shoes by Gulf Air. Indians are now going to these places in numbers now, as clerks, accountants, vegetable sellers. So I was told by the girl— an Anglo-Indian, as I learnt, and a former model—whom I met at the flat of the photographer, with Rahul Singh. She herself has been working in Sharja for two years and is back on holiday. The rats playing at night around the Gateway of India. At first they had seemed to be scuttling; but then I realized that they were playing like baby rabbits; they were not looking for shelter.

It is tenser in Delhi, they say. Here people still talk openly. But the newspapers are to be read in a special way. They are full of stories of raids on grain merchants who have been hoarding grain, cinema managers who have been holding back on entertainment tax, brothel keepers who have been arrested, civil servants who have been dismissed. The journalists are demoralized. The Illustrated Weekly which sold 260,00 (rising in 1969 from 80,000) is now going to decline.

The photographer and the model: the Picasso theme.

August 21

The *Express* this morning; more cryptic paragraphs about arrests and raids. But the people arrested seem small fry. A dull paper. There is a quality about censored newspapers; it can be amusing to decipher them. But this is as boring as the news on AIR [All India Radio]. In between the [main] news, though, there are items that are more interesting: engineering exports last year up to 375 crores of rupees; the steel plant at Rourkela made a profit for the first time. It was a holiday, Rakhi Bandan; when brothers are given

...as tokens of regard of sisters. The Prince of Wales Museum was full of ordinary people, people like those [who] fill the breasts of goddesses smooth and hard the pair of Shiva & Uma. The collection was grander than I had expected, the range of miniatures quite fantastic. It takes time to learn to look at India: to arch the art the sculpture, the architecture. I had never before studied the architecture of Bombay: these Victorian-Indian-Gothic which was seen to have a great charm. We wandered around the Gateway of India in the afternoon, a during & sunset had (a cinema make of trumpet chime & temple bells) and a religious prayer of some sort going on below the arch. The white wall of India, the windows picked out of the ornament light red & green & pillars of saris. The naked divers. But the holidays of Maharashtra have been cut down to three now.

There is a package tour in the hotel, which as a result seems fuller than yesterday. It is a European package tour.

At seven we went to the Bombay Republican Club. In the funny, half-lit light of dark this overcast day. And sat in the verandah that lies about flat to the level green expanse of playing field (full of flowers in the leafy light) below the fans that whipped up my muscle aches. Then Jha, of the Times of India was there. He is fatter now than he was six years ago. His wife died six years ago in Benares, during an Israeli air raid on the city; she was a doctor & had been asked to spend a day or two else in the city. She left a daughter, who is now aged ten; and then Jha said that for the past two months or so he had been thinking of getting married again. He said that democracy had begun to break down since ... age, people had lost confidence the ballot box and had

wristlets as tokens of regard by sisters. The Prince of
Wales Museum was full of ordinary people; people like
these polish the breasts of goddesses smooth and touch the
groins of Shiva and Uma. The collection was grander than
I had expected, the range of miniatures quite fantastic. It
takes time to learn & look at India; to enter the art, the
sculpture, the architecture. I had never before studied the
architecture of Bombay: this Victorian-Indian-Gothic
which now seems to have a great charm. The crowds
wandered around the Gateway of India in the afternoon, a
drumming & trumpet band (a curious mixture of trumpet,
drums and temple bells) and a religious puja of some sort
going on below the arch. The white crowd of India, the
whiteness picked out by the occasional bright reds &
greens & yellows of saris. The naked divers. But the
holidays of Maharashtra have been cut down to three now.
There is a package tour in the hotel, which as a result
seems fuller than yesterday. It is a European package tour.
At seven we went to the Bombay Gymkhana Club. In the
pearly, half-livid light of dusk this overcast day. And sat in
the veranda that lies almost flat to the level green expanse
of playing field (full of players in the half light) below the
fans that whipped up my muscle aches. Prem Jha of the
Times of India was there. He is fatter now than he was
seven years ago. His wife died two years ago in Damascus,
during an Israeli air raid on the city; she was a dancer and
had been asked to spend a day or two extra in the city. She
left a daughter, who is now aged six, and Prem Jha said
that for the past two months or so he had been thinking of
getting married again. He said that democracy had begun
to break down three years ago; people had lost confidence
in the ballot box and had

4

begun to talk of the street. Until the Monday, he said, the
road outside the Taj India office was regularly blocked by
processions, trade union agitations. This had begun to decay
enormously one class ago; the students were being hustled. There
was a "package" — the main point of which seemed to be the
abolition of price controls, which damaged industry — let not
the people on top know this, by were also aware of opposition from
the people — small traders etc — who benefited from price
controls and who were able to present the case for controls as the
case for socialism. But PJ's attitude was as apathetic as
it raised to me eight years ago: the new & pervasive frenzy,
the non-class frenzy. He said there was great cynicism the
civil service, that people puffed in their paper, and smiled when
ideas were put to them, and showed the reason why nothing
should be done. This is an attitude I understand too: it
was exemplified for me some time ago by Romila Thapar who
always knew why things would fail, like technology by
satellite.

The other man said, when I asked him: Yes, we all
criticise the system, but it is what keeps us here, we like
this. The third man was a boo-wallah, who had very
good reasons for Indian inaction over issues like East
Africa.

Dinner afterwards with Rachel & Pinky at Kebab korner
in the Nataraj.
Friday April 22   Awoke 10.30 and went for a fitting to
Burlington in the Taj. The trousers were far too narrow around
the waist & hips. At 12.30 Shirish Patel came, small & attractive,
and as past I thought him younger than myself. He was dressed
in white & carrying the rakhi that had been posted to him

begun to take to the streets. Until the other day, he said, the road outside the Times of India office was regularly blocked by processions, trade union agitations. Things had begun to decay economically some time ago; the statistics were being twisted. There was a 'package'—the main point of which seemed to be the abolition of price controls, which damaged industry—but though the people on top knew this, they were also aware of opposition from the people—small traders etc—who benefited from price controls and were able to present the case for controls as the case for socialism. But PJ's attitude was as negative as it seemed to me eight years ago. The newspaperman's frenzy, the non-doer's frenzy. He said there was great cynicism in the civil service, that people puffed on their pipes and smiled when ideas were put to them, and showed the reasons why nothing should be done. This is an attitude I understand too: it was exemplified for me some time ago by R_ T_, who always knew why things would fail, like teaching villages by satellite.

The other man said, when I asked him: Yes, we all criticize the system, but it is what keeps us here, living like this. The third man was a box wallah, who had very good reasons for Indian inaction over issues like East Africa. Dinner afterwards with Rahul and Pinky at Kebab Korner in the Nataraj.

Friday August 22

Awoke 10.30 and went for a fitting to Burlingtons' in the Taj. The trousers were far too narrow around the waist & hips. At 12.30 Shirish Patel came, small & attractive, and at first I thought him younger than myself. He was dressed in white and carrying the rakhi that had been presented to him . . .

NAIPAUL'S DIARY REPRODUCED COURTESY OF THE UNIVERSITY OF TULSA

IMAGINED WORLDS
FREEMAN DYSON

One hundred years after H. G. Wells visited the future in *The Time Machine*, Freeman Dyson marshals his uncommon gifts as a scientist and storyteller to show us where science and technology, real and imagined, may be taking us. The stories he tells—about "Napoleonic" versus "Tolstoyan" styles of doing science, the coming era of radioneurology and radiotelepathy, the works of writers from Aldous Huxley to Michael Crichton to William Blake—come from science, science fiction, and history. Sharing in the joy and gloom of these sources, Dyson seeks out the lessons we must learn from all three if we are to understand our future and guide it in hopeful directions. Jerusalem-Harvard Lectures

27 halftones
$22.00 / £14.50 cloth

THE ANATOMY OF DISGUST
WILLIAM IAN MILLER

William Miller embarks on an alluring journey into the world of disgust, showing how it both horrifies us and brings order and meaning to our lives. Our notion of the self depends on it; cultural identities have frequent recourse to its boundary-policing powers; love depends on overcoming it. Imagine aesthetics without disgust for tastelessness and vulgarity; imagine morality without disgust for evil, hypocrisy, stupidity, and cruelty. Miller traverses literature, philosophy, history, political theory and psychology to show how disgust animates our world.

$24.95 / £16.50 cloth

DISPATCHES FROM THE FREUD WARS
Psychoanalysis and Its Passions
JOHN FORRESTER

In this engaging collection of essays, noted historian and philosopher of science John Forrester raises a provocative issue: no matter how you feel about Freud, you can't escape the influence of his theories. Through questions central to our century's ways of thinking Forrester explores dreams, history, ethics, political theory, and psychoanalysis as a scientific movement. He gives us a sense of the ethical surprises and epistemological riddles that a century of tumultuous psychoanalytical debate has often obscured.

$27.95 / £18.50 cloth

Harvard University Press

US: 800 448 2242
UK: 0171 306 0603
www.hup.harvard.edu

Art: from "Invitation," by Michael Sowa, Courtesy of Inkognito, from the jacket of *The Anatomy of Disgust*

NIRAD CHAUDHURI
MY HUNDREDTH YEAR

ROGER HUTCHINGS/NETWORK

NIRAD CHAUDHURI was born in rural Bengal in 1897 and can remember
the excitement in his neighbourhood when the news reached it that
Japan had defeated Russia in the war of 1905, the first Asian victory
over modern Europe. He has lived in England since 1970. His books
include *The Autobiography of an Unknown Indian*, *A Passage to England*,
The Continent of Circe, *Hinduism* and *Thy Hand, Great Anarch*.

W hy do writers write? My acquaintances often ask me: 'How did the idea of writing come to you?' I give them an answer which could be regarded as flippant. I ask in my turn: 'Why don't you ask a tiger: "How did the idea of hunting come to you?"'

But I mean it seriously. To my thinking, no writer writes from choice; he writes because he cannot help it. He is under an irresistible compulsion to write.

The compulsion, however, is different for different kinds of writers. It is of one kind for those who may be called 'vocational' writers, and of another kind for those who proclaim themselves and are recognized by the great majority of readers as 'professional' writers. They, of course, far outnumber the 'vocationals'.

The obvious fact about the motivation of vocational writers is that they have no motive at all. They give expression to what comes to their mind without thought of money, position, fame, or even attention. In stark contrast, the professionals want all these, will not write otherwise, and are clever enough to secure them. I shall indicate their social affiliation by citing the great Bengali novelist, Bankim Chandra Chatterji (1838–94). He created an eccentric character, something of a wag, who was summoned as a witness in a court case. The plaintiff's lawyer asked him: 'What is your profession?'

He retorted angrily: 'Profession! Am I a prostitute or a lawyer that I should have a profession?'

He was an authentic traditionalist in his brusqueness. As Kipling wrote in his story 'On the City Wall': 'Lalun is a member of the most ancient profession in the world. Lilith was her very-great-grandmama, and that was before the days of Eve.'

Over and above, writers can be classified zoologically. Actually, all vocations and professions may be placed within the zoological taxonomy. Members of each one of them can be regarded as an animal of a distinct species—say, a lion, a horse, a dog, or cat.

There is, however, a fundamental difference between the zoological correlatives of writers and those of all other professions. Members of all professions are one animal, differing among themselves only by their standing as that particular animal.

For instance, a successful barrister in a high court may be an Arab horse, while lawyers of lowly rank in a court of the lowest jurisdiction will be a hackney.

But writers, zoologically classified, are not one animal; they are different animals. That is to say, if one writer can be regarded as a lion or horse, another will be a bullock, or donkey, or a monkey, or even a skunk. Therefore no one can form a correct idea of what a particular writer is or does by simply considering him as a writer. This is a very vague description and too wide in its scope to be of value.

I shall not proclaim myself any particular animal as a writer, but leave it to the reader to place me in the zoological hierarchy. I shall only describe how I write and what conception I have of the business of writing.

First, considering myself as a 'vocational' writer, I certainly set down in writing whatever comes into my mind. But I do not regard it primarily as a product of my own mind, i.e. as an idea or a sense impression of my own.

I try to convert my mind into a camera to take the impression of whatever it is exposed to, and thus create the equivalent of a photographic negative. My personal work is to develop this negative and then make a print. I do not allow anything that was not present in the untouched negative to be in the print for the sake of pictorial effect.

I have next to explain the methodology of my writing. The basic realization which dictates my method is that language is something to be heard, not merely to be looked at. Thus I consider what is written by way of literary work to be the exact equivalent of a musical score, and when writing I always behave like a musical composer; I never write without sounding what I am writing in my ear.

I did not learn English from Englishmen, nor hear it as spoken by native speakers of the language till late in life. Till 1910 I learned it at my birthplace, Kishanganj, a small town in East Bengal, from my Bengali teachers. From 1910 to 1914 (when I passed the matriculation examination) I learned it in Calcutta, also from Bengali teachers. This gave me a mastery of English syntax, idioms and also an adequate vocabulary so that when I entered university life in 1914 I did not have to consult dictionaries for the meaning of words and could concern myself with the subject matter of what I had to read, both as to information and ideas. Nonetheless an acute anxiety troubled me when I was writing my first book, *The Autobiography of an Unknown Indian,* in 1947 and 1948. I asked myself whether what I was writing would sound like English to those who were born to the language. I knew, unless it did, no English publisher would accept my book.

I adopted a special method to rid myself of the worry. I read what I had written aloud and then also read a passage from some great book of English prose in the same way. If the two sound effects agreed I passed my writing. The prose writers I selected were very diverse, e.g. from Richard Hooker (sixteenth century) to George Moore (twentieth century). There is no such thing as one standard rhythm of English prose. English prose rhythms are bewilderingly diverse, but all are authentic English rhythms. There is variation even in one writer. No one (unless totally deaf to sound) will say that Sir Thomas Browne's *Religio Medici* is in the same rhythm as is his *Hydriotaphia.* Dryden in his prose (which I admired), as well as Gibbon in his, were equally authentic to me, in spite of the latter's assertive Gallicisms. I might add that George Moore, in his *Esther Waters,* was not the same writer as he was in one of his later books, *The Brook Kerith.* His *Hail and Farewell* I found to be captivatingly limpid.

This method proved itself. When, after the publication of my book in England on 8 September 1951, the BBC read out certain passages from it, I said to myself: 'That was the sound I had in my mind's ear.'

The habit of writing by sounding has led me to another basic discovery in regard to diction. I have found that the mood and temper created in me by anything I see or feel control the rhythm and tempo of what I write. For instance, if my mood is excited and dramatic, my diction at once becomes staccato in rhythm and allegro or even presto in tempo; whereas when I am contemplative these become legato and adagio or even lento.

All these correlations are spontaneous and unselfconscious. No self-conscious striving after effect succeeds in moving readers.

Another realization which has come to me is that the substance of a piece of writing cannot be separated from its style. There is no such thing in literary works as good substance spoilt by a bad style, or poor substance undeservedly accompanied by a good style. To believe in such theories is to have the stupidity which is dead to matter and the vulgarity which is dead to form. The old proverb says that the style is the man himself. I would say that the style is the subject itself.

With all these explanations, I have done with my methodology. But method is only a means to an end. Does my method have any end in view? I shall try to answer that very natural, yet baffling question.

At the outset, I have to state that my writing life has extended so far over seventy-one years from 1925 to 1996. I am sure it is the longest in history. In its course I have written fourteen books, in English as well as Bengali, and poured out hundreds of articles and broadcasts. I have been more a journalist than a man of letters. But to what end? My countrymen have left no room for doubt as to their view of it. They have ceaselessly proclaimed that my purpose has always been to settle my score with them, the score of an unsuccessful, embittered and soured life, by denigrating them, their life, and their civilization. I have never contradicted them in words.

At first I did not understand why there was such a hostile reaction to my first book from my countrymen. But Sir John Squire, who as publisher's reader reported on the book, expected this. In a letter written on 5 December 1950 to an Indian friend of his he wrote: 'If the book comes out it may put India into an uproar, and he might possibly find a refuge in England . . . '

This has come true and after considering the question deeply I have understood why the Indian reaction was ferociously adverse.

The dedication to the 'memory of the British Empire in India' did provoke them. But that was due to their failure to understand its significance. It was really a condemnation of the British rulers for not treating us as equals. It was an imitation of what Cicero said about the conduct of Verres, a Roman proconsul of Sicily who oppressed the Sicilian Roman citizens, although in their desperation they cried out: '*Civis Romanus Sum.*'

Next, I gave offence to fellow Indians by writing objectively about the personality of my parents. No Hindu does this; he utters hagiographical platitudes.

Last of all I wrote in an English style which was not accessible to the general run of educated Indians. Sir John Squire detected this. He wrote: 'His English is so good that one is tempted to think he must have had a translator; but a translator as good as that would never have been bothered about translation, but written great works of prose of his own.' I think all this explains the hostility.

But I have contradicted my dectractors by my actions. I have been, so to speak, a man of action through my writings. I have always been what is called an *engagé*. I have never shrunk from getting involved in all that I have seen and experienced and reacting to it in writing.

Furthermore, I have frankly admitted that in the last stage of my writing I became a dogmatist and theorizer. I have written two books which are clearly dogmatic. I admitted that by describing the subject of one book in a borrowed phrase, *De Rerum Indicarum Natura.* I also confessed my dogmatism by quoting the following biblical passage: 'I will pour out my spirit upon all flesh; and your sons and daughters shall prophesy, your old men shall dream dreams, your young men shall see visions.'

Thus I have been something other even than a journalist; I have really been a preacher. I have said to myself: 'I applied my mind to know wisdom and my mind has great experience of wisdom and knowledge.'

But my countrymen have not taken my preaching at my valuation. They have set it down as mere *bavardage*. Perhaps it is so in form. Nonetheless, I would say that all this *babil* of mine shows no absence of clarity and honesty, and also no absence, if not of courage, at least of boldness.

Here ends the apology for my writings.

On stepping into my hundreth year... 23 November 1996

□

PHILLIP KNIGHTLEY
AN ACCIDENTAL SPY

imprint

THE BEST OF BOOKS EVERY MONTH

PHILLIP KNIGHTLEY's work for the London *Sunday Times*, for which he was twice named Journalist of the Year in the British Press Awards, included investigations of Kim Philby, Robert Maxwell and the Thalidomide affair. His books include *The First Casualty*, on war correspondents, and *The Second Oldest Profession*, about intelligence agencies. 'The Accidental Spy' is an extract from his autobiography, *A Hack's Progress*, which will be published by Jonathan Cape in August.

Iarrived in Bombay on 13 December 1960. I was thirty-one years old, free and on my way home to Australia after working for a fruitless couple of years in London as a journalist. India, I had decided, would just be another brief port of call. I had sixty-five pounds in traveller's cheques, ten American dollars and a ticket for the next ship to Sydney—which, I discovered, did not leave for another five months. Could I last out? On that very first day I moved in with an Australian artist, Roy Dalgarno, and his wife Betty. Roy was art director of Lintas, the international advertising agency, and Betty represented a German film company in India.

They swept me immediately into the fantasy world of the Bombay film and racing crowd—morning coffee at Gaylords in Churchgate, talking in lakhs (hundreds of thousands) of rupees when I did not have hundreds, then a swim at Breach Candy with the English jockeys down for the winter season. We had absolutely nothing in common, but I cherished a hope that one would slip me a tip that would win me a fortune at Mahalaxmi racecourse on Saturday afternoon. It was exciting but unreal, a prolonged holiday that I felt must have a delayed reckoning. Then, surprisingly, I got a job. A new English-language literary magazine called *Imprint* was about to start, and I was offered the post of managing editor—1,200 rupees a month, four weeks' annual holiday and a return airline ticket to Australia.

Three months after I had arrived I was living in a two-bedroom flat in Colaba, the most fashionable part of the city. I had acquired a German girlfriend, an Indian manservant and an account at the tailor's. Since India was then in the grip of prohibition, I also had liquor permit number ZO 4035 entitling me, as a 'foreign alcoholic by birth', to four bottles of whisky or thirty-six bottles of beer a month. This was not enough, so I had also acquired a bootlegger who delivered regular supplies of 'country liquor', a concoction made out of banana skins, which was drinkable if mixed with lime juice and soda but which, nevertheless, produced excruciating hangovers.

In an emotional depression following an attack of dysentery exacerbated by a country liquor hangover, came a revelation. I was living like an expatriate, a sahib, and apart from the different physical surroundings, I might as well have been back in London.

India was slipping away from me. It was Dr Massa who changed my life.

Dr Massa was an Italian, a spiritual easterner who happened to have been born in the West. He was vague about his background and never properly explained how he came to be in India. One of his patients said that Massa had been touring India when the Second World War started and he had spent the war years in an internment camp. Trained in orthodox western medicine, he had spent these years studying homeopathy. When I went to see him, he was practising a blend of all known medical systems.

He was the first and only doctor I have known who treated a patient as a whole human being instead of a collection of symptoms. His consulting room was the living room of his flat. He sat on the sofa with you, and you chatted and had tea together. His prescription for the dysentery was brief. Drugs will cure it, but you will probably get it again. In the long term it is better to help your body to cope with it. You need less food in India than in Europe, so eat sparingly. Don't drink alcohol before meals and keep up the afternoon-nap habit. 'Man was not made for work alone,' he said. 'Everyone needs a consuming interest outside his work. Find yourself a hobby or a sport, something you can do every day, something you can look forward to during office hours. See life as a whole in which work is only a small part.'

It seemed to be a recipe for living like an Indian, so I moved out of my Colaba apartment and took a 150-rupee a month room with a Parsi family and a crow that came through the window each morning to wake me up. I ate nothing for breakfast, dhal and chapatti for lunch and had a light dinner. I bought a motor scooter (I considered a bicycle, but everyone said that would be going too far), wore Gandhian handloom clothes, took up tennis, cut my living allowance to one pound a day and never felt better in my life. I got my lunch from a colleague at work, Dolly Irani, whose grandmother sent her tiffin all the way from Bombay Central. Dolly's grandmother made the best dhal in India: thick, deep yellow, scattered with burnt onion and with little patches of ghee glistening on the top.

In the office, I took more interest in my colleagues. Why had Mr Khatri become an accountant? Where had Devidas Gawaskar learned to draw? What was life like for Sheila Trace in the Indian YWCA? Soon I knew more Indians than Europeans: the mechanic who fixed my motor scooter, the leather worker who made my belts, the juice squeezer outside the cinema, the *jamadar* who cleaned the office. I made a point of trying to negotiate Indian life without an intermediary to shield me from its stresses. I queued for hours to take my scooter-riding test. I spent a whole day at the docks clearing a parcel from Australia. I visited the magistrates' courts, wrote letters to newspapers and was caught in a prohibition raid on a private party. (The Indian in a white dhoti on whom I had been pressing drinks turned out to be an inspector in the Anti-Corruption Squad.)

I began writing film scripts, first for a small production company, then for the Government of India Films Division: how to understand metric weights; why farmers should use fertilizer; and then in that traumatic month of November 1962, 'give your blood for Indian soldiers on the Indo-Chinese frontier'. I began to feel Indian, aggressively defensive over the 'liberation' of Goa, fiercely patriotic over the border trouble with China and patronizingly tolerant of the first tourists on twenty-one-day package tours, who would never know the real India.

In September 1962 I went to Delhi to make a documentary for the Second Punjab Regiment, the oldest in the Indian Army, which was celebrating its two-hundredth anniversary. It was a fortnight of rehearsals and drill, interspersed with an endless round of parties, music recitals, films, cocktail parties and formal dinners. Every surviving British officer was brought at the regiment's expense from retirement to take part. The presentation of colours was followed by a ball and then the Junior Commissioned Officers' dinner at a table creaking under silver collected over two centuries, and—could I have imagined it?—a young Sikh captain steadily munching his way around the rim of a champagne glass until only the stem was left. 'Take no notice of him,' his wife said. 'He does it at every party.'

From Delhi I took the third-class sleeper to Pathankot and then a bus to Srinagar in Kashmir. The road had been washed away and the journey took two days. At lunch on the second day, at some roadside hotel, the South Indian couple at my table found that the waiter, not surprisingly, spoke no Tamil and no English. They, on the other hand, spoke English but no Hindi. I surprised myself by interpreting for them. I spent a week sightseeing in Gulmarg, longing for the plains, and then took the train back to Bombay. The ticket cost fifty-six rupees, and I remember thinking that if I saved furiously for a while I could spend the rest of my life on the road like Kim, travelling the railways of India, eating toast that dribbled with butter and drinking endless cups of incomparable railway tea.

Meanwhile my work at *Imprint* had been taking some strange turns. The original idea seemed an admirable one: western books in India were prohibitively expensive so *Imprint* would condense four or five best-sellers and publish them in the magazine which, because it also carried advertising, would sell for only one rupee a copy. It could overcome nationwide distribution problems by soliciting subscriptions by direct mail. The mailshot, one of the first in India, produced an enormous response, something like a twenty-five per cent success rate. We even had letters from people complaining that we had not written to them:

> My neighbour, a Jain, has had an offer from you to subscribe to your new magazine, *Imprint*, the best of books each month. I have had no such offer. Is this because you are discriminating against Muslims? Please advise.

My job was to condense the books, read the proofs and answer readers' letters. I loved the letters.

> Contrary to your usual policy, you have not condensed *To Kill a Mockingbird* into one part but into three. This did not greatly concern me because I could look forward to three nectaries instead of one. Part one arrived on schedule, as did part three. But part two did not arrive at all, thus totally fucking the continuity.
>
> Yours sincerely, . . .

It was pleasant, relaxing work, and the editor, Glorya Hale, and her husband, Arthur, who ran the business side of the venture, were amusing cosmopolitan Americans and fun to work for. They lived on the fifth floor of Bakhtavar, a modern high-rise apartment block that looked out over the approaches to Bombay Harbour. They installed *Imprint* on the sixth floor and since there was plenty of space suggested I should live in one suite and turn it into an editorial office by day. Sitting on the balcony one evening after everyone had gone home, enjoying a quiet beer and watching the lights of the small fishing boats come on as the light faded, I became aware that someone in the next block was doing the same thing. We nodded to each other and raised glasses. Then he called across the gap, 'What are you drinking?' When I told him it was beer, he said, 'Come over and try vodka.' I did. I went down in the lift, across the courtyard and up in the lift in the next block to the sixth floor where I noticed that a sign on the bell I was about to ring said SOVEXPORT FILM.

Inside I met Igor—I never got to know his other name and even if I had, it was probably not his real one. Ostensibly Igor represented the Soviet film industry in India. He tried to persuade Indian distributors to show Soviet films and kept an eye open for Indian films that might do well in the Soviet Union. He was not very busy which was fortunate because he also had another agenda which slowly revealed itself to me over the next six months. He would invite me to Soviet consulate parties to celebrate various national days or just to get drunk. One of his colleagues, who lived in some style on Malabar Hill, one of Bombay's smartest suburbs, had been a tank commander in the battle for Moscow and could tell gripping stories about the Great Patriotic War. The drinking at his parties was, even for India, formidable, and would go on long after all the women guests had left and the sun was beginning to creep through the slats of the venetian blinds. The Indians would pass out first, quietly crumpling to sleep in armchairs or on rugs on the marble floors. The British would creep off to find unoccupied bedrooms until, with unconscious bodies everywhere, the whole flat looked like a first-aid station on the Western Front circa 1915. Finally, there were only Russians and Australians upright, and then the Australians would crash where they stood, Roy Dalgarno on one occasion bringing down with him a heavy brocade curtain complete with all its rods and drawstrings, and crushing under him an elaborate, pierce-carved Burmese side table. It was the only time I saw the tank commander angry. As we carried a semi-conscious Dalgarno through the front door, apologizing for the accident, the commander kept saying, 'Not accident. Deliberate anti-Soviet act.'

Eventually Igor came to the point. He invited me to his flat, sent his wife out of the room, put a bottle of vodka, two bottles of mineral water and two glasses on the table and said, 'I have something to confess to you. I want to be a journalist. I want you to teach me.' I said I saw no problem, but I knew nothing about Soviet newspapers or magazines or what sort of articles might interest them.

'Leave that side to me,' Igor said. 'You and I will write articles on India. Political articles. True stories with inside information. I will sell them to the Soviet press, and we will divide the income equally.'

We shook hands on the deal. Our first article was about the India that Bulganin and Khrushchev would not see on their impending visit: the poverty-stricken shacks, the notorious caged prostitutes of Bombay, the illicit liquor stills, the villages given over entirely to gold smuggling.

Igor placed it with surprising speed. Again he invited me to his flat where he showed me the cutting. Then he produced a small wad of rupee notes and a sheet of paper with several sentences typewritten in Russian. 'I must send the editor a receipt showing that the fee has been received and properly divided. You know bureaucrats. Please sign here.' The faint tinkling of alarm began deep in my head, and I hesitated. As I did so, Igor looked simultaneously eager and shifty. 'Look, Igor,' I said, 'I don't really need the extra money.' As I said this I took a quick look at the figures, the only part of the receipt I could read. The amount was large enough to be tempting but not so large as to create suspicion. This confirmed my decision, and I pressed on. 'Please give my share to the children's hospital.'

Igor looked at me, very disappointed, but was professional enough not to press me. We finished the vodka, and I left promising to meet again soon. He never invited me anywhere again and dodged all my invitations to him.

I learned later that Igor's pitch was typical not only of the

KGB but of most intelligence services. If I had accepted the money then I would have crossed a barrier. The next payment would have been bigger, and the third bigger still, until I came to rely on the extra money. If I wanted to pull out, there would have been my signatures on receipts, something I would have found hard to explain. Our joint articles would have delved deeper into areas of Indian affairs that should not have concerned us, and if I had complained that the sort of information Igor's Soviet 'editors' wanted was not readily available, he would then have suggested that we try to find an Indian who did have access to such information and pay him for it. I could have found myself a principal agent running a ring of subagents for Igor. I had quit just in time.

If I had been naive about Igor's intentions then I was simply stupid about *Imprint*. Arthur Hale went to Delhi regularly in order, he said, to argue our case for an increased newsprint allocation. I thought nothing about these trips. I knew that Hale had been in Burma during the Second World War in psychological warfare operations. It did not click. Odd Americans dropped by en route from Saigon to Delhi or Hong Kong and stayed with the Hales. I never gave them a second glance. When I look back now over those early copies of *Imprint* I see that many of the books we chose to condense lauded the American way of life and painted a grim picture of the lack of freedom in the Soviet Union. I did not notice that at the time.

Then there was this subsidiary publishing operation. At the Hales' request I was writing short histories of American folk heroes—Johnny Appleseed, Casey Jones, Davy Crockett—which *Imprint* was publishing as lavishly illustrated children's books and putting on the Indian market at ridiculously low prices. It seemed a nice, innocent idea. There was one incident that puzzled me briefly, something that stirred a tiny tremor of unease. I was out sailing one Saturday afternoon with Arthur Hale, and we were talking about the rights and wrongs of the Indian border dispute with China. I said that, hard though it was for me to admit it, perhaps there was more to China's case than we knew. I said I had heard about an Indian academic, a Professor J. G. Ghose, who had been working in the national archives in Delhi when he had accidentally come across a survey map which the British had drawn up in the nineteenth century. The map clearly showed the disputed territory as being within China's borders. Hale appeared to absorb this without much interest. But back at the landing at the Gateway of India, he said, a little too casually, 'What were that Professor Ghose's initials again?'

Twenty years later I was in Washington working on a documentary film about the exploits of the notorious British traitor Kim Philby, the British Secret Intelligence Service officer who was, all along, an agent of the KGB. The film crew and I had travelled to Virginia to have lunch with Harry Rositzke, former head of the Soviet Bloc division of the CIA. Rositzke was sitting at the head of the table, and I was on his right. I became aware that down at the other end of the table, Mrs Rositzke was talking about India with the production assistant. I said casually to Rositzke, 'Were you and Mrs Rositzke in India at some stage?'

He said, '1960 to 1964. I was at the embassy.'

I said, 'Oh. What were you doing?'

He looked at me, a bit puzzled, presumably because he thought I would have researched his career before coming to see him.

'CIA station chief,' he said. 'We were very interested in India in those days. Delhi was friendly but in bed with Moscow, and that made India one of the few places in the world where we had any interface with the Soviets.'

I told him that I too had been in India in the early Sixties.

'Yes?' Rositzke said. 'And what were you doing?'

I said, 'I was with a little magazine in Bombay, a literary magazine called *Imprint*.'

Rositzke grinned. 'I knew it well,' he said. 'It was one of my little operations. Shake hands with your ex-boss.'

I must have turned pale, because he added with some concern, 'Didn't you know?' And then he explained it all to me. The CIA had become concerned about Soviet influence in India in the early 1960s. Not only was the government friendly with Moscow, but the bazaars of India were being flooded with cheap but beautifully produced and lavishly illustrated children's books about Soviet folk heroes, published not only in English but in many of the regional languages. 'A whole generation of Indian kids were growing up to believe that the only heroes in the world were Russian ones,' Rositzke said. 'We had to get in there with some American folk heroes.' The obvious answer would have been to have published the books in America and then shipped them to India. But the CIA did not work like that. Since—as is usually the case with intelligence operations—money did not matter, the CIA decided to set up a whole publishing operation in India to produce the books. Once that was agreed, the idea just grew. Why not also publish a magazine with a subtle pro-American slant? The spin-offs from having a genuine publishing house in Bombay clinched it—a legitimate bank account which could provide funds for covert activities; a safe house for visiting officers and agents; a listening post for all the snippets of political and social gossip that go to make up raw intelligence. I suppose that, as intelligence operations go, it was one of the more benign ones, but it was still something of a shock to learn that, however unwittingly, I had been employed by the CIA.

Now Igor's attempt to recruit me made sense. He was not after an Australian itinerant journalist who was passing through Bombay; he was after an employee of the CIA front. He must have known. It could not have been coincidence that the KGB's front operation in Bombay, Sovexport Film, was right next door to the CIA's front operation in Bombay: *Imprint*. What a joke it all was. What a waste of time, money and talent. Or was it? Indian film-goers got to see some Russian masterpieces thanks to Sovexport Film. Thirty thousand Indian subscribers got to read a few good books that they could not otherwise have afforded thanks to *Imprint*. And I got to spend two years in Bombay, one of the great cities of the world. □

DAYANITA SINGH
MOTHER INDIA

'For eight years I worked as a photographer in India catering to western perceptions of what India is. I got fed up working in worlds that I did not truly belong to—I could empathize with but never really understand what it means, say, to be a Bombay prostitute or a child labourer. I wanted to look at the India I come from, at the changing styles and relationships which are taking place inside well-off families who live in big cities, and particularly my own city, Delhi. When I showed this new work to some American editors, they couldn't believe it was India (or if it was, then I had a gall to be photographing such people in a poverty-ridden country!). That just made me more determined. There are many versions of India, and this is mine.'   DAYANITA SINGH

Four generations, New Delhi

Tahira Kochar performs for her mother and grandmother, New Delhi

Rasik and Samara Chopra (aged thirteen) the night before Rasik left to study in the US

Arvind and Mini at their new bungalow, New Delhi

Bhopal family

Minni Boga, furniture designer, with her poodles

Mrs Bijli in her bedroom, New Delhi

*Shahnaz Hussain,
herbal queen
of India, in her
dressing room*

MUKIWA

A WHITE BOY IN AFRICA

'Marvellous'
William Boyd
Sunday Times

'A classic'
Sunday Telegraph

PETER GODWIN

WINNER OF THE *ESQUIRE/WATERSTONE'S* NON-FICTION AWARD

NOW IN PAPERBACK

PICADOR

GRANTA

AMIT CHAUDHURI
WAKING

AMIT CHAUDHURI was born in Calcutta in 1962 and grew up in
Bombay. He has published two books: *A Strange and Sublime Address*,
which won the Betty Trask Award, and *Afternoon Raag*, which won the
Encore Prize. 'Waking' is taken from his next novel, *Freedom Song*, to
be published in the UK by Picador.

When afternoon came to Vidyasagar Road, wet clothes—
Piyu's dresses, Bhaskar's pyjamas and kurtas, even a few
soggy towels—hung from a clothes line that stretched across the
veranda of the first floor. The line, which had not been tightly
drawn anyway, sagged with the pressure of the heavy wet clothes
that dripped, from sleeves and trouser ends, a curious grey water
on to the floor in the middle; it curved downwards as if a smile
were forming. To the people in the house, the clothes formed a
screen or curtain which threw shadows and provided bewitching
glimpses of the speedy criss-crosses of the grille, and, through
those criss-crosses, bits of the balcony of the house opposite, the
sky and the *shajana* tree. The slow leaking of the drops of water
from the clothes and their casual, flirtatious flutter with every
breeze would not have been noticed by the passer-by on the road,
who, if he had looked beyond the remaining leaves on the *shajana*
tree and the iron pattern of the grille, would have seen them
suspended there, like colourful ghosts. Who had put them there?
To know that, one would have had to be present at half-past two,
when Haridasi, the servant, helped by Bhaskar's mother and
watched regally by his sister, Piyu, had hung up the clothes one by
one, till the passer-by would have seen all the figures, including
Piyu in the doorway, gradually consumed by the clothes that they
were hanging up.

Winter changed Calcutta. It gave its people, as they wore their
sweaters and mufflers, a feeling of having gone somewhere else, a
slight sense of the wonder and dislocation of being in a foreign
city. Even the everyday view from their own houses was a little
strange. Smoke travelled everywhere, robbing the sunlight of its
fire. Afternoon, with its gentle orange-yellow light, was the
warmest time of day, though the wet clothes, assisted by a breeze,
dried more slowly than in the summer. And as the orange light fell
on the brickwork and the sides of the houses, it was easier to tell,
from the flushed rose centre that appeared now on a terrace and
now a parapet, that its origins lay in fire.

On the street, Tommy the dog haunted the rubbish heap again,
probing, in a concerned way, its bright smelly edges with his muzzle.
When someone cranked the handle of the tube well, it creaked and
twanged like a one-stringed instrument. Crows, sometimes alighting

on a window sill or a banister, clamoured as usual, comforting the child in every human figure in the house, those who were half-asleep or awake, bringing up memories of other human, beloved faces, or creating the expectation of homecomings. Their cries had something to do with hope and return and the continuance of human business. Bhaskar's mother, turning in her sleep, grew full with the return of her son in the evening.

She was sleeping with Piyu on the bed; her husband, Bhola, lay sleeping on the divan in the next room. He was snoring, but gently compared to his night-time snores, so that one would not have heard it from the bed where Piyu and her mother slept, though, moving closer to the doorway, one might have been distracted by a faraway sound that was hardly a sound at all, trapped, urgent, but private. Then, abruptly, one would have realized what it was, and the body with its small belly and bald patch, clothed in kurta and pyjamas, and the frowning mouth and big nose, would have formed around the snore.

On Bhaskar's mother's outstretched hand, on the shining dark brown skin, there was, near the thumb and the index finger, a large pink spot like a rose where the skin had peeled off after one drop of boiling oil had leapt on it while she was frying *luchis*. The yellow Burnol paste that she put there timidly and perfunctorily after stubborn exhortations from Piyu had now faded into what looked like healing dabs of turmeric. She was dark and slept intensely, while Piyu, beside her, was fair and fresh-faced, a plant that had been nurtured in this garden, in the shadow of pillows, cupboards, shelves, clothes horses, untouched as yet by life. Let it always be so, the house around her seemed to say, the four walls and the beam on the ceiling, let us always keep her as she is. Let her not leave us. She breathed gently. The sun came in through the clothes line and printed the wall and the blue bedcover with triangles and rectangles.

Haridasi, small Haridasi, barely four feet six inches tall, had cleared the dining table, first cupping her endlessly compliant palm and pushing bits of moist rice and salt that had littered the table into its dark cave, to rest there among her heart line and her lifeline, collecting bits of fish bone as well to deposit them there, and then curling her fingers as if she were holding a secret and throwing the debris into the kitchen basin, though she had been told not to. She wiped the table after this with a wet cloth. Then she sat in one corner of the kitchen, the only one awake in the house, a guest, a stranger, a friend, and ate from a plate with a heap of rice and a puddle of dhal and vegetables on one side. She was quiet as a mouse. Without being aware of it, she tried to mix the puddle of dhal uniformly with the huge quantity of rice. She loved rice.

It was today, in the evening, that Bhaskar's mother would take her husband to the doctor for his annual check-up. For about two weeks she had been persuading him to go, but something else always came up instead. Now, at last, they had a free evening ahead of them. It was a short journey by car, past the Lake Market in Rashbehari Avenue, turning into a lane at whose entrance wheat and grain were piled in open heaps by the roadside. Once the visit was over they immediately went to the Fern Road Pharmacy, bought the medicines that had been prescribed and proceeded without further delay to a relative's house.

Bhaskar's father had a great, childlike respect for this doctor. Though he was himself an engineer, the doctor was what in his youth some of the brightest young men went on to be: a Fellow of the Royal College of Physicians from London. Those were the days when young men went to England, not America, and came back with degrees and sometimes even an English wife in a sari. The letters FRCP made Bhaskar's father feel that both he and India were suddenly, completely, though temporarily, young again. Each time he went for an appointment, he signed his name on the compounder's slip and sat in the waiting room with his wife and the other patients as shyly as if he were visiting his in-laws, flicking through, meanwhile, old copies of *Span* magazine. Once they were inside, he loved listening to the doctor's diagnosis and asking questions about the prescription, not because he doubted the doctor but because he always wished, whenever he had the opportunity, to widen his own limited, though not negligible, knowledge of medicine. The doctor was a mild, slightly boring man whom time had passed by; he wore black-framed bifocal spectacles and had small tufts of black and grey hair coming out of his ears. He was content to see fewer patients these days and sit behind his old wooden table with its green leather top, his arms resting behind a glass paperweight with little flecks of pink and blue suspended in its strange, crystalline atmosphere, and talk in a leisurely way about his son who was studying at Caltech and, in winter, about all the marriages that were now under way in the city. Behind him, on the wall, there were two framed photographs—the class of '49 in Calcutta Medical College and the class of '53 in London, the students all men, with smart, close-cropped haircuts.

Now an interminable mail train passed on the railway tracks that formed the horizon visible in the gap between the houses on the other side of Vidyasagar Road. For a while, all other local and habitual noises, of birds and cars, were subsumed under the long, swelling note of the mail-train whistle, which, with its lone trumpeting, made the air vibrate around one. Yet they slept in that vibrating air. Then, when the train had gone, the air was cleansed, and the room was as quiet as its reflection in the dressing-table mirror, with Oil of Ulay, Lactocalamine, Vaseline, Ponds Dream Flower Talc and two lipsticks arranged carefully, with all devotion and seriousness, on the shelf before it. Very slowly, like town officials who had respectfully ceased their transactions for a minute, the crows and sparrows began again, but sounding more distant now, even chastised, perhaps in comparison with the grand interlude of the train whistle. In this new, petty, semi-silent, post-whistle moment came the postman to Vidyasagar Road, dressed in civilian clothes, a dark red sweater and black trousers with bottoms that were wide and floppy; on his shoulder there was a handwoven cotton sling bag such as college students swing casually and thoughtlessly by their sides, crammed with neat, though uneven, stairways of letters, a small blue aerogramme climbing up to a broad brown-paper envelope, which rose again to a disproportionately small inland postcard. This frail man, eclipsed almost entirely by his sweater and his trousers, now, retrieving more and more piles from his shoulder bag, seemed the paradigm of modest but real generosity, as he, without any special demonstrativeness or affection, left at least one letter in every letter box on his progress from one house to another. Into the yellow-green letter box by the gate to Bhaskar's house, there came a wedding invitation with '*Shubho Bibaho*' inscribed on the envelope: on the card inside, embossed in fine gold lines on a red background, a wedding procession moved forward, looking as wedding processions might once have looked, with a palanquin and red-and-gold revellers in profile, wearing turbans and blowing pipes and beating drums and making an infernal racket. There was another card, announcing a funeral, with '*Ganga*' printed in Bengali on the envelope. Lying on it was a yellow postcard from Bangladesh, sent by a distant relative; one half of the square, divided by a vertical line from the other, had clean horizontal lines that had been meticulously loaded with Bhaskar's father's name and his address, and the numbers of the postcode imprisoned inside tiny printed boxes. The letter, written in blue ink, began on this side with pleasantries and general reminiscences and then came, in its tidy persistent way, to occupy all of the other side, ending with a plea for financial help for a daughter's marriage. Like a house which shelters sons, daughters, grandparents, servants, frustrations, expectations, a whole world under its roof, the postcard, with not one inch of it wasted, gave whatever space it could to words that expressed both necessary sentiments and urgent requirements. And there was a letter from Robi, a nephew in Pennsylvania, with photographs of his daughter, now seven, enclosed. He had once lived in this house as a student. The one-dollar postage stamp, with Lincoln's picture on it, would be acquired by Mohit for his collection.

On the first floor of the house, on the double bed where Piyu and her mother were now sleeping, a grandmother had lived twenty years ago. She was Bhaskar's father's mother; from time to time her seven children, who were scattered with their families in different parts of India, would visit this house to see their mother, who was eccentric and did not have much to say to them any more; she had brought them up and now her duties, she had decided, were over. Bhaskar's father and his sister, Khuku, who was only a year older than him, often called their mother *Goonga*. The bed on which Piyu and her mother were now sleeping was her bed; it was also her divan, armchair and footstool. In the morning her quilt and pillows were banked on one side of the bed, the bed beaten with a *jhata* by Durga, her old maidservant, and then draped with a bedcover. She, wearing her white sari, for her husband had died thirty years ago, sat peering at the *Amrita Bazaar Patrika* through her reading glasses, beginning at the first paragraph on the first page and ending at the last. No one dared bother her but the children, among whom she was only openly affectionate towards Piyu, who could still barely walk and was regarded by everyone, including six-year-old Bhaskar, as a discovery, a curiosity and especially amusing in the way she imitated certain grown-up gestures. The grandmother's lunch was laid out on a table before the bed by Nando, who worked then in this house in white shirt and pyjamas, his hair oiled, and his face demon-like. 'Ei Nando,' she would shout. 'Bring the salt and the oil!' And Nando would rush back with salt on a plate and a bowl of mustard oil. She had died a few years later. The pomelo tree by her window, whose fruit she ate with mustard oil, secretly adding sugar, had blossomed again this winter, its fruit picked and stolen by a new generation of urchins and scallywags who looked exactly like the ones who had climbed the tree twenty years ago. Some of her children, in those twenty years, had grown old and died as well, leaving Khuku, Bhola and two more brothers, including the eldest, who, though hunched now and forgetful of names, still found time to get angry about umpires' decisions in cricket matches.

It was an old house, a hospitable house. Bhaskar now had more or less to himself the big room on the second floor, where he engaged in animated discussions or restful gossip with comrades from the Party—shy men with moustaches whose frail chests suddenly expanded during these discussions. On the large bed in this room Bhaskar and his brother Manik, who was now in Germany, used to sleep once. In the summers then Khuku's elder sister would arrive from the hills of Assam where, in a town with a funny name that sounded like a kitchen utensil, she was headmistress of a girls' school. Reading everything from *Beowulf* to puja annuals at the oddest of angles—for she would lie sideways and let the magazine dangle from the fingers of one outstretched hand, moving grudgingly only when it dawned on her that it was impossible to turn the page without the aid of the hand that was trapped beneath her—reading everything at such angles had given her eye a squint, and her an incongruous lost and searching look. Incongruous, for, despite being widowed when she was thirty-four, she had raised her children robustly, feeding them well and twisting their ears. During those summers, on the bed on the second floor, she told Bhaskar and Manik stories about ancient Rome and the last days of Pompeii. At present, the bed upstairs was empty, with winter sunlight falling upon it, obstructed only by the mullions in the windows, and Bhaskar was away at the factory in Howrah— but once he had lain there on his stomach with a new book before him and seen *rakkhoshes* with fangs and noserings drink the blood of innocent kings, *rakkhoshes* who married female *rakkhoshes* and produced hordes of fearful little *khokkhoshes* with small fangs and round eyes. Durga had told Bhaskar and Manik when to be careful of ghosts—between two and three o'clock in the afternoon, when grown-ups slept or were away at work, and even real objects threw no shadows; and at night, during the pregnant hours that preceded dawn. If they sensed anything unearthly, Bhaskar and Manik promptly muttered to themselves the lines they knew by heart:

> Ghoul's my daughter,
> Ghost's my son.
> Ram's in my heart,
> And no harm can be done.

When the children were born, they came to the house like guests. Their parents and Durga welcomed them and took them out of their first wondering, semi-conscious state. Once, when Bhaskar was seven and Manik five, they saw from their bed at three or four in the morning a woman who was not Durga or their mother hanging clothes to dry in the bathroom; then they fell asleep again. It was an old house; a family had lived in it before their parents had moved in, and Bhaskar was certain that a woman in that family had died. He hinted, but never admitted, that the woman he and Manik had seen was the same woman.

This house had been a wedding gift from Bhola's father-in-law, part of a dowry. Since then it had gone through changes, for the worse and then for the better, but its red stone floors and stairs, and its bottle-green windows with slats, and the small prayer room upstairs had remained the same. The kitchen had been painted; new shelves had been fitted; and the earthen oven, dust-coloured, hollow, into whose sides Durga pushed wood and coal, had been put in the shed at the back of the house where the coal and wood used to be kept. Durga herself had returned to her village.

At four o'clock Bhaskar's mother woke as surely as if an alarm clock had gone off inside her. Her eyes, in a face puffed with sleep, opened, red and unfocused. For fifteen years she would get up thus at half-past six in the morning and, with her eyes still small and red, walk towards the bed where Manik and Bhaskar were sleeping and push them by their shoulders, for they always slept on their sides, curled up, one side of their face sunk in the pillow, so that, waking up, their cheeks would be lined with pillow marks. Manik had always been shorter and fairer than Bhaskar until, when he was fourteen, he shot up, and they were both the same height, though Manik, much thinner, sometimes looked taller. And Manik, wandering joyously with his friends in the sun, grew darker, till he was brown as a roasted nut. In the morning, their mother would shake their rather bony frames (look at them, she would think in disgust, not a bit of flesh on them, just like urchins) and say in a loud whisper, 'Ei, Manik! Ei, Bhaskar! Get up! Get up!' while they clutched their pillows tightly and grew more and more angry in their sleep. When they had any spare time, these two were always arguing and fighting, till, each wrestling titanically with the other, they fell rolling upon the bed. They were separated and brought to their senses by two sharp slaps and smart tugs of the hair administered by their mother.

'You idiots! Look at yourselves! Why don't you fight on the streets—that's where you should be!' Then she would turn to Bhaskar. 'And you . . . I know very well you're the one who starts it . . . this other one's an idiot, but you . . . you're a mischievous devil!'

'What did I do?' Bhaskar would wail, wiping his eyes and about to cry.

'And look at your face . . . Every day it's getting longer, till it's begun to look like a slipper! You don't eat anything, you don't do any work, all you can do is tease this fool.'

These days the house was quieter. School had been one of the

243

most difficult of times for everyone, getting up in the morning,
coming back in the evening and doing homework, buying a new
white uniform every year, the white shorts being replaced by
trousers, Bhaskar, Manik and Piyu swigging down glasses of milk
each morning as quickly as if it were medicine, lifting their faces
from their glasses with uneven white moustaches around their lips.
How their mother suffered for them, what tension, sewing buttons
and pushing them towards the school bus on time, the rice still
unfinished on their plates—'Tell him to wait!' Piyu would shout,
rinsing her mouth at the basin, 'tell him to wait!'—while the bus
engine rumbled sullenly in the lane; she—their mother—had gone
nearly mad coping with it. Yet now it was silent, lives took shape,
things changed and widened, unused spaces vacated by children
wandered about the house, Manik had gone to Germany, and it
seemed there had been a certain innocence and neglect about that
time. She wanted to witness it again; she wanted Bhaskar to marry
now and have children and that whole maddening bustle to resume.

   She got up and walked to the basin and sprinkled her face
with cold water from the tap. She would, before going to the
doctor's with her husband, prepare a snack—Chinese noodles with
bits of vegetable and perhaps chicken in it—to amuse Piyu and
Bhaskar and make herself happy. She called it 'chow mein'. Her
husband would demand some, and then finally have to beg for it,
but she would deny him the noodles that evening because he was
putting on weight, and that was bad at his age. Bhaskar and Piyu
would chant: 'Chow mein! Chow mein!' like children, as if the
name made them hungry and also satisfied their appetites, and if
her husband got a small ration on a plate he would say that it was
as good if not better than what you got in restaurants. They would
shovel up the noodles with tablespoons after they had put some of
Han's Chilli Sauce in it, thumping the end of the bottle with the
palm of their hands until their palms became red, and thick drops
of the sauce, pale green, like something that flows in drains, had
fallen out sluggishly. She had started making these steaming
diversions—noodles and soups—playfully about ten years ago.
And now she dialled the number of the house where her niece lived
with Mohit, her son. It was picked up by Mohit's cousin, Sameer,
who was eleven—three years younger than him.

'Hello!' he said, hoarse and loud. He sounded urgent and ready, as if he had been shouting all this time at the top of his voice.

'Hello,' said Bhaskar's mother.

The female voice took Sameer aback. A note of wonder came to his voice.

'Yes?' he said softly (though he found it difficult to speak softly).

'Can I speak to Mohit?'

There was a stunned silence. Then Sameer found his voice; he shouted at his normal volume—'Ei Mohit,' and Mohit's voice in the background, slightly superior and heavy after it had recently broken, wanted peevishly to know, 'What is it?' Sameer was like the boy who cried 'wolf' at every opportunity, and no one took his shouts seriously any more. But this time Sameer sounded vindicated, for he had important news: 'It's a girl, she wants to talk to you.' There was silence again. Then, tense and prepared, Mohit's voice came on the phone; and it was easy to visualize Sameer's wide eyes, open mouth and pricked-up ears behind it.

'Yes!'

'Can you recognize me?'

'Are you sure,' said Mohit in his knowledgeable way, 'that you have the right number?'

'So you don't recognize me.'

'Is this a joke?' asked Mohit stiffly.

'I'm Didimoni.'

There was an embarrassed sigh. Then Mohit cried: 'Didimoni, why didn't you say so to Sameer? This donkey said you were "a girl".'

'Eh Ram!' could be heard from Sameer in the background.

'Never mind that. You two come today for chow mein at my house.'

So that was agreed. They would tell Mohit's mother, and all three would arrive together in the evening, in an auto-rickshaw. □

Sampāti

*A Petrarchan sonnet
based on a character
in the Ramayana*

' Why
do
you
cry? '
' I
flew
too
high.
Un-
done,
all
see
me
fall. '

VIKRAM SETH

In the magic forest of the *Ramayana*, the early Indian epic, Sampāti, 'the king of the vultures', tells the story of how he lost his wings, in a tale that resembles the Greek myth of Icarus.

> My brother and I were racing each other and we flew up to the sun. Higher and higher we flew, faster and faster in spirals. When the sun had reached the middle of the sky, Jatayu grew tired. I saw that he was almost fainting from the heat, so I spread my wings over him and shielded him. My wings were burnt off, and I fell here, on top of the Vindhya mountain. I have lived here since then but have had no news of my brother.

The *Ramayana* is thought to date from between 700 and 500 BC.

246

What we lost

The interior love poem
the deeper levels of the self

dates when the abandonment
of certain principles occurred

The role of courtesy—how to enter
a forest, how to touch
a master's feet before lesson or performance

The art of the drum. The art of eye-painting.
How to cut an arrow. Gestures between lovers.
The pattern of teeth marks on skin
drawn by a monk from memory

The limits of betrayal. The five ways
a lover could mock an ex-lover

The skill in tentative messages
which included yes and no
but never the direct maybe

Nine finger and eye gestures
to signal key emotions

The small boats of solitude

Lyrics that rose
from love
back into air

naked with guile
and praise

Our works and days

We knew how monsoons
(south-west, north-east)
would govern behaviour

and when to discover
the knowledge of the dead

hidden in clouds
in rivers, in unbroken rock

All this was burnt

or traded for power and wealth
from the eight compass points of vengeance

from the two levels of envy

MICHAEL ONDAATJE

247

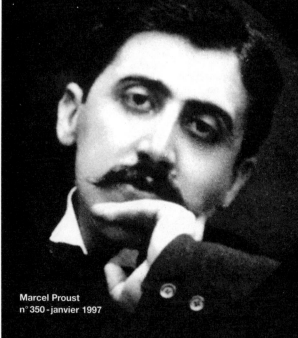

JAN MORRIS
CLIVE'S CASTLE

Powis Castle   TOPHAM

JAN MORRIS is the author of numerous travel books, including *Venice, Sydney, Hong Kong* and *Wales: The First Place*, and of *Pax Britannica*, a three-volume history of the British Empire. Her most recent book is *Fisher's Face*. She lives in Wales.

Robert Clive

On a low ridge near the market town of Welshpool (Y Trallwng to Welsh-speakers) stands the red sandstone castle of Powis, Y Castell Goch, set among formal terraced gardens in a wide and wooded park. It is only a mile or two from the English border and began life in the Middle Ages as a Welsh fortress; but down the centuries, in the hands of the cultivated Herbert family, Earls of Powis, it mutated into a delectable country house— gatehouse, bailey, keep and all absorbed into an ambience of elegant and cultivated comfort.

Today the castle belongs to the National Trust, and in summer streams of visitors are shown over it. Most of the tour is of a kind familiar to habitués of National Trust properties: the statutory Chippendale furniture, the family portraits, the Bellotto view of Verona, magnificent tapestries, fine carpets, ormolu clocks sustained by figures of Cupid and Psyche—all that kind of thing. At the far end of the ballroom, however, in the north side of the outer ward, is something very different. A door opens, the light shifts, and there is revealed . . . an oriental treasure chamber. Sabres glitter alongside ranks of ivory-filled exhibition cases, ancient armour shines, there is a nabob's palanquin and a marvellous hookah embedded with gems, there are glorious textiles and fly whisks; all is a sheen of gold and bone and silver, lotus forms and lions' heads, shields of lacquered hide, painted ivory playing cards and betel-nut cutters shaped like mythical beasts.

There in the green Welsh countryside, among the serene gardens, in that beautifully civilized house, a hoard of Indian booty! It was assembled by Robert Clive, 'the heaven-born general' of eighteenth-century British India, and his son Edward, governor of Madras, who married into the Herbert family in 1784 and presently, in the absence of a male Herbert heir, became Earl of Powis himself, leaving his progeny to live happily in the castle ever after. This is not only one of the great moments of country-house tourism; it is a supreme paradigm of Britain's imperial connection with India, which linked the two countries in a fantastic association for 300 years and is only now fading in the national consciousness of them both.

Jan Morris

M ost visitors to Powis, I am told, are rather taken aback by
the Clive hoard. It is not what they expect. Some are
repelled by what they see as an exhibition of imperialist rapacity;
others are simply baffled to find such a dazzling pile of foreign
treasure there at the end of the library. Their grandparents would
not have been so surprised. This display is no different in kind,
only in scale, splendour and historic significance, from a thousand
collections of Indian curios, found in their time in houses grand
and modest in every part of Britain. I can remember them
myself—the Benares brass tables, the ivory elephants, the lovingly
folded fabrics, the quaint hubble-bubbles and silver-embossed
walking sticks which brought the same sudden flash of the Orient
into so many an aunty drawing room then. They certainly did not
include the tiger-headed sword of Tipu Sultan, or the gilded
palanquin abandoned by Siraj-ud-Daula on the battlefield of
Plassey; the hubble-bubbles were not set with diamonds and
rubies; but no less vividly than Clive of India's trophies, they were
reminders of young British lives lived exotically in places far away.

England in those days was infused with the idea of Empire,
and especially the idea of what later generations have learned to
call the Raj. That colossal possession on the other side of the
world was part of the national idiom. What would the trade figures
be without India? How would England face up to Russia without
the Indian Army? What would politics be without an Indian
Question? Who would fill the obituary columns, if not the old
India hands? Good God, was not His Majesty Emperor of India
too? Scattered across the country were reminders of the grand
connection. There were exotic houses, like Sezincote in the
Cotswolds, or the Prince Regent's fabulous pavilion at Brighton.
There were the graves of generals, and heroic memorials of Indian
wars. There were the venerable offices of Anglo-Indian firms
(London and Calcutta, By Appointment to the Viceroy), and the
ever-crowded East India Docks, and the ships of the British India
Line, and Indian cricketers at Lords, and Camp Coffee, and
drinking wells endowed by charitable maharajas. England without
India was unthinkable: like the British lion without its unicorn, or
the drawing-room cabinet without the dancing figure of Shiva in
it—the figure your great-grandmother brought home from the

Punjab heaven knows how many years ago, oh I don't know, dear, before you and I were born, anyway.

So the Powis collection might have astonished our grand-parents by its magnificence, but it would not have surprised them by its existence. Until the middle of our century it was perfectly natural for Britons, especially Britons of the upper middle classes, to make careers for themselves in India, with luck returning to the Mother Country honoured, self-satisfied and well-off.

On the other hand, I suppose, to the Welsh border peasantry of the eighteenth century, the arrival of the Clives at Powis was like a magic visitation. They knew the Herberts well, after several centuries of landlordship, but these colossal nabobs, father and son, rolling up with their cartloads of gold and their resplendent reputations of war and avarice, must have been like glittering aliens from another world. India? Where was India?

India never did grip the British working classes as it seized the imagination of the bourgeoisie. It was not a settlement colony, like Australia or Canada, and there were few jobs for ordinary Britons out there—working men might go soldiering in India, and that was about all. Nor did it in general attract the landowning upper classes, who understandably preferred to enjoy their happy privileges at home: by and large English aristocrats went to India only as viceroys or governors, or in later years as sporting guests and tourists. The British presence in India was, as Kipling saw, overwhelmingly middle-class, and it was above all in middle-class homes that one saw the general run of Indian curios, together with the inscribed pig-sticking cups, the insignia of British-Indian orders of chivalry, and topied groups of regimental officers in silver frames on mantelpieces. The very people who visit Powis nowadays went to India then.

It was an empire, by and large, without ideology. Except for Christian missionaries, during the three centuries of the imperial rule few British men and women went east with any more than a vague misconception of mission—to do good in general terms, to spread the notion of fair play and extend to the natives the blessings of technique. For the most part their loftiest motive was Clive's loftiest too—the patriotic motive—and their basest was his too—to get rich quick. In between, most of those run-of-the-mill

Jan Morris

imperialists wanted only to earn a decent living from an interesting job in another climate, attended by servants.

A young maharaja once paid a visit to Kedleston Hall in Derbyshire, from whose palatial rooms George Curzon had departed to be Viceroy of India. The maharaja was almost as baffled as today's visitors to Powis. How could a man like Curzon leave such a place, when he could have spent his life there, playing the flute and watching the rabbits?

Actually, Curzon's motives were transparent enough. He genuinely wished, as he said, to feel that among the subject millions of British India he had 'left a little justice or happiness'. At the same time he was one of the most ambitious men alive: he sought not only (as his self-composed epitaph said) to serve his country, but also 'to add honour to an ancient name'. Though they may not recognize it, and probably have no ancient name to add honour to, modern Englishmen share many of the same impulses as their predecessors. Their motives may be more vaguely recognized. Their energies may be muted by comparison, or emasculated by contemporary ideas of correctness. But when a modern English money broker flies off to Asia to make his million out of slightly dubious speculations in the exchange markets, how different is he from the young Robert Clive, son of an impecunious gentleman farmer, when in 1744 he sailed away to Bengal to make his fortune out of the Calcutta trade?

Almost all the imperial intentions are still being fulfilled by Britons today, when the British Empire exists no more. The money broker may well get rich in his eastern markets almost as fast as the young gentlemen of the East India Company turned themselves into nabobs. There is adventure still to be enjoyed, fame still to be won—if not by deposing Tipu Sultans or beating the French and Dutch to Indian domination, at least by sailing single-handed across oceans. The old aspiration to do good, and thus to feel good, is pursued by a thousand imperialists manqués, though they do not often recognize themselves as such as they drive ambulances in war zones, deliver charitable supplies through hostile roadblocks, nurse orphans or feed indigents. Most commonly of all, who has not looked out of a window in the

254

Britain of the 1990s, to peer through the glowering drizzle while Radio Four drones on with another testy political interview, or another analysis of social-security arrangements—who has not thought, on such a morning, how wonderful it would be to run down to the travel agent and book a ticket to some other, sunnier kind of place, where the air would be scented with strange scents, lovely dark people would be smiling in the evening, and nothing would be altogether predictable.

All this was the force behind the British dominion of India, a terrific historical adventure which satisfied many a British desire and did some great things for the Indians too. This is the treasure of Powis! And this was the old urge of the Raj that overcame me when I went back to the castle myself the other day—an urge hardly to be whispered nowadays. The long drive was infested with admonitory notices telling me the opening hours, forbidding me to picnic, warning me that some parts of the estate were Out of Bounds, directing me to a permissible car park or the Way Out. What a relief it would be, I thought then, to escape from all the petty restrictions of British life, the dos and the don'ts, the not heres and over theres, the conventions, the sticking to the rules, the traffic wardens, the Inland Revenue, the drab web of social conformity and inescapable prohibitions, into a distant society where one would be de facto a member of the ruling class! Free to swagger, free to be shameless, free to drink a couple of bottles of claret a night, make a bit under the counter with disreputable but agreeable associates, and look forward with confidence to tax-free treasures in this world if not in the next. These were the improper aspirations, I do not doubt, that Clive of India knew, and generations of British imperialists after him. □

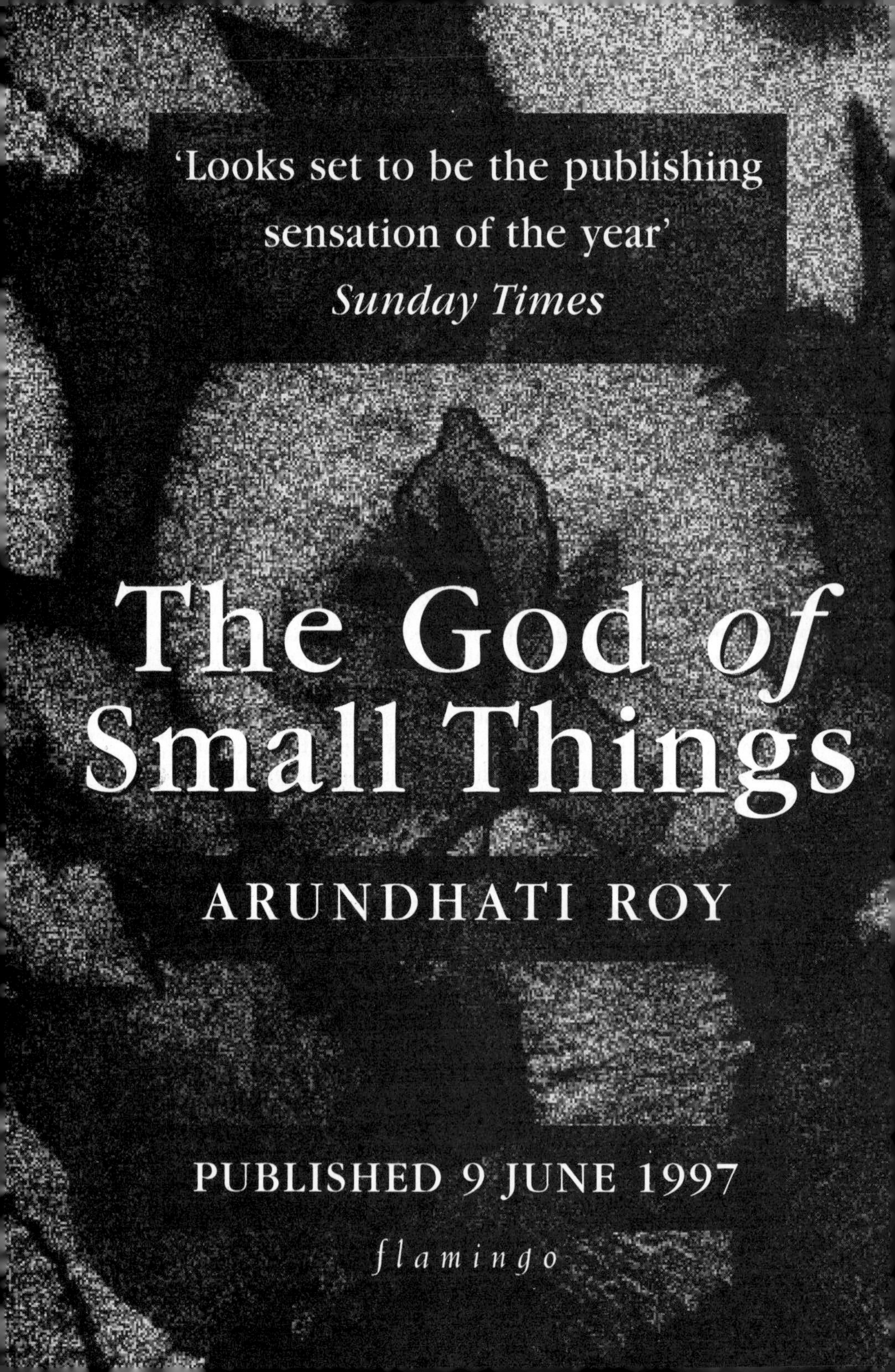

'Looks set to be the publishing
sensation of the year'
Sunday Times

The God *of* Small Things

ARUNDHATI ROY

PUBLISHED 9 JUNE 1997

flamingo

GRANTA

ARUNDHATI ROY
THINGS CAN CHANGE IN A DAY

PRADIP KRISHEN

ARUNDHATI ROY grew up in Kerala, in south-west India, and trained as an architect. 'Things Can Change in a Day' is taken from her first novel, *The God of Small Things*, to be published later this year by Flamingo in London and Random House in New York.

From the dining-room window where she stood, with the wind in her hair, Rahel could see the rain drum down on the rusted tin roof of what used to be her grandmother's pickle factory.

Paradise Pickles and Preserves.

It lay between the Ayemenem house and the river.

They used to make pickles, squashes, jams, curry powders and canned pineapples. And banana jam (illegally) after the FPO (Food Products Organization) banned it because according to their specifications it was neither jam nor jelly. Too thin for jelly and too thick for jam. An ambiguous consistency, they said.

As per their books.

Looking back now, to Rahel it seemed as though this difficulty that her family had with classification ran much deeper than the jam–jelly question. Perhaps Ammu, her mother, and Estha, her twin brother, and she were the worst transgressors. But it wasn't just them. It was the others too. They all broke the rules. They all crossed into forbidden territory. They all tampered with the laws that lay down who should be loved and how. And how much. The laws that make grandmothers grandmothers, uncles uncles, mothers mothers, cousins cousins, jam jam and jelly jelly.

It was a time when uncles became fathers, mothers lovers, and cousins died and had funerals.

It was a time when the unthinkable became thinkable and the impossible really happened.

It would probably be correct to say that it all began when Sophie Mol came to Ayemenem. Perhaps it's true that things can change in a day. That a few dozen hours can affect the outcome of whole lifetimes. And that when they do, those few dozen hours, like the salvaged remains of a burnt house—the charred clock, the singed photograph, the scorched furniture—must be resurrected from the ruins and examined.

Equally, it could be argued that it actually began thousands of years ago. Long before the Marxists came. Before the British took Malabar, before the Dutch Ascendancy, before Vasco da Gama arrived, before the Zamorin's conquest of Calicut. It could be argued that it began long before Christianity arrived in a boat and seeped into Kerala like tea from a tea-bag.

That it really began in the days when the Love Laws were made. The laws that lay down who should be loved, and how. And how much.

However, for practical purposes, in a hopelessly practical world . . . it was a skyblue day in December '69 (the nineteen silent). A skyblue Plymouth, with the sun in its tailfins, sped past young rice fields and old rubber trees, on its way to Cochin. Further east, in a small country with similar landscape (jungles, rivers, rice fields, communists), enough bombs were being dropped to cover all of it in six inches of steel. Here, however, it was peacetime, and the family in the Plymouth travelled without fear or foreboding.

The Plymouth belonged to Mammachi, Rahel and Estha's grandmother, and the twins were on their way to Cochin to see *The Sound of Music* for the third time. They knew all the songs.

After that they were all going to stay at Hotel Sea Queen with the oldfood smell. Bookings had been made. Early next morning they would go to Cochin Airport to pick up Chacko's ex-wife—their English aunt, Margaret Kochamma—and their cousin, Sophie Mol, who were coming from London to spend Christmas at Ayemenem. Earlier that year, Margaret Kochamma's second husband, Joe, had been killed in a car accident.

When Chacko heard about the accident he invited them to Ayemenem. He said he couldn't bear to think of them spending a desolate Christmas in England. In a house full of memories.

Ammu said that Chacko had never stopped loving Margaret Kochamma. Mammachi disagreed. She liked to believe that he had never loved her in the first place.

Rahel and Estha had never met Sophie Mol. They'd heard a lot about her, though, that last week. From their grand aunt, Baby Kochamma, and even from Mammachi. None of them had met her either, but they all behaved as though they already knew her. It had been the *What Will Sophie Mol Think?* week.

That whole week Baby Kochamma eavesdropped relentlessly on the twins' private conversations, and whenever she caught them speaking in Malayalam she levied a small fine which was deducted at source. From their pocket money. She made them write lines—'impositions' she called them—*I will always speak in English, I will always speak in English.* A hundred times each. When they were done, she scored them out with her red pen to make sure that old lines were not recycled for new punishments.

She had made them practise an English car song for the way back. They had to form the words properly and be particularly careful about their pronunciation. Prer *NUN* sea ayshun.

> Rej-Oice in the Lo-Ord Or-Orlways
> And again I say rej-Oice,
> RejOice,
> RejOice,
> And again I say rej-Oice.

Estha's full name was Esthappen Yako. Rahel's was Rahel. For the Time Being they had no surname because Ammu was considering reverting to her maiden name, though she said that choosing between her husband's name and her father's name didn't give a woman much of a choice.

Estha was wearing his beige and pointy shoes and his Elvis puff. His Special Outing Puff. His favourite Elvis song was 'Party'. '*Some people like to rock, some people like to roll,*' he would croon, when nobody was watching, strumming a badminton racket, curling his lip like Elvis. '*But moonin' an' a-groonin' gonna satisfy mah soul . . . less have a pardy . . .* '

Estha had slanting, sleepy eyes, and his new front teeth were still uneven on the ends. Rahel's new teeth were waiting inside her gums, like words in a pen. It puzzled everybody that an eighteen-minute age difference could cause such a discrepancy in front-tooth timing.

Most of Rahel's hair sat on top of her head like a fountain. It was held together by a Love-in-Tokyo—two beads on a rubber band, nothing to do with Love or Tokyo. In Kerala Love-in-Tokyos have withstood the test of time, and even today if you were to ask for one at any respectable A1 Ladies' Store, that's what you'd get. Two beads on a rubber band.

Rahel's toy wristwatch had the time painted on it. Ten to two. One of her ambitions was to own a watch on which she could change the time whenever she wanted to (which according to her was what Time was meant for in the first place). Her yellow-rimmed red plastic sunglasses made the world look red. Ammu said that they were bad for her eyes and had advised her to wear them as seldom as possible.

Her Airport Frock was in Ammu's suitcase. It had special matching knickers.

Chacko was driving. He was four years older than Ammu. His room was stacked from floor to ceiling with books. He had read them all and quoted long passages from them for no apparent reason. Or at least none that anyone else could fathom. Chacko had been a Rhodes Scholar at Oxford and was permitted excesses and eccentricities nobody else was.

He claimed to be writing a Family Biography that the Family would have to pay him not to publish. Ammu said that there was only one person in the family who was a fit candidate for biographical blackmail and that was Chacko himself.

Of course that was then. Before the terror.

In the Plymouth Ammu was sitting in front, next to Chacko. She was twenty-seven, and in the pit of her stomach she carried the cold knowledge that, for her, life had been lived. She had had one chance. She made a mistake. She married the wrong man.

Ammu finished her schooling the same year that her father retired from his job in Delhi and moved to Ayemenem. Pappachi insisted that a college education was an unnecessary expense for a girl, so Ammu had no choice but to leave Delhi and move with them. There was very little for a young girl to do in Ayemenem other than to wait for marriage proposals while she helped her mother with the housework. Since her father did not have enough money to raise a suitable dowry, no proposals came Ammu's way. Two years went by. Her eighteenth birthday came and went. Unnoticed, or at least unremarked upon by her parents. Ammu grew desperate. All day she dreamed of escaping from Ayemenem and the clutches of her ill-tempered father and bitter, long-suffering mother. She hatched several wretched little plans. Eventually, one worked. Pappachi agreed to let her spend the summer with a distant aunt who lived in Calcutta.

There, at someone else's wedding reception, Ammu met her future husband.

He was on vacation from his job in Assam where he worked as an assistant manager of a tea estate. His family were once-wealthy landlords who had migrated to Calcutta from East Bengal after Partition.

He was a small man, but well-built. Pleasant-looking. He wore old-fashioned spectacles that made him look earnest and completely belied his easygoing charm and juvenile but totally disarming sense of humour. He was twenty-five and had already been working on the tea estates for six years. He hadn't been to college, which accounted for his schoolboy humour. He proposed to Ammu five days after they first met. Ammu didn't pretend to be in love with him. She just weighed the odds and accepted. She thought that *anything*, anyone at all, would be better than returning to Ayemenem. She wrote to her parents informing them of her decision. They didn't reply.

Ammu had an elaborate Calcutta wedding. Later, looking back on the day, Ammu realized that the slightly feverish glitter in her bridegroom's eyes had not been love, or even excitement at the prospect of carnal bliss, but approximately eight large pegs of whisky. Straight. Neat.

When Ammu and her husband moved to Assam, Ammu, beautiful, young and cheeky, became the toast of the Planters' Club. She wore backless blouses with her saris and carried a silver lamé purse on a chain. She smoked long cigarettes in a silver cigarette holder and learned to blow perfect smoke rings. Her husband turned out to be not just a heavy drinker but a full-blown alcoholic with all of an alcoholic's deviousness and tragic charm. There were things about him that Ammu never understood. Long after she left him, she never stopped wondering why he lied so outrageously when he didn't need to. *Particularly* when he didn't need to. In a conversation with friends he would talk about how much he loved smoked salmon when Ammu knew he hated it. Or he would come home from the club and tell Ammu that he'd seen *Meet Me in St Louis*, when they'd actually screened *The Bronze Buckaroo*. When she confronted him about these things, he never explained or apologized. He just giggled, exasperating Ammu to a degree she never thought herself capable of.

Ammu was eight months pregnant when war broke out with

China. It was October of 1962. Planters' wives and children were evacuated from Assam. Ammu, too pregnant to travel, remained on the estate. In November, after a hair-raising, bumpy bus ride to Shillong, amid rumours of Chinese occupation and India's impending defeat, Estha and Rahel were born. By candlelight. In a hospital with the windows blacked out. They emerged without much fuss, within eighteen minutes of each other. Two little ones, instead of one big one. Twin seals, slick with their mother's juices. Wrinkled with the effort of being born. Ammu checked them for deformities before she closed her eyes and slept.

She counted four eyes, four ears, two mouths, two noses, twenty fingers and twenty perfect toenails.

She didn't notice the single Siamese soul. She was glad to have them. Their father, stretched out on a hard bench in the hospital corridor, was drunk.

Ammu loved her children (of course), but their wide-eyed vulnerability, and their willingness to love people who didn't really love them, exasperated her and sometimes made her want to hurt them—just as an education, a protection.

To Ammu her twins seemed like a pair of small bewildered frogs engrossed in each other's company, lolloping arm in arm down a highway full of hurtling traffic. Entirely oblivious of what trucks can do to frogs. Ammu watched over them fiercely. Her watchfulness stretched her, made her taut and tense. She was quick to reprimand her children, but even quicker to take offence on their behalf.

Within the first few months of her return to her parents' home, Ammu quickly learned to recognize and despise the ugly face of sympathy. Old female relations with incipient beards and several wobbling chins made overnight trips to Ayemenem to commiserate with her about her divorce. They squeezed her knee and gloated. She fought off the urge to slap them. Or twiddle their nipples. With a spanner. Like Chaplin in *Modern Times*.

When she looked at herself in her wedding photographs, Ammu felt the woman that looked back at her was someone else. A foolish, jewelled bride. Her silk sunset-coloured sari shot with gold. Rings on every finger. White dots of sandalwood paste over her arched eyebrows. Looking at herself like this, Ammu's soft mouth would twist into a small, bitter smile at the memory—not of the wedding itself so much as the fact that she had permitted herself to be so painstakingly decorated before being led to the gallows. It seemed so absurd. So futile.

Like polishing firewood.

She went to the village goldsmith and had her heavy wedding ring melted down and made into a thin bangle with snakeheads that she put away for Rahel.

For herself she knew that there would be no more chances. There was only Ayemenem now. An old house. A front veranda and a back veranda. A hot river and a pickle factory. And in the background, the constant, high, whining mewl of local disapproval.

On the back seat of the Plymouth, between Estha and Rahel, sat Baby Kochamma. Ex-nun and incumbent baby grand aunt. In the way that the unfortunate sometimes dislike the co-unfortunate, Baby Kochamma disliked the twins, for she considered them doomed, fatherless waifs. Worse still, they were Half-Hindu Hybrids whom no self-respecting Syrian Christian would ever marry. She was keen for them to realize that they (like her) lived on sufferance in the Ayemenem House, their maternal grandmother's house, where they really had no right to be. Baby Kochamma resented Ammu, because she saw her quarrelling with a fate that she, Baby Kochamma herself, felt she had graciously accepted. The fate of the wretched Man-less woman.

She subscribed wholeheartedly to the commonly held view that a married daughter had no position in her parents' home. As for a *divorced* daughter—according to Baby Kochamma, she had no position anywhere at all. And as for a *divorced* daughter from a *love* marriage, well, words could not describe Baby Kochamma's outrage. As for a *divorced* daughter from an *intercommunity* love marriage—Baby Kochamma chose to remain quiveringly silent on the subject.

The twins were too young to understand all this, so Baby Kochamma grudged them their moments of high happiness when a dragonfly they'd caught lifted a small stone off their palms with its legs, or when they had permission to bathe the pigs, or they found an egg—hot from a hen. But most of all she grudged them the comfort they drew from each other. She expected from them some token unhappiness. At the very least.

Chacko said that going to see *The Sound of Music* was an extended exercise in Anglophilia.

Ammu said, 'Oh come on, the whole world goes to see *The Sound of Music*. It's a World Hit.'

'Nevertheless, my dear,' Chacko said in his Reading Aloud voice. 'Never. The. Less.'

Mammachi often said that Chacko was easily one of the cleverest men in India. 'According to whom?' Ammu would say. 'On *what* basis?' Mammachi loved to tell the story (Chacko's story) of how one of the dons at Oxford had said that in his opinion, Chacko was brilliant, and made of prime ministerial material.

To this, Ammu always said, 'Ha! Ha! Ha!' like people in comics.

She said:

(a) Going to Oxford didn't necessarily make a person clever.

(b) Cleverness didn't necessarily make a good prime minister.

(c) If a person couldn't even run a pickle factory profitably, how was that person going to run a whole country?

And, most important of all:

(d) All Indian mothers are obsessed with their sons and therefore poor judges of their abilities.

Chacko said:

(a) You don't *go* to Oxford. You *read* at Oxford.

And:

(b) After *reading* at Oxford, you *come down*.

'Down to earth, d'you mean?' Ammu would ask. '*That* you definitely do.'

It was Chacko's idea to have the Paradise Pickles billboard installed on the Plymouth's roof-rack. On the way to Cochin now, it rattled and made fallingoff noises.

Near Vaikon they had to stop to buy some rope to secure it more firmly. That delayed them by another twenty minutes. Rahel began to worry about being late for *The Sound of Music*.

Then, as they approached the outskirts of Cochin, the red-

265

and-white arm of the railway level-crossing gate went down. Rahel knew that this had happened because she had been hoping that it wouldn't.

She hadn't learned to control her Hopes yet. Estha said that that was a Bad Sign.

So now they were going to miss the beginning of the picture. When Julie Andrews starts off as a speck on the hill and gets bigger and bigger till she bursts on to the screen with her voice like cold water and her breath like peppermint.

The red sign on the red-and-white arm said STOP in white.

'Pots,' Rahel said.

A yellow hoarding said BE INDIAN, BUY INDIAN in red.

'Naidni yub, naidni eb,' Estha said.

The twins were precocious with their reading. They had raced through *Old Dog Tom*, *Janet and John* and their *Ronald Ridout Workbooks*. Baby Kochamma, who had been put in charge of the twins' formal education, had read them a version of *The Tempest* abridged by Charles and Mary Lamb.

'*Where the bee sucks, there suck I,*' Estha and Rahel would go about saying. '*In a cowslip's bell I lie.*'

So when Baby Kochamma's Australian missionary friend, Miss Mitten, gave Estha and Rahel a baby book—*The Adventures of Susie Squirrel*—as a present when she visited Ayemenem, they were deeply offended. First they read it forwards. Miss Mitten, who belonged to a sect of born-again Christians, said that she was a Little Disappointed in them when they read it aloud to her backwards.

'*ehT serutnevdA fO eisuS lerriuqS. enO gnirps gninrom eisuS lerriuqS ekow pu.*'

They showed Miss Mitten how it was possible to read both *Malayalam* and *Madam I'm Adam* backwards as well as forwards. She wasn't amused, and it turned out that she didn't even know what Malayalam was. They told her it was the language everyone spoke in Kerala. She said she had been under the impression that it was called Keralese. Estha, who had by then taken an active dislike to Miss Mitten, told her that as far as he was concerned it was a Highly Stupid Impression.

Miss Mitten complained to Baby Kochamma about Estha's

rudeness, and about their reading backwards. She told Baby Kochamma she had seen Satan in their eyes. *nataS* in their *seye*.

They were made to write *In future we will not read backwards. In future we will not read backwards.* A hundred times. Forwards.

A few months later Miss Mitten was killed by a milk van in Hobart, across the road from a cricket oval. To the twins there was hidden justice in the fact that the milk van had been *reversing*.

The Waiting filled Rahel until she was ready to burst. She looked at her watch. It was ten to two. She thought of Julie Andrews and Christopher Plummer kissing each other sideways so that their noses didn't collide. She wondered whether people always kissed each other sideways. She wondered whom to ask.

Then a distant trainrumble seeped upwards from the frog-stained road. The yam leaves on either side of the railway track began to nod in mass consent. *Yesyesyesyesyes.* The train slammed past under a column of dense black smoke. A gossamer blanket of coaldust floated down like a dirty blessing and gently smothered the traffic.

Chacko started the Plymouth. A carbreeze blew. Greentrees and telephone poles flew past the windows. Still birds slid by on moving wires, like unclaimed baggage at the airport.

A pale daymoon hung hugely in the sky and went where they went. As big as the belly of a beer-drinking man.

Abhilash Talkies advertised itself as the first cinema hall in Kerala with a seventy-millimetre CinemaScope screen. To drive home the point, its façade had been designed as a cement replica of a curved CinemaScope screen. On top (cement writing, neon lighting) it said ABHILASH TALKIES in English and Malayalam.

The toilets were called HIS and HERS. HERS for Ammu, Rahel and Baby Kochamma. HIS for Estha Alone, because Chacko had gone to see about the bookings at the Hotel Sea Queen.

'Will you be OK?' Ammu said, worried.

Estha nodded.

Through the red Formica door that closed slowly on its own, Rahel followed Ammu and Baby Kochamma into HERS. She turned to wave across the slipperoily marble floor, at Estha Alone (with a comb), in his beige and pointy shoes. Estha waited in the dirty marble lobby with the lonely, watching mirrors till the red door took his sister away. Then he turned and padded off to HIS.

In HERS, Ammu suggested that Rahel balance in the air to piss. She said that Public Pots were Dirty. Like Money was. You never knew who'd touched it. Lepers. Butchers. Car Mechanics. (Pus. Blood. Grease.)

Once, when the cook, Kochu Maria, took her to the butcher's shop, Rahel noticed that the green five-rupee note that he gave them had a tiny blob of red meat on it. Kochu Maria wiped the blob away with her thumb. The juice left a red smear. She put the money into her bodice. Meat-smelling blood money.

Rahel was too short to balance in the air above the pot, so Ammu and Baby Kochamma held her up, her legs hooked over their arms. Her feet pigeon-toed in Bata sandals. High in the air with her knickers down. For a moment nothing happened, and Rahel looked up at her mother and baby grand aunt with naughty (now what?) question marks in her eyes.

'Come on,' Ammu said. 'Sssss . . . '

Sssss for the sound of Soo-soo. Mmmmm for the Sound of Myooozick.

Rahel giggled. Ammu giggled. Baby Kochamma giggled. When the trickle started, they adjusted her aerial position. Rahel was unembarrassed. She finished, and Ammu had the toilet paper.

'Shall you or shall I?' Baby Kochamma said to Ammu.

'Either way,' Ammu said. 'Go ahead. You.'

Rahel held her handbag. Baby Kochamma lifted her rumpled sari. Rahel studied her baby grand aunt's enormous legs. (Years later during a history lesson being read out in school—*The Emperor Babur had a wheatish complexion and pillar-like thighs*—this scene would flash before her. Baby Kochamma balanced like a big bird over a public pot. Blue veins like lumpy knitting running up her translucent shins. Fat knees dimpled. Hair on them. Poor little tiny feet to carry such a load!) Baby Kochamma waited for half of half a moment. Head thrust forward. Silly smile. Bosom swinging low. Melons in a blouse. Bottom up and out. When the gurgling, bubbling sound came, she listened with her eyes. A yellow brook burbled through a mountain pass.

Rahel liked all this. Holding the handbag. Everyone pissing in front of everyone. Like friends. She knew nothing then of how precious a feeling this was. *Like friends.* They would never be together like this again. Ammu, Baby Kochamma and she. When Baby Kochamma finished, Rahel looked at her watch. 'So long you took, Baby Kochamma,' she said. 'It's ten to two.'

Ammu did hers in a whisper. Against the side of the pot so you couldn't hear.

Estha Alone in HIS had to piss on to naphthalene balls and cigarette stubs in the urinal. To piss in the pot would be Defeat. To piss in the urinal, he was too short. He needed Height. He searched for Height, and in a corner of HIS, he found it. A dirty broom, a squash bottle half-full of a milky liquid (phenyl) with floaty black things in it. A limp floorswab, and two rusty tin cans of nothing. They could have been Paradise Pickle products. Pineapple chunks in syrup. Or slices. Pineapple slices. His honour redeemed by his grandmother's cans, Estha Alone organized the rusty cans of nothing in front of the urinal. He stood on them, one foot on each, and pissed carefully, with minimal wobble. Like a Man. The cigarette stubs, soggy then, were wet now, and swirly. Hard to light. When he finished, Estha moved the cans to the basin in front of the mirror. He washed his hands and wet his hair. Then, dwarfed by the size of Ammu's comb that was too big for him, he reconstructed his puff carefully. Slicked back, then pushed forward and swivelled sideways at the very end. He returned the comb to his pocket, stepped off the tins and put them back with the bottle and swab and broom. He bowed to them all. The whole shooting match. The bottle, the broom, the cans, the limp floorswab.

'Bow,' he said and smiled because when he was younger, he had been under the impression that you had to say 'Bow' when you bowed. That you had to *say* it to do it. 'Bow, Estha,' they'd say. And he'd bow and say, 'Bow,' and they'd look at each other and laugh, and he'd worry.

Estha Alone of the uneven teeth.

Outside, he waited for his mother, his sister and his baby grand aunt. When they came out, Ammu said 'OK, Esthappen?'

Estha said 'OK' and nodded his head carefully to preserve his puff. He put the comb back into her handbag. Ammu felt a sudden clutch of love for her reserved, dignified little son in his

Arundhati Roy

beige and pointy shoes, who had just completed his first adult assignment. She ran loving fingers through his hair. She spoilt his puff.

The Man with the steel Ever-Ready Torch said that the picture had started, so to hurry. They had to rush up the red steps with the old red carpet. Red staircase with red spit stains in the red corner. The Man with the Torch scrunched up his *mundu* and held it tucked under his balls, in his left hand. As he climbed, his calf muscles hardened under his climbing skin like hairy cannonballs. He held the torch in his right hand. He hurried with his mind.

'It started longago,' he said.

So they'd missed the beginning. Missed the rippled velvet curtain going up, with light bulbs in the clustered yellow tassels. Slowly up, and the music would have been 'Baby Elephant Walk' from *Hatari!*. Or Colonel Bogey's March.

Ammu held Estha's hand. Baby Kochamma, heaving up the steps, held Rahel's. Baby Kochamma, weighed down by her melons, would not admit to herself that she was looking forward to the picture. She preferred to feel that she was only doing it for the children's sake. In her mind she kept an organized, careful account of Things She'd Done For People, and Things People Hadn't Done For Her.

She liked the early nun-bits best, and hoped they hadn't missed them. Ammu explained to Estha and Rahel that people always loved best what they *Identified* most with. Rahel supposed she Identified most with Christopher Plummer who acted as Captain von Trapp. Chacko didn't Identify with him at all and called him Captain von Clapp-Trapp.

Rahel was like an excited mosquito on a leash. Flying. Weightless. Up two steps. Down two. Up one. She climbed five flights of red stairs for Baby Kochamma's one.

> I'm Popeye the sailor man   dum dum
> I live in a cara-van   dum dum
> I op-en the door
> And Fall-on the floor
> I'm Popeye the sailor man   dum dum

Up two. Down two. Up one. Jump, jump.

270

'Rahel,' Ammu said, 'you haven't learned your Lesson yet. Have you?'

Rahel had: *Excitement Always Leads to Tears*. Dum dum.

They arrived at the Princess Circle lobby. They walked past the Refreshment Counter where the orangedrinks were waiting. And the lemondrinks were waiting. The orange too orange. The lemon too lemon. The chocolates too melty.

The Torch Man opened the heavy Princess Circle door into the fan-whirring, peanut-crunching darkness. It smelt of breathing people and hairoil. And old carpets. A magical, *Sound of Music* smell that Rahel remembered and treasured. Smells, like music, hold memories. She breathed deep, and bottled it up for posterity.

Estha had the tickets. Little Man. He lived in a cara-van. Dum dum.

The Torch Man shone his light on the pink tickets. Row J. Numbers seventeen, eighteen, nineteen, twenty. Estha, Ammu, Rahel, Baby Kochamma. They squeezed past irritated people who moved their legs this way and that to make space. The seats of the chairs had to be pulled down. Baby Kochamma held Rahel's seat down while she climbed on. She wasn't heavy enough so the chair folded her into itself like sandwich stuffing, and she watched from between her knees. Two knees and a fountain. Estha, with more dignity than that, sat on the edge of his chair.

The shadows of the fans were on the sides of the screen where the picture wasn't.

Off with the torch. On with the World Hit.

The camera soared up in the skyblue (car-coloured) Austrian sky with the clear, sad sound of church bells.

Far below, on the ground, in the courtyard of the abbey, the cobblestones were shining. Nuns walked across it. Like slow cigars. Quiet nuns clustered quietly around their Reverend Mother. They gathered like ants around a crumb of toast. Cigars around a Queen Cigar. No hair on their knees. No melons in their blouses. And their breath like peppermint. They had complaints to make to their Reverend Mother. Sweetsinging complaints. About Julie Andrews, who was still up in the hills, singing 'The Hills are Alive with the Sound of Music', and was once again late for Mass.

> She climbs a tree and scrapes her knee

the nuns sneaked musically.

> Her dress has got a tear.
> She waltzes on her way to Mass
> And whistles on the stair . . .

People in the audience were turning around.
'Shhh!' they said. Shh! Shh! Shh!

> And underneath her wimple
> She has curlers in her hair!

There was a voice from outside the picture. It was clear and true,
cutting through the fan-whirring, peanut-crunching darkness. There
was a nun in the audience. Heads twisted around like bottle caps.
Black-haired backs of heads became faces with mouths and
moustaches. Hissing mouths with teeth like sharks. Many of them.

'Shhh!' they said together.

It was Estha who was singing. A nun with a puff. An Elvis
Pelvis Nun. He couldn't help it.

'Get him out of here!' the Audience said, when they found him.
Shutup or Getout. Getout or Shutup.

The Audience was a Big Man. Estha was a Little Man, with
the tickets.

'Estha, for heaven's sake, shut UP!' Ammu's fierce whisper
said.

So Estha shut UP. The mouths and moustaches turned away.
But then, without warning, the song came back, and Estha
couldn't stop it.

'Ammu, can I go and sing it outside?' Estha said (before
Ammu smacked him). 'I'll come back after the song.'

'But don't ever expect me to bring you out again,' Ammu
said. 'You're embarrassing *all* of us.'

But Estha couldn't help it. He got up to go. Past angry Ammu.
Past Rahel concentrating through her knees. Past Baby Kochamma.
Past the Audience that had to move its legs again. Thiswayandthat.
The red sign over the door said EXIT in a red light. Estha EXITed.

In the lobby, the orangedrinks were waiting. The lemondrinks were waiting. The melty chocolates were waiting. The electric blue foamleather car-sofas were waiting. The *Coming Soon!* posters were waiting.

Estha Alone sat on the electric blue foamleather car-sofa, in the Abhilash Talkies Princess Circle lobby, and sang. In a nun's voice, as clear as clean water.

> But how do you make her stay
> And listen to all you say?

The Man behind the Refreshments Counter, who'd been asleep on a row of stools, waiting for the interval, woke up. He saw, with gummy eyes, Estha Alone in his beige and pointy shoes. And his spoiled puff. The Man wiped his marble counter with a dirtcoloured rag. And he waited. And waiting he wiped. And wiping he waited. And watched Estha sing.

> How do you keep a wave upon the sand?
> Oh, how do you solve a problem like Maree . . . yah?

'Ay! *Eda cherukka!*' the Orangedrink Lemondrink Man said, in a gravelly voice thick with sleep. 'What the hell d'you think you're doing?'

> How do you hold a
> moonbeam
> in your hand?

Estha sang.

'Ay!' the Orangedrink Lemondrink Man said. 'Look, this is my Resting Time. Soon I'll have to wake up and work. So I can't have you singing English songs here. Stop it.' His gold wristwatch was almost hidden by his curly forearm hair. His gold chain was almost hidden by his chest hair. His white Terylene shirt was unbuttoned to where the swell of his belly began. He looked like an unfriendly, jewelled bear. Behind him there were mirrors for people to look at themselves in while they bought cold drinks and refreshments. To reorganize their puffs and settle their buns. The mirrors watched Estha.

'I could file a Written Complaint against you,' the Man said to Estha. 'How would you like that? A Written Complaint?'

273

Estha stopped singing and got up to go back in.

'Now that I'm up,' the Orangedrink Lemondrink Man said, 'Now that you've woken me up from my Resting Time, now that you've *disturbed* me, at least come and have a drink. It's the least you can do.'

He had an unshaven, jowly face. His teeth, like yellow piano keys, watched little Elvis the Pelvis.

'No thank you,' Elvis said politely. 'My family will be expecting me. And I've finished my pocket money.'

'*Porketmunny?*' the Orangedrink Lemondrink Man said with his teeth still watching. 'First English songs and now *Porket-munny*! Where d'you live? On the moon?'

Estha turned to go.

'Wait a minute!' the Orangedrink Lemondrink Man said sharply. 'Just a minute!' he said again, more gently. 'I thought I asked you a question.'

His yellow teeth were magnets. They saw, they smiled, they sang, they smelt, they moved. They mesmerized.

'I asked you where you lived,' he said, spinning his nasty web.

'Ayemenem,' Estha said. 'I live in Ayemenem. My grand-mother owns Paradise Pickles and Preserves. She's the Sleeping Partner.'

'Is she now?' the Orangedrink Lemondrink Man said. 'And who does she sleep with?' He laughed a nasty laugh that Estha couldn't understand. 'Never mind. You wouldn't understand.'

'Come and have a drink,' he said. 'A Free Cold Drink. Come. Come here and tell me all about your grandmother.'

Estha went. Drawn by the yellow teeth.

'Here. Behind the counter,' the Orangedrink Lemondrink Man said. He dropped his voice to a whisper. 'It has to be a secret because drinks are not allowed before the interval. It's a Theatre Offence.'

'Cognizable,' he added after a pause.

Estha went behind the Refreshments Counter for his Free Cold Drink. He saw the three high stools arranged in a row for the Orangedrink Lemondrink Man to sleep on. The wood shiny from sitting.

'Now if you'll kindly hold this for me,' the Orangedrink

Lemondrink Man said, handing Estha his penis through his soft white muslin dhoti. 'If you could just hold this, I'll get you your drink. Orange? Lemon?'

Estha held it because he had to.

'Orange? Lemon?' the Man said. 'Lemonorange?'

'Lemon, please,' Estha said politely.

He got a cold bottle and a straw. He held a bottle in one hand and a penis in the other. Hard, hot, veiny. Not a moonbeam.

The Orangedrink Lemondrink Man's hand closed over Estha's. His thumbnail was long like a woman's. He moved Estha's hand up and down. First slowly. Then fastly.

The lemondrink was cold and sweet. The penis hot and hard.

The piano keys were watching.

'So your grandmother runs a factory?' the Orangedrink Lemondrink Man said. 'What kind of factory?'

'Many products,' Estha said, not looking, with the straw in his mouth. 'Squashes, pickles, jams, curry powders. Pineapple slices.'

'Good,' the Orangedrink Lemondrink Man said. 'Excellent.'

His hand closed tighter over Estha's. Tight and sweaty. And faster still.

> Fast faster fest
> Never let it rest
> Until the fast is faster,
> And the faster's fest.

Through the soggy paper straw (almost flattened with spit and fear), the liquid lemon sweetness rose. Blowing through the straw (while his other hand moved), Estha blew bubbles into the bottle. Stickysweet lemon bubbles of the drink he couldn't drink. In his head he listed his grandmother's produce.

PICKLES	SQUASHES	JAMS
Mango	Orange	Banana
Green pepper	Grape	Mixed fruit
Bitter gourd	Pineapple	Grapefruit marmalade
Garlic	Mango	
Salted lime		

Then the gristly-bristly face contorted, and Estha's hand was wet

275

and hot and sticky. It had egg white on it. White egg white. Quarter-boiled.

The lemondrink was cold and sweet. The penis was soft and shrivelled like an empty leather change purse. With his dirt-coloured rag, the man wiped Estha's other hand.

'Now finish your drink,' he said, and affectionately squished a cheek of Estha's bottom. Tight plums in drainpipes. And beige and pointy shoes. 'You mustn't waste it,' he said. 'Think of all the poor people who have nothing to eat or drink. You're a lucky rich boy, with porketmunny and a grandmother's factory to inherit. You should Thank God that you have no worries. Now finish your drink.'

And so, behind the Refreshments Counter, in the Abhilash Talkies Princess Circle lobby, in the hall with Kerala's first seventy-millimetre CinemaScope screen, Esthappen finished his free bottle of fizzed, lemon-flavoured fear. His lemontoolemon, too cold. Too sweet. The fizz came up his nose. He would be given another bottle soon (free, fizzed fear). But he didn't know that yet. He held his sticky Other Hand away from his body.

It wasn't supposed to touch anything.

When Estha finished his drink, the Orangedrink Lemondrink Man said, 'Finished? Goodboy.'

He took the empty bottle and the flattened straw, and sent Estha back into *The Sound of Music*.

Back inside the hairoil darkness, Estha held his Other Hand carefully (upwards, as though he was holding an imagined orange). He slid past the Audience (their legs moving thiswayandthat), past Baby Kochamma, past Rahel (still tilted back), past Ammu (still annoyed). Estha sat down, still holding his sticky orange.

And there was Captain von Clapp-Trapp. Christopher Plummer. Arrogant. Hardhearted. With a mouth like a slit. And a steelshrill police whistle. A captain with seven children. Clean children, like a packet of peppermints. He pretended not to love them, but he did. He loved them. He loved her (Julie Andrews), she loved him, they loved the children, the children loved them. They all loved each other. They were clean, white children, and their beds were soft with Ei. Der. Downs.

The house they lived in had a lake and gardens, a wide

staircase, white doors and windows, and curtains with flowers.

The clean white children, even the big ones, were scared of the thunder. To comfort them, Julie Andrews put them all in her clean bed, and sang them a clean song about a few of her favourite things. These were a few of her favourite things.

(1) Girls in white dresses with blue satin sashes.

(2) Wild geese that flew with the moon on their wings.

(3) Bright copper kettles.

(4) Doorbells and sleighbells and schnitzel with noodles.

(5) Etc.

And then, in the minds of certain members of the audience in Abhilash Talkies, some questions arose that needed answers:

(a) *Did Captain von Clapp-Trapp shiver his leg?*
    He did not.

(b) *Did Captain von Clapp-Trapp blow spit bubbles? Did he?*
    He did most certainly not.

(c) *Did he gobble?*
    He did not.

Oh Captain von Trapp, Captain von Trapp, could you love the little fellow with the orange in the smelly auditorium?

He's just held the Orangedrink Lemondrink Man's soo-soo in his hand, but could you love him still?

And his twin sister? Tilting upwards with her fountain in a Love-in-Tokyo? Could you love her too?

Captain von Trapp had some questions of his own.

(a) *Are they clean white children?*
    No. *(But Sophie Mol is.)*

(b) *Do they blow spit bubbles?*
    Yes. *(But Sophie Mol doesn't.)*

(c) *Do they shiver their legs? Like clerks?*
    Yes. *(But Sophie Mol doesn't.)*

(d) Have they, either or both, ever held strangers' soo-soos?
    N . . . Nyes. *(But Sophie Mol hasn't.)*

'Then I'm sorry,' Captain von Clapp-Trapp said. 'It's out of the question. I cannot love them. I cannot be their Baba. Oh no.'

Captain von Clapp-Trapp couldn't.

Estha put his head in his lap. 'What's the matter?' Ammu said. 'If you're sulking again, I'm taking you straight home. Sit up please. And watch. That's what you've been brought here for.'

Finish the drink.

Watch the picture.

Think of all the poor people.

Lucky rich boy with porketmunny. No worries.

Estha sat up and watched. His stomach heaved. He had a greenwavy, thickwatery, lumpy, seaweedy, floaty, bottomlessbottomful feeling.

'Ammu?' he said.

'Now WHAT?' The *WHAT* snapped, barked, spat out.

'Feeling vomity,' Estha said.

'Just feeling or d'you want to?' Ammu's voice was worried.

'Don't know.'

'Shall we go and try?' Ammu said. 'It'll make you feel better.'

'OK,' Estha said.

OK? OK.

'Where're you going?' Baby Kochamma wanted to know.

'Estha's going to try and vomit,' Ammu said.

'Where're you going?' Rahel asked.

'Feeling vomity,' Estha said.

'Can I come and watch?'

'No,' Ammu said.

Past the Audience again (legs thiswayandthat). Last time to sing. This time to try and vomit. Exit through the EXIT. Outside in the marble lobby, the Orangedrink Lemondrink Man was eating a sweet. His cheek was bulging with a moving sweet. He made soft, sucking sounds like water draining from a basin. There was a green Parry's wrapper on the counter. Sweets were free for this man. He had a row of free sweets in dim bottles. He wiped the marble counter with his dirtcoloured rag that he held in his hairy watch hand. When he saw the luminous woman with polished shoulders and the little boy, a shadow slipped across his face. Then he smiled his portable piano smile.

'Out again sosoon?' he said.

Estha was already retching. Ammu moonwalked him to the Princess Circle bathroom. HERS.

He was held up, wedged between the notclean basin and Ammu's body. Legs dangling. The basin had steel taps and rust stains. And a brownwebbed mesh of hairline cracks, like the road map of some great, intricate city.

Estha convulsed, but nothing came. Just thoughts. And they floated out and floated back in. Ammu couldn't see them. They hovered like storm clouds over the Basin City. But the basin men and basin women went about their usual basin business. Basin cars and basin buses still whizzed around. Basin Life went on.

'No?' Ammu said.

'No,' Estha said.

No? No.

'Then wash your face,' Ammu said. 'Water always helps. Wash your face, and let's go and have a fizzy lemondrink.'

Estha washed his face and hands and face and hands. His eyelashes were wet and bunched together.

The Orangedrink Lemondrink Man folded the green sweet wrapper and fixed the fold with his painted thumbnail. He stunned a fly with a rolled-up magazine. Delicately he flicked it over the edge of the counter on to the floor. It lay on its back and waved its feeble legs. 'Sweetboy this,' he said to Ammu. 'Sings nicely.'

'He's my son,' Ammu said.

'Really?' the Orangedrink Lemondrink Man said, and looked at Ammu with his teeth. 'Really? You don't look old enough!'

'He's not feeling well,' Ammu said. 'I thought a cold drink would make him feel better.'

'Of course,' the Man said. 'Ofcourseofcourse. Orangelemon? Lemonorange?'

Dreadful, dreaded question.

'No thank you.' Estha looked at Ammu. Greenwavy, seaweedy, bottomless-bottomful.

'What about you?' the Orangedrink Lemondrink Man asked Ammu.

'Coca-ColaFanta? IcecreamRosemilk?'

'No. Not for me. Thank you,' Ammu said. Deep-dimpled, luminous woman.

'Here,' the Man said, with a fistful of sweets, like a generous air hostess. 'These are for your little Mon.'

'No thank you,' Estha said, looking at Ammu.

'Take them, Estha,' Ammu said. 'Don't be rude.'

Estha took them.

'Say Thank you,' Ammu said.

'Thank you,' Estha said.

'No mention,' the Orangedrink Lemondrink Man said in English.

'So!' he said. 'Mon says you're from Ayemenem?'

'Yes,' Ammu said.

'I come there often,' the Orangedrink Lemondrink Man said. 'My wife's people are Ayemenem people. I know where your factory is. Paradise Pickles, isn't it? He told me. Your Mon.'

He knew where to find Estha. That was what he was trying to say. It was a warning.

Ammu saw her son's bright feverbutton eyes.

'We must go,' she said. 'Mustn't risk a fever. Their cousin is coming tomorrow,' she explained to the Orangedrink Lemondrink Man. And then, added casually, 'from London.'

'From London?' A new respect gleamed in his eyes. For a family with London connections.

'Estha, you stay here with Uncle. I'll get Baby Kochamma and Rahel,' Ammu said.

'Come,' the Orangedrink Lemondrink Man said. 'Come and sit with me on a high stool.'

'No, Ammu! No, Ammu, no! I want to come with you!'

Ammu, surprised at the unusually shrill insistence from her usually quiet son, apologized to the Orangedrink Lemondrink Man.

'He's not usually like this. Come on then, Esthappen.'

The back-inside smell. Fan shadows. Backs of heads. Necks. Collars. Hair. Buns. Plaits. Ponytails.

A fountain in a Love-in-Tokyo. A little girl and an ex-nun.

Captain von Trapp's seven peppermint children had had their peppermint baths, and were standing in a peppermint line with their hair slicked down, singing in obedient peppermint voices to the woman the Captain nearly married. The blonde Baroness who shone like a diamond.

The hills are alive
with the sound of music

'We have to go,' Ammu said to Baby Kochamma and Rahel.

'But Ammu!' Rahel said. 'The Main Things haven't happened yet! He hasn't even *kissed* her! He hasn't even torn up the Hitler flag yet! They haven't even been *betrayed* by Rolf the Postman!'

'Estha's sick,' Ammu said. 'Come on!'

'The Nazi soldiers haven't even come!'

'Come on,' Ammu said. 'Get up!'

'They haven't even done "*High on a hill was a lonely goatherd*"!'

'Estha has to be well for Sophie Mol, doesn't he?' Baby Kochamma said.

'He doesn't,' Rahel said, but mostly to herself.

'What did you say?' Baby Kochamma said, getting the general drift, but not what was actually said.

'Nothing,' Rahel said.

'I *heard* you,' Baby Kochamma said.

Outside the Orangedrink Lemondrink Man was reorganizing his bottles. Wiping with his dirtcoloured rag the ring-shaped water stains they had left on his marble Refreshments Counter. Preparing for the Interval. He was a Clean Orangedrink Lemondrink Uncle. He had an air hostess's heart trapped in a bear's body.

'Going then?' he said.

'Yes,' Ammu said. 'Where can we get a taxi?'

'Out the gate, up the road, on your left,' he said, looking at Rahel. 'You never told me you had a little Mol too.' And holding out another sweet, 'Here, Mol—for you.'

'Take mine!' Estha said quickly, not wanting Rahel to go near the man.

But Rahel had already started towards him. As she approached him, he smiled at her and something about that portable piano smile, something about the steady gaze in which he held her, made her shrink from him. It was the most hideous thing she had ever seen. She spun around to look at Estha.

She backed away from the hairy man.

Estha pressed his sweets into her hand and she felt his fever-hot fingers whose tips were as cold as death.

"Bye, Mon,' Uncle said to Estha. 'I'll see you in Ayemenem sometime.'

So, the redsteps once again. This time Rahel lagging. Slow. No I don't want to go. A ton of bricks on a leash.

'Sweet chap, that Orangedrink Lemondrink fellow,' Ammu said.

'Chhi!' Baby Kochamma said.

'He doesn't look it, but he was surprisingly sweet with Estha,' Ammu said.

'So why don't you marry him then?' Rahel said petulantly.

Time stopped on the red staircase. Estha stopped. Baby Kochamma stopped.

'Rahel,' Ammu said.

Rahel froze. She was desperately sorry for what she had said. She didn't know where those words had come from. She didn't know that she'd had them in her. But they were out now, and wouldn't go back in. They hung about that red staircase like clerks in a government office. Some stood, some sat and shivered their legs.

'Rahel,' Ammu said. 'Do you realize what you have just done?'

Frightened eyes and a fountain looked back at Ammu.

'It's all right. Don't be scared,' Ammu said. 'Just answer me. Do you?'

'What?' Rahel said in the smallest voice she had.

'Realize what you've just done?' Ammu said.

Frightened eyes and a fountain looked back at Ammu.

'D'you know what happens when you hurt people?' Ammu said. 'When you hurt people, they begin to love you less. That's what careless words do. They make people love you a little less.'

A cold moth with unusually dense dorsal tufts landed lightly on Rahel's heart. Where its icy legs touched her, she got goose bumps. Six goose bumps on her careless heart.

A little less her Ammu loved her.

And so, out of the gate, up the road, and to the left. The taxi stand. A hurt mother, an ex-nun, a hot child and a cold one. Six goose bumps and a moth.

The taxi smelt of sleep. Old clothes rolled up. Damp towels.

Armpits. It was, after all, the taxi driver's home. He lived in it. It was the only place he had to store his smells. The seats had been killed. Ripped. A swathe of dirty yellow sponge spilt out and shivered on the back seat like an immense jaundiced liver. The driver had the ferrety alertness of a small rodent. He had a hooked, Roman nose and a Little Richard moustache. He was so small that he watched the road through the steering wheel. To passing traffic it looked like a taxi with passengers but no driver. He drove fast, pugnaciously, darting into empty spaces, nudging other cars out of their lanes. Accelerating at zebra crossings. Jumping lights.

'Why not use a cushion or a pillow or something?' Baby Kochamma suggested in her friendly voice. 'You'll be able to see better.'

'Why not mind your own business, sister?' the driver suggested in his unfriendly one.

Driving past the inky sea, Estha put his head out of the window. He could taste the hot, salt breeze in his mouth. He could feel it lift his hair. He knew that if Ammu found out about what he had done with the Orangedrink Lemondrink Man, she'd love him less as well. Very much less. He felt the shaming churning heaving turning sickness in his stomach. He longed for the river. Because water always helps.

The sticky neon night rushed past the taxi window. It was hot inside the taxi, and quiet. Baby Kochamma looked flushed and excited. She loved not being the cause of ill feeling. Every time a pyedog strayed on to the road, the driver made a sincere effort to kill it.

The moth on Rahel's heart spread its velvet wings, and the chill crept into her bones.

In the Sea Queen car park, the skyblue Plymouth gossiped with other, smaller cars. *Hslip Hslip Hsnooh-snah.* A big lady at a small ladies' party. Tailfins aflutter.

'Room numbers 313 and 327,' the man at the reception said. 'Non-airconditioned. Twin beds. Lift is closed for repair.'

The bellboy who took them up wasn't a boy and hadn't a bell. He had dim eyes and two buttons missing on his frayed maroon coat. His greyed vest showed. He had to wear his silly bellhop's cap tilted sideways, its tight plastic strap sunk into his sagging dewlap. It seemed unnecessarily cruel to make an old man wear a cap sideways like that and arbitrarily reorder the way in which age chose to hang from his chin.

There were more red steps to climb. The same red carpet from the cinema hall was following them around. Magic flying carpet.

Chacko was in his room. Caught feasting. Roast chicken, finger chips, sweetcorn and chicken soup, two parathas and vanilla ice cream with chocolate sauce. Sauce in a sauceboat. Chacko often said that his ambition was to die of overeating. Mammachi said it was a sure sign of suppressed unhappiness. Chacko said it was no such thing. He said it was Sheer Greed.

Chacko was puzzled to see everybody back so early, but pretended otherwise. He kept eating.

The original plan had been that Estha would sleep with Chacko, and Rahel with Ammu and Baby Kochamma. But now that Estha wasn't well, and Love had been reapportioned (Ammu loved her a little less), Rahel would have to sleep with Chacko, and Estha with Ammu and Baby Kochamma.

Ammu took Rahel's pyjamas and toothbrush out of the suitcase and put them on the bed.

'Here,' Ammu said.

Two clicks to close the suitcase.

Click. And click.

'Ammu,' Rahel said, 'shall I miss dinner as my punishment?'

She was keen to exchange punishments. No dinner, in exchange for Ammu loving her the same as before.

'As you please,' Ammu said. 'But I advise you to eat. If you want to grow, that is. Maybe you could share Chacko's chicken.'

'Maybe and maybe not,' Chacko said.

'But what about my punishment?' Rahel said. 'You haven't given me my punishment!'

'Some things come with their own punishments,' Baby Kochamma said. As though she was explaining a sum that Rahel couldn't understand.

Some things come with their own punishments. Like bedrooms with built-in cupboards. They would all learn more about punishments soon. That they came in different sizes. That some were so big they were like cupboards with built-in bedrooms. You could spend your whole life in them, wandering through dark shelving.

Baby Kochamma's goodnight kiss left a little spit on Rahel's cheek. She wiped it off with her shoulder.

'Gooodnight Godbless,' Ammu said. But she said it with her back. She was already gone.

'Goodnight,' Estha said, too sick to love his sister.

Rahel Alone watched them walk down the hotel corridor like silent but substantial ghosts. Two big, one small, in beige and pointy shoes. The red carpet took away their feet sounds.

Rahel stood in the hotel room doorway, full of sadness.

She had in her the sadness of Sophie Mol coming. The sadness of Ammu's loving her a little less. And the sadness of whatever the Orangedrink Lemondrink Man had done to Estha.

A stinging wind blew across her dry, aching eyes.

Chacko put a leg of chicken and some finger chips on to a quarter plate for Rahel.

'No thank you,' Rahel said, hoping that if she could somehow effect her own punishment, Ammu would rescind hers.

'What about some ice cream with chocolate sauce?' Chacko said.

'No thank you,' Rahel said.

'Fine,' Chacko said. 'But you don't know what you're missing.'

He finished all the chicken and then all the ice cream.

Rahel changed into her pyjamas.

'Please don't tell me what it is you're being punished for,' Chacko said. 'I can't bear to hear about it.' He was mopping the last of the chocolate sauce from the sauceboat with a piece of paratha. His disgusting, after-sweet sweet. 'What was it? Scratching your mosquito bites till they bled? Not saying Thank you to the taxi driver?'

'Something much worse than that,' Rahel said, loyal to Ammu.

'Don't tell me,' Chacko said. 'I don't want to know.'

He rang for room service, and a tired bearer came to take away the plates and bones. He tried to catch the dinner smells, but they escaped and climbed into the limp, brown hotel curtains.

A dinnerless niece and her dinnerful uncle brushed their teeth together in the Hotel Sea Queen bathroom. She, a forlorn, stubby

285

convict in striped pyjamas and a Fountain in a Love-in-Tokyo. He, in his cotton vest and underpants. His vest, taut and stretched over his round stomach like a second skin, went slack over the depression of his belly button.

When Rahel held her frothing toothbrush still and moved her teeth instead, he didn't say she mustn't.

He wasn't a fascist.

They took it in turns to spit. Rahel carefully examined her white Binaca froth as it dribbled down the side of the basin, to see what she could see.

What colours and strange creatures had been ejected from the spaces between her teeth?

None tonight. Nothing unusual. Just Binaca bubbles.

Chacko put off the Big Light. In bed, Rahel took off her Love-in-Tokyo and put it by her sunglasses. Her fountain slumped a little but stayed standing.

Chacko lay in bed in the pool of light from his bedside lamp. A fatman on a dark stage. He reached over to his shirt lying crumpled at the foot of his bed. He took his wallet out of the pocket, and looked at the photograph of Sophie Mol that Margaret Kochamma had sent him two years ago.

Rahel watched him, and her cold moth spread its wings again. Slow out. Slow in. A predator's lazy blink.

The sheets were coarse, but clean.

Chacko closed his wallet and put out the light. Into the night he drew on a red-tipped Charminar and wondered what his daughter looked like now. Nine years old. Last seen when she was red and wrinkled. Barely human. Three weeks later, Margaret his wife, his only love, had cried and told him about Joe.

Margaret told Chacko that she couldn't live with him any more. She told him that she needed her own space. As though Chacko had been using *her* shelves for *his* clothes. Which, knowing him, he probably had.

She asked him for a divorce.

Those last few tortured nights before he left her, Chacko would slip out of bed with a torch and look at his sleeping child. To learn her. Imprint her on his memory. To ensure that when he thought of her, the child that he invoked would be accurate. He memorized the brown down on her soft skull. The shape of her puckered, constantly moving mouth. The spaces between her toes. The suggestion of a mole. And then without meaning to, he found himself searching his baby for signs of Joe. The baby clutched his index finger while he conducted his insane, broken, envious, torchlit study. Her belly button protruded from her satiated satin stomach like a domed monument on a hill. Chacko laid his ear against it and listened with wonder at the rumblings from within. Messages being sent from here to there. New organs getting used to each other. A new government setting up its systems. Organizing the division of labour, deciding who would do what.

She smelt of milk and urine. Chacko marvelled at how someone so small and undefined, so vague in her resemblances, could so completely command the attention, the love, the *sanity*, of a grown man. When he left, he felt that something had been torn out of him. Something big.

But Joe was dead now. Killed in a car crash. Dead as a doorknob. A Joe-shaped hole in the universe.

In Chacko's photograph, Sophie Mol was seven years old. White and blue. Rose-lipped, and Syrian Christian nowhere. Though Mammachi, peering at the photograph, insisted she had Pappachi's nose.

'Chacko?' Rahel said. 'Can I ask you a question?'

'Ask me two,' Chacko said.

'Chacko, do you love Sophie Mol Most in the World?'

'She's my daughter,' Chacko said.

Rahel considered this.

'Chacko? Is it *necessary* that people HAVE to love their own children Most in the World?'

'There are no rules,' Chacko said. 'But people usually do.'

'Chacko, for example,' Rahel said. 'Just for *example*, is it possible that Ammu can love Sophie Mol more than me and Estha? Or for you to love me more than Sophie Mol, for *example?*'

'Anything's possible in Human Nature,' Chacko said in his Reading Aloud voice. Talking to the darkness now, suddenly insensitive to his little fountain-haired niece. 'Love. Madness. Hope. Infinite joy.'

Of the four things that were Possible in Human Nature, Rahel thought that *Infinnate Joy* sounded the saddest. Perhaps because of the way Chacko said it.

Infinnate Joy. With a church sound to it. Like a sad fish with fins all over.

A cold moth lifted a cold leg.

The cigarette smoke curled into the night. And the fat man and the little girl lay awake in silence.

A few rooms away, while his baby grand aunt snored, Estha Alone walked weavily to the bathroom. He vomited a clear, bitter, lemony, sparkling, fizzy liquid. The acrid aftertaste of a Little Man's first encounter with Fear. Dum dum.

He felt a little better. He put on his shoes and walked out of his room, laces trailing, down the corridor, and stood quietly outside Rahel's door.

Rahel stood on a chair and unlatched the door for him.

Chacko didn't bother to wonder how she could possibly have known that Estha was at the door. He was used to their sometimes strangeness.

He lay like a beached whale on the narrow hotel bed. His thoughts returned to Margaret Kochamma and Sophie Mol. Fierce bands of love tightened around his chest until he could barely breathe. He lay awake and counted the hours till they drove to the airport.

On the next bed, his niece and nephew slept with their arms around each other. A hot twin and a cold one. He and She. We and Us. Somehow, not wholly unaware of the hint of doom and all that waited in the wings for them.

They dreamed of their river.

Of the coconut trees that bent into it and watched, with coconut eyes, the boats slide by. Upstream in the mornings. Downstream in the evenings. And the dull, sullen sound of the boatmen's bamboo poles as they thudded against the dark, oiled boatwood.

It was warm, the water. Greygreen. Like rippled silk.

With fish in it.

With the sky and trees in it.

And at night, the broken yellow moon in it. ☐